The Talmadge Girls

ALSO BY ANITA LOOS

The Talmadge Girls

A Memoir

Anita Loos

The Viking Press  New York

First published in 1978 by The Viking Press
625 Madison Avenue, New York, N.Y. 10022

Published simultaneously in Canada by
Penguin Books Canada Limited

LIBRARY OF CONGRESS CATALOGING IN PUBLICATION DATA

Loos, Anita, 1894–
The Talmadge girls.

1. Talmadge, Constance, 1900–1973   2. Talmadge,
Norma, 1897–1957   3. Moving-picture actors and
actresses—United States—Biography.   I. Title.
PN2287.T14L6   791.43'028'0922 [B]   78-15449
ISBN 0-670-69302-2

Printed in the United States of America
Set in VIP Garamond

CONTENTS

The Talmadge Girls

Norma and Constance and Natalie and Peg

B ack in the heyday of the silent film there were two stars of the first magnitude who happened to be sisters. Their careers flourished as long as dialogue was printed in subtitles. When sound came in, a number of other stars were able to storm the Tower of Babel; the early talkies of Greta Garbo, Lillian Gish, Joan Crawford, and Gloria Swanson have now become museum pieces. But the Talmadge girls, although generally included in the picture albums that grace today's coffee tables, exist for the most part only in the memories of those old enough to have seen their silent films.

Actually, Norma rounded out her career with three sound pictures. The first, in 1929, entitled *New York Nights,* was an elaborate soap opera directed by Lewis Milestone, who later crashed into film history with *All Quiet on the Western Front.* Its cast boasted Gilbert Roland (Norma's sweetheart at that time, both on screen and off) as well as Lilyan Tashman, Roscoe Karns, and John Wray—all of them gone now except for Gilbert Roland, who is still trim and dark-haired and has recently been filming in Spain.

CHAPTER ONE

New York Nights was released at the beginning of the Great Depression, when people were skimping on the bare necessities of life in order to buy entertainment, turning those years into the golden age of the talkies. Nevertheless, Norma's first sound picture was a failure and, in reviewing it, the critic for *Time* magazine reported that its star spoke like an elocution pupil. In 1930 Norma attempted a more elaborate project called *Du-Barry, Woman of Passion*, and the same *Time* critic granted that Norma showed improvement; she now spoke like an elocution *teacher*. Actually, Norma's voice was not in the least disagreeable and she had no trace of a Brooklyn accent. But the heroines she played were noble creatures, and Norma's intonation lacked nobility.

While Norma was trying to correct her enunciation in New York, Constance, who had abandoned her career for marriage, was sparkling as one of London's Bright Young People. When she read the criticism of her sister's voice, she cabled Norma: "Quit pressing your luck, baby. The critics can't knock those trust funds Mom set up for us."

Norma took that sisterly advice and gave up acting forever. She could well afford to. Her first husband had settled a fortune on her at the time of their divorce, in addition to which she had earned over five million dollars during her years as a star.

I wrote scripts for both Talmadges from 1916 through 1925—scripts that were filmed on the movie stages of both New York and Hollywood. But even before the girls retired, I deserted movies to write other things, while they became short-term wives of a series of husbands, who didn't have to be rich because their wives were so well-heeled but who generally were, supplementing those trust funds very nicely indeed. As time went on the girls and I met only sporadically. Show business is like that; we had been tied to each other by our jobs, but new occupations took us into other fields.

Early in the fifties, I had a memorable encounter with Constance in New York. I happened to be crossing the street in front of the Drake Hotel when I noticed that a smartly dressed young woman just ahead of me was unsteady on her feet. Suddenly she fell smack onto the asphalt. As I stopped in shock, a traffic cop hurried to pick her up. The lady was not too tight to thank him graciously, at which the officer remarked, "Don't mention it, Mrs. Giblin."

"I won't if you don't!" said she, and as they joined in a friendly laugh over her drinking problem, I recognized Constance Talmadge.

By then in her early fifties, Constance had changed very little from the old days. She still had the same girlish figure and pretty face, the same bright tawny hair and spirited laugh as she joked with the neighborhood cop. I was embarrassed for my old-time chum and tried to pass by unnoticed, but Constance spotted me and, totally unabashed, exclaimed, "Well, if it isn't Buggie!"

Calling Constance by her nickname, I answered, "Hi, Dutch." Then, in a foolish attempt at conversation, I added, "Let's have lunch some day."

"Yes, let's!" she said eagerly, at which point the Drake doorman took over from the cop and started to steer her into the hotel. At the doorway Dutch turned to call back, "I'm going up to Anne Robinson's tomorrow to dry out. I'll phone you when I get home." (Anne Robinson's was a health spa in Croton-on-Hudson that was popular with the drinking set.) Of course Dutch forgot to phone.

It was not more than a year later when I saw Norma for the last time. She was accompanied by Dutch and we all met in front of the same hotel, where Constance lived with her fourth husband, Walter Giblin, a mild-mannered and adoring Wall Street broker.

Norma was visiting Dutch from Florida, where she had retired with a third husband, who was to be her last, Dr. Carvel James. Norma was still romantically beautiful but she walked with a cane and her eyes were shining with a sort of unnatural glitter. After greeting me fondly Norma said, "Are you still pushing a pencil across all that yellow paper?" I told her I found it a good way to put in time. "Oh well—every girl to her own taste," said she. And then, as she chuckled over her feeble joke, the muscles of Norma's face started to twitch beyond control.

Dutch, to keep me from further studying Norma's drugged condition, quickly spoke up. "Come along, honey," said Dutch, at which she led Norma into the hotel and out of my life forever.

I have known any number of actresses who yearned and burned to be movie stars but who were just as tiresome as they were ambitious. Norma and Dutch, however, their feet firmly planted on the scaffold of fame, kicked the whole thing apart and were the best of company. Even so, the girls were no match for the engaging woman who gave them birth.

Promoting the career of many a stage or screen star is that matronly nuisance, the "stage mother." But Margaret Talmadge, known throughout the movie world as Peg, was a rare specimen of the breed; Peg caused all her nuisance value to pay off in laughs.

The remarkable beauty of Peg's daughters was hard to account for. They certainly didn't take after their mother, whose features were dominated by the type of scoop nose adorning Bob Hope or, more classically, the archaic stone faces of Easter Island. Peg's blue eyes were small and wishy-washy; her pepper-and-salt hair looked like a neglected bird's nest; and although Peg wasn't exactly fat, her silhouette was sort of lumpy, like an overstuffed shopping bag. Her general appearance was too ordinary to provoke much comment. Peg couldn't have cared less.

The girls' good looks were possibly inherited from their father, but he had disappeared long before they became famous. And I pause here to paraphrase the sad old song "Where Have All the Flowers Gone?" to wonder "Where Have All the Fathers Gone?" for who knows anything about a Mr. Gish, a Mr. Pickford, a Mr. Crawford, a Mr. Swanson, a Mr. Goddard, or even a Mr. Streisand? Stage mamas are legion, but who ever heard of a stage father? In any event, Mr. Talmadge had disappeared somewhere and no one ever seemed to notice.

Norma was the oldest of three girls, a brunette of glowing beauty, with the black Irish temperament of her forebears, which sometimes gave out danger signals. (On that day of our last meeting, they were flying high.)

Constance, three years younger than Norma, couldn't have been more unlike her sister. Along with a spontaneous wit went an almost childish love of fun. Both off screen and on she was a delectably pretty clown. Because as a child Constance was blonde and chubby, Peg called her "Dutch," a nickname that stuck throughout her life.

There was a middle sister, Natalie (let's call her Nate as everyone always did), who was born in 1899, a year before Dutch. A brunette, Nate bore a certain resemblance to Norma, but she had a sort of pinched look, as if she harbored the same genes that produced her radiant sisters but had simply failed to blossom into full, lush bloom. Peg tried to organize a career for Nate through bit parts in her sisters' movies, but she soon came to grips with Nate's lack of star potential and settled for marrying her off instead. Peg chose Buster Keaton as Nate's husband—that mini-Molière of filmdom whose slapstick comedies were works of art. Peg had schooled Nate to look down on her husband as a mere substitute for a career, but in my opinion the chance to wake up in the morning and look across a pillow into that fabulous face should have been fulfillment enough for any girl.

The best of the Talmadge movies were produced by Norma's first husband, Joseph M. Schenck, but once they had run their course, Joe allowed them to filter into dust. The preservation of movies is a tricky business; film dampens, buckles, and gets glued together in fuzzy, unintentional double exposures, or it dries out and crumbles. The technicians who restore old films have got to be in love with their jobs, and they invariably are. But during those early years we had little respect for a métier that we looked down on as a mere passing fad. Nobody ever dreamed that those images would one day start to speak, that Shakespeare could be brought to life through them. Those of us whom the movies were making rich were bent only on cashing in before the craze died out.

But little by little those old silent films began to gain respectability. In New York, The Museum of Modern Art (MOMA) undertook to make a collection of them. For a long while MOMA tried to track down the Talmadge films without any luck. Then, miraculously, a copy of Norma's most popular movie, *Smilin' Through*, was unearthed in Czechoslovakia. ("Whenever we can't find an old movie," says Lillian Gerard of MOMA's film department, "we contact a museum in Prague which started collecting early American films even before we did.") The Prague museum supplied MOMA with a copy of *Smilin' Through*, thanks to which Norma Talmadge can once again be seen playing an Irish beauty with the improbable name of Moonyeen. At the end of the picture she holds a tryst with the spirit of her departed sweetheart, carrying on an eternal love affair that nothing but double exposure could supply.

Another image out of that silent past occasionally comes to view whenever D.W.Griffith's *Intolerance* is run. That tousled gamine of ancient Babylon driving a chariot and munching on a fistful of scallions is none other than Constance Talmadge.

The driving power behind Norma's habitual self-restraint and Dutch's razzmatazz was their mama, and although Peg had all the impact of a force of nature, she could joke about her situation. "I've spent years driving those two wild horses to a trough," she would declare, "and I'll be damned if I don't make the bastards drink!" But Peg spoke with affection, and the term "bastard" was poetic license, for her daughters were as legitimate as a Jersey City marriage license could make them.

When I was writing scripts for the girls, I was like a member of the family. I accompanied them on location and sometimes we all took holiday jaunts together, either here or abroad. Wherever we went, Peg's wisecracks gave a special accent to our ventures. I recall an evening in Paris when Norma and Joe Schenck were newlyweds and Joe took us all to the Folies Bergères. We girls had recently acquired a manicurist at the Hotel Crillon, a certain Mme. Gerbel, whose daughter was in the chorus of the Folies. That night we watched the lovely creature posing nude on a gigantic crystal chandelier. Joe pointed her out and asked if I knew her age. When I told him that she was eighteen, Peg let out a snort. "She lies in her teeth! No girl could get her knees that dirty in only eighteen years!" (Later I paraphrased Peg's remark in *Gentlemen Prefer Blondes*.)

Although Joe would always be passionately in love with his ravishing wife, he was a film producer and had to be on the lookout for star material. Mlle. Gerbel's beauty was of Hollywood caliber, including her well-scrubbed knees. But the next day during a lunch party at the Ritz, I heard Joe remark to Sam Goldwyn, "Don't every import any French girls to Hollywood, Sam. They never wash their knees."

Such was Peg Talmadge's power of suggestion.

Any Blind Alley Might Lead to Hollywood

W hen the Talmadge girls reached the point of having their own companies, the picture industry was still anchored in New York. Most of our movies were produced by Norma's bridegroom, Joe Schenck, and filmed in an old warehouse on East Forty-eighth Street that Joe had converted into a studio. It was ramshackle to a degree, but we all lived in great opulence at the Ambassador Hotel on Park Avenue. Peg, Nate, and Dutch occupied a large apartment, while Norma, with a solidarity that was the family's chief trait, had steered her bridegroom into the honeymoon suite under the very same roof with his snoopy mother-in-law.

The two stars drove to work every morning in a custom-built Cadillac accompanied by Nate, for whom Peg requisitioned a job answering fan mail. Thus Peg was left alone for long stretches. Unlike most movie mothers, she didn't choose to hang around the studio, for she looked on movie-making as rep-etitious and boring. Her visits to the studio were generally to pick up the girls' weekly paychecks.

Peg didn't read novels, play cards, haunt the shops, frequent beauty parlors, or indulge in martinis. Her favorite diversion was gossip. My afternoons were free because I did my writing in the morning, so we used to spend long hours lolling among the marabou cushions of Peg's Louis XVI divan, dishing up the day's quota of scandal. Then, Peg would sometimes dredge memories out of her lowly past, and I came to understand what she meant by "dragging those two wild horses to a trough." In lamenting the girls' atrocious behavior, Peg would often wince, close her eyes and utter a favorite plaint, "May God give me strength!"

I recall Peg's account of a typical blooper committed by Norma. It had taken place recently at St. Patrick's Cathedral during a funeral for the ninety-five-year-old father of a Tammany Hall big shot. The church was swarming with VIPs, including New York's Governor Al Smith, whose jaunty brown derby, on him, looked impressive. Mayor Jimmy Walker was resplendent in frock coat and striped pants, and Joe Schenck, whose influence with Tammany came to the rescue whenever scandal erupted in the film industry, was an honored pallbearer.

Norma had begged off, arguing that Joe's tribute of an Irish harp in rosebuds would make up for her absence. And besides, she was due for a fitting at Mme. Frances's. But viewing herself in a mirror, she decided that her new dress deserved an audience. So over she traipsed to the funeral. "The ceremony was just getting under way," said Peg, "when I heard a stir among the mourners. I looked back and there was Norma, coolly meandering down the aisle in a bright red hobble skirt. Cameramen were galloping toward her from every point of the compass, and Norma was saluting them with a big, friendly hello."

Peg paused to gain equilibrium and then continued. "Tammany Hall will always blame Joe for letting his wife steal the limelight away from that corpse! *May God give me strength!*" sighed Peg.

(In writing *Gentlemen Prefer Blondes* I sometimes paraphrased Peg in the dialogue of Dorothy. This led to a rumor that the original Dorothy was Peg Talmadge. But I had other Dorothys among my girl friends, and indeed one of them was a certain gentleman who designed our hats.)

One day, harking back to earlier calamities, Peg took up the subject of her husband, and for the first time I got a line on Mr. Talmadge. Generally referring to him as "that skunk," Peg described some of the rough deals he'd put them through when he was still a resident father. She told me about a time they lived in a frame cottage on Fenimore Street in Brooklyn. For over a year things had been going from bad to worse, and when Christmas morning broke, there was nothing in the house to eat. The girls, aged seven, eight, and ten, woke their father up to whimper that they were hungry. But Pop Talmadge, rising jauntily above his hangover, said, "Don't worry, kiddies. I'll just step out and buy you some hamburgers."

Peg, having already gone through his pockets, was not impressed. (She had her own word for money, calling it "eagles," after the picture of that bird on greenbacks and perhaps also for its ability to fly away.) "And what will you use for eagles?" asked Peg.

Summoning his considerable machismo, Fred announced, "I'll stop at the corner tavern and borry a dollar." ("I could never get the ignoramus to say 'borrow,'" Peg complained, "but he sure had plenty of practice mispronouncing it!" However, she spoke more in tolerance than in abuse.)

The kids waited all morning for Santa to come down the chimney with those hamburgers. He never showed. Neither did Pop. "I had a sneaky feeling the skunk had gone for good," Peg told me, and she was right. But as the afternoon wore on, Peg rallied. She had hidden a bagful of soda crackers, bought from a neighboring factory at half price because they were broken. Peg arranged the fractured morsels in a pan, together with salt, pepper, aqua pura, and a few residues of margarine, and added several pinches of sage to give the mixture a vague flavor of turkey stuffing. Then Peg shoved it in the oven, browned it to a crisp, and that was the Talmadge Christmas celebration.

It seemed that when Peg married Fred Talmadge she had to break off with her family, who took a dim view of him. Peg's father held an honored post in the Affiliated Association of Plumbers and Pipe Fitters, in addition to which he was presiding officer of the Jersey City Knights of Columbus. But to the teenage Peg, life seemed a deadly routine. No self-deceiver, Peg realized she lacked the beauty that might provide the glamour for which she yearned, but Fred Talmadge already possessed glamour to a flamboyant degree. Fred belonged to a faith that had produced, among many other outcasts, the fabulous Wandering Jew. Without a legitimate profession, he went from one makeshift job to another, most of them vaguely connected with the entertainment industry.

While courting Peg, Fred held down a job as salesman for the souvenirs used by street fair and carnival companies; he could thus present his sweetheart with such items as pink-plush teddy bears and enormous Kewpie dolls.

But though he possessed all the flashy charm his job required, Fred needed alcohol to sustain it, and that made his services highly expendable. By the time his bride found herself pregnant, Fred had already been out of work for weeks. In later years it suited Peg's notion of romance to say that Norma was born in Niagara Falls, but actually the girls were all born and brought up in Brooklyn, where Peg and Fred had moved shortly after their marriage.

Irritated by the presence of his crusty wife, Fred hung out in saloons, except on Thursdays, when *The Saturday Evening Post* appeared. Feigning illness, he would take to his couch and read the *Post* from cover to cover. One day Peg, fed up with his hypochondria, took it on herself to investigate an appeal for workers at a neighborhood cannery. "It'll be a makeshift until things pick up," she urged her uninterested spouse. "All you'd have to do is unload some cans of tomatoes into the labeling department." Fred visualized himself daintily handling those cans one at a time, but on finding he had to lug heavy trays full of them, he cashed his paycheck and vanished into the mystery of a binge.

It was his first disappearance after their marriage, and Peg refused to report it to a family that would only say "We told you so!" She began a career of self-survival. Her pregnant state didn't interfere with a "home laundry," which had the further advantage of requiring no capital. Then on Saturday afternoons, Peg taught a class of artistic housewives to paint Orpheus and Eurydice on black-velvet panels, copying an original by Peg herself that hung in the hall.

"Sometimes," Peg told me in reminiscence, "that skunk would land a job and come home to flaunt it in my teeth." (She failed to comment that during those visits Fred engendered two more babies.)

Expenses mounted as the years rolled by, but Peg was able to rent out her hall bedroom to a responsible Austrian waiter, whose six dollars every week paid for the kids' milk. And as a sideline, Peg canvassed the neighborhood, taking orders for a line of cosmetics.

Peg's tenant loved the children and in time he developed sentimental feelings for their spunky young mother. When he was alone in his room Peg could hear him pouring his heart out, crooning Viennese love songs accompanied by a zither.

During one of Fred's longer absences, Peg's tenant offered her the security of a future marriage. But at that crucial moment a letter arrived from Sandusky, Ohio, enclosing a two-dollar greenback, together with the boast, "I am now on tour with the colossal Jones Brothers' Carnival Company, in charge of publicity for all the man-eating animals!" Peg was able to grin over her husband's boast, but it turned the tide in his favor. Even as a rat, Fred was debonair, whereas her suitor was heavyhearted. In time Peg's suitor got discouraged and returned to his native Austria, but Fred continued to visit his family for short periods until that gloomy Christmas when he disappeared.

Peg's hand laundry remained a reliable standby, but her most popular cosmetic item, an antiwrinkle mask, was belied by the deepening furrows on Peg's brow. "Don't judge this product by me, Modom!" she'd explain. "My husband is a nature crank and he won't allow me to use any beauty aids." (This at a time when she was without a husband who, in turn, had never given a thought to nature.)

It was increasingly hard to keep up with changing conditions; painting on velvet went "out" and etching on suede with an electric stylus came "in." So Peg valiantly updated her art lessons and sold the necessary equipment to her students at a meager profit. Another plus was that Norma had grown big enough to pick up and deliver laundry.

But there was an even larger plus; it was becoming evident that both Norma and Dutch were going to be beauties. Different as they were in coloring, they had both inherited their father's large brown eyes that gazed at the world through abnormally long lashes. Strangers used to stop Peg in the street to comment on Norma's dark beauty and Dutch's tawny loveliness while little Nate stood meekly by, never mentioned in the compliments.

Peg's daydream of providing better lives for the girls than she had done for herself began slowly to gain substance. One day she told me about the first definite turning point in family history. It occurred on a rainy Saturday when she roused Norma from sleep. "Wake up, you little slut," said Peg. "We've got a big day ahead of us." I'm sure her intonation was affectionate, as it usually was, but Norma, at fourteen, was already the full-blown laggard she remained all her life.

"Don't bother me, Peg!" she grumbled. "Nobody will be out today in this weather."

"That's what you think," Peg argued, "but the best time to hustle is when other folks stay home."

Norma herself was responsible for being disturbed that morning. A few weeks earlier she had come home late from school and Peg, chiding her, had asked, "Have you been letting some boy or other make free?"

Norma brushed the crack aside as one of her Mom's frequent plugs for chastity. "The teacher made us girls stay after class," she explained.

"But why?" asked Peg.

"On account of Hazel Converse. She's in trouble, so we're supposed to keep her company and take her mind off the boys."

At which Peg, taking another swipe at sex, remarked, "When a trollop's born with round heels, nothing's going to keep her perpendicular!"

"But Peg, it isn't Hazel's fault the boys chase her. You see, she's a model."

"A model for *what?*" asked Peg.

"For illustrated song slides. Hazel poses for them at a photographer's over in Union Hill."

Peg's mind started to churn. "How old is this Converse girl?" she demanded.

"I don't know; about sixteen, maybe."

Peg said not another word, but after the kids left for school, she phoned a onetime pal of Fred's who tended bar in Union Hill to ask if he knew of such a photographer. Sure enough, the man sometimes dropped in for a beer.

"Will you ask him for an interview with my sixteen-year-old daughter, Norma?" asked Peg.

"Good grief, that kid of Fred's ain't sixteen yet!" came the response.

"I can age her," said Peg evasively. "And, while you're at it, find out what those jobs pay."

A few days later the barkeeper landed an interview for Norma and also reported that the salary was a whopping five dollars for a day's work.

But while she was getting Norma ready for the interview, Peg began to have qualms; the child scarcely looked her real age of fourteen. Optimistically, Peg combed Norma's hair into a lofty pompadour and topped it with her own "peach-basket" hat, decorated by a satin peach, stuffed and hand-painted by Peg. But Norma still looked so immature that Peg touched up her face with some of the cosmetics she sold.

Peg's devices fooled the bleary-eyed photographer only too well, for squinting at Norma, he said, "Your daughter's too urban for this job."

"*Urban?*" Peg repeated. "And what does *that* mean?"

"It means . . . sophisticated."

"It's this hat!" Peg said in panic, and started to yank it off.

"Don't bother," the photographer told Peg. "There's a girl coming in tomorrow who's just right."

At this point the phone rang. While Peg stalled to keep from facing defeat, the photographer suddenly turned from the phone to address her. "Don't go away, lady," said he. Then after hanging up, he explained. "They're waiting for these slides over in Tin Pan Alley. I've got to shoot 'em today."

While Peg looked on frozen in suspense, the photographer started to experiment with Norma. He let down the pompadour, took out a grimy handkerchief, and wiped off the purple eye shadow. Then he finally said, "Tell you what, if you'll settle for three dollars, the job's yours." And Peg was so weakened by tension that she gave in without a hassle.

Stepping to a back door, the photographer called downstairs. "Marvin! Come up here."

"All right, Papa," came an answer.

While he was waiting, the photographer cranked up a Gramophone. "I'll play you the song number," he told Norma, "so you'll know what the action's about."

The machine began to squeak out a lyric titled "Stop, Stop, Stop," which concerned a country girl's attempt to fend off the advances of a city slicker. A youth, whose profound effeminacy was increased by a mop of oily hair, now entered, and Norma's "seduction" began in front of a blank screen on which rustic backgrounds would be filled in later by double exposure.

In due time Peg took her girls to a matinee to see Norma's "performance." The song was delivered by a fat, middle-aged soloist who stood to the left of the screen. When she sang her plea of "Stop, Stop, Stop," Norma's ordinarily languid expression actually seemed to register alarm. As she watched, Peg's heart started to race.

In describing the situation to me, Peg wisecracked, "There wasn't much point in Norma telling the guy to stop, when she was the wrong sex to even get him started." A few years later I remember repeating Peg's crack to the youthful author of the lyric, one Irving Berlin.

That fateful day, when Peg led her kids out through the theater lobby, she stopped to buy them the five-cent bag of popcorn she thought she couldn't afford on their way in. The children were much more excited over the popcorn than their sister's debut, but to Peg it meant she'd found a pathway out of destitution: Norma was an actress! And there was only one more step for her to take from those static song slides onto a *moving picture screen.*

Hollywood was far away and not yet the film capital of the world. But it so happened that the Vitagraph Motion Picture Studio was located in Flatbush, a mere trolley ride from the Talmadges' front door.

Peg wangled a set of the song slides from Marvin's father and betook herself to Flatbush. But she went alone; her stratagem was to flash those slides as proof that her child was a bona fide professional. This would whet interest in Norma and lead to her grand entrée in the flesh later on.

On reaching the end of the trolley line Peg had a thrilling foretaste of the prosperity that might lie in store for them. The studio was an impressive complex occupying two city blocks. A three-story administration building faced the street; looming up behind it were five enormous structures that resembled conservatories, complete with glass walls to make full use of daylight. (This was before the first arc lamps would begin to provide stage lighting.) There was a lofty building for the construction of sets and a stable for horses, which were constantly in use for Westerns or for transportation. And there was a spacious costume department.

Out front a motor bus was about to take off for location, loaded with aluminum reflecting screens and other paraphernalia, including actors whose faces were covered with a pasty white goo, over which their eyes were smeared on in black. The troupe wore fashionable attire, and one actress, in an enormous picture hat, was provoking giggles as she tried to get onto the bus in a long, slinky ball gown. Peg gave a start as she recognized the famous star Florence Turner. But comparing her to Norma, Peg considered Miss Turner frowsy. Her hair, an indifferent shade of brown, was rather sloppy, while her pale eyes and pastel coloring lacked the dash that brunette Norma possessed. Norma could make her look like Miss Halloween of 1898, decided Peg.

Entering the lobby in high gear, Peg approached a young man at a desk who was checking in a group of employees.

"Can you tell me where I'll find the casting office?" Peg inquired.

"Have you got a pass?" the young man asked.

". . . Well, no."

"You'll have to get one."

"Where'll I do that?"

"Try writing in," was his rebuff, which was obviously intended to end the interview.

Firmly standing her ground, Peg argued, "I'm here representing my daughter." Then, handing him the packet of slides, she continued, "You're probably familiar with her work. She poses for illustrated songs." The man showed a flicker of interest, so Peg ventured, "She'd like to get into work that's more of a challenge."

Returning the slides, the young man picked up a questionnaire. "She can fill this out and mail it back with two cabinet-sized photos."

"But—"

"Stand aside please, and let the folks in."

"But—"

"You'll hear from us if there's an opening!" By this time Peg was pushed out of line and there was nothing to do but retreat.

Unswerved, Peg proceeded to obey instructions. She induced Marvin's father to come through with the cabinet photos at a "professional" rate and mailed them, special delivery, to the studio along with the questionnaire, which had become largely a pack of lies. There followed endless days of waiting at home, with Peg's ear cocked toward a phone that never gave a tinkle.

After a couple of weeks, Peg decided to board the trolley for Flatbush again, this time with Norma in tow. Once more Peg roused her child at dawn.

"Why do we have to start so early?" Norma whimpered.

"Sh!" answered Peg. "We've got to be there while folks are arriving for work."

"But why, Peg? We haven't got any job!"

"Okay! We can mix with the mob and try to get past the gate."

Peg so often made sense that Norma's protests subsided. And, because Peg had read a recent ruling aimed at keeping kiddies out of show business, she again disguised her child as an adult.

Once inside the crowded lobby, Peg remained discreetly in the background until a last-moment rush of employees milled around the barrier, at which point she pulled Norma through unchallenged.

The two wandered along corridors until Peg spotted a door marked "Casting." An office girl, fooled by the fact that they'd overcome outer obstacles, ushered them in to her boss.

The boss proved to be a bullet-headed male who was engaged in an angry argument on the phone. "Look here, Breta," he was barking, "you attend to *your* department and let me attend to mine!" Slamming down the receiver he turned to Peg and belted out, "Yes? What *is* it?"

"I mailed you some photos of my daughter Norma," Peg spoke up, "but I thought it might be better if you met her in person."

Without even looking at Norma, the man snapped, "Yeah? Well, I'll call you if there's an opening."

"Thanks," said Peg, trying to appear grateful.

But when they reached the door, that hatchet man added a warning. *"Don't bring your daughter back here unless we call you!"* Sensing his words to be the kiss of a cobra, Peg retreated.

Peg and Norma made their way down the hall, at which point two office workers appeared and one of them, hailing the other, called out, "Hi, Breta!" The name "Breta" was unusual; she must be the object of that casting director's fury. Instantly Peg took hold and, stopping the woman, asked, "Do you work here, Modom?"

"Yes. I'm the scenario editor."

"What a coincidence!" exclaimed Peg. "I'm looking for a really *professional* opinion on my daughter." She tilted Norma's chin to bring her face into prominence.

Norma's budding beauty seemed to impress the woman, who now asked, "Have you taken her to our casting director?"

Making a wry face Peg answered, *"That amateur?"* Peg knew that among show folks "amateur" is the terminal insult.

And Breta, in a fine spirit of revenge on her enemy, said, "Come with me!"

Breta Breuill led her charges to a stage where filming was about to begin. The set represented an artist's studio, and the scene required his jealous wife to barge in and discover that a pair of attractive female feet were visible below the portiere. The director was about to order his script girl to fill in for the job when Mrs. Breuill persuaded him to use Norma. And at the end of the day, Peg collected two dollars and fifty cents for her child's labor.

It didn't matter that Norma's beauty was hidden by a portiere. Peg had succeeded in outwitting that tough casting director. Her most fervent prayer had been answered. *"God grant me a toehold!"*

Constance (left) *and Norma Talmadge in their silent films of the 1920s were objects of desire for men; for women they were models to emulate. In this study, New York's most stylish photographer, Charlotte Fairchild, caught the lively banter, the lack of pretension, and the total absence of rivalry between the two. (The Museum of Modern Art/Film Stills Archive)*

Above: *The other Talmadge sister, Natalie, nicknamed Nate, couldn't make the grade as a star, and her resilient mama decided on a career as wife and mother for her. In due course Nate and husband Buster Keaton supplied Peg with her first grandson.*

Opposite: *In appearance Peg Talmadge (shown here with Nate and grandson Joseph Keaton) gave no intimation of Norma's and Dutch's peerless beauty. Her pale blue eyes were small, and she had a scooped nose and an overstuffed figure. But Peg, having placed all her bets on Norma and Dutch, didn't much care what she looked like.*

Although the script of our first success with Norma, The Social Secretary, required her to disguise herself as a homely girl, Norma's image on screen always smacked more of socialite than secretary. (*The Museum of Modern Art/Film Stills Archive*)

Joe Schenck and Norma (opposite, above) on their honeymoon on Long Island. Joe had already become more than Norma's bridegroom. He was her Pygmalion, Santa Claus, and Sugar Daddy—and the son-in-law of Peg Talmadge's fondest dreams. In this snapshot, taken in Bayside, Joe had briefly annexed a neighbor's child, who was to be as much of a family as Norma would ever grant Joe or any other husband.

Opposite, below: *In movies the Talmadge girls might sparkle with spangles, but in real life they had a natural bright glimmer all their own.*

The team responsible for A Virtuous Vamp (above) *tried in vain to appear casual for this photograph. Director John Emerson, at left, carefully arranges his favorite profile above his scenarist and unofficial fiancée, A. Loos. Dutch pretends an interest in the script held by Assistant Director Sidney Franklin, and at far right is our young cameraman, Oliver, brother of the silent star Mae Marsh. Oliver Marsh had gotten his job through influence but he eventually developed into one of Hollywood's ace cameramen. (The Museum of Modern Art/Film Stills Archive)*

Opposite, top left: *Joe Schenck's first choice as a leading man for his wife was Eugene O'Brien. This photo shows Gene and Norma in* Graustark, *filmed in 1925. (Courtesy of Lester Glassner)*

Opposite, top right: *Irving Berlin and I were photographed here in Baden-Baden, where we had gone for a "cure," but Dutch was cavorting far away, which supplied no cure for Irving.*

Opposite, below: *At the time Peg was trying to get Joe Schenck to annex me on Dutch's behalf, I was under contract to Doug Fairbanks, who was in his second year of stardom. I had written most of Doug's scripts from the beginning, but he was getting fed up with depending on a small female scrivener, and I was yearning to get to New York. And thus began seven years of hoopla with the Talmadge clan.*

Nathan Gibson, our favorite New York milliner and very precious friend, kept up with fashion trends through tax-exempt trips abroad. Here Gibby studies the fashions in feathers as worn by the pigeons of Venice.

Sweet Are the Uses of Perversity

So Peg had outsmarted that enemy casting director and, thanks to the connivance of Breta Breuill, Norma was able to keep her toehold at Vitagraph. Peg made it a practice to board the trolley to Flatbush when the kids were safely in school. There she took up a post in Breta's office, where she had a permanent toehold of her own.

Breta found Peg an antidote for many of the troubles that plagued her. The studio abounded in sons, daughters, in-laws, nieces, and nephews of its flamboyant head, J. Stuart Blackton. As none of them had either talent or looks, they all wrote scenarios. Peg, forever on the watch for a possible opening for her child, used to read those scripts, and she earned Breta's loyalty by criticizing their authors. "Those sons-of-bitches could even louse up *Cinderella*!"

Breta enjoyed a wholesome entente with the entire staff of Vitagraph directors, and she was able to usher Norma into a group of "regulars" who got first call on extra work and sometimes even played bit parts. When such a plum fell her way, Peg allowed Norma to skip school. "Why waste time learning that the capital of Kansas is Topeka, when there's good money to be earned in Flatbush?" Peg would ask herself, knowing the answer full well.

Norma's apprenticeship had gone on for over a year, during which she had appeared in over one hundred short subjects, including *A Tale of Two Cities,* when at last opportunity rang a bell. It came about through the fact that occasionally the script department ran short of story material, at which times Breta, inspired by any best-selling novel of the moment, would take to her typewriter and whack out an "original." J. Stuart would immediately rush the purloined story into production and thus beat the best seller to the silver screen.

Time came when an overcrowded schedule found all the studio's featured players busy in other productions, and Breta, still bent on proving that she could recognize talent better than that smart-ass casting director, wangled her chum's daughter into the film's leading role.

Actually Norma had a real contribution to make to silent movies. The technique of film acting is based on understatement. The camera so exaggerates that the mildest expression registers in a close-up as a grimace. Unrestrained emotion can frighten children in an audience; worse still, it can cause grown-ups to snicker.

The actors J. Stuart hired from Broadway had to forget the technique of projection they had learned on the legitimate stage. But it turned out that Norma, with her poker face, had nothing to unlearn.

Movie stars were created by audiences, who would focus on some new image and bombard the studio with fan mail. J. Stuart would then follow through and sign the promising actor or actress for his stock company. It consisted of about eighty regular members, who earned from twenty-five to forty dollars a week. A few, like Florence Turner and Maurice Costello, got slightly more—Maurice because he'd earned a certain standing in the legitimate theater and Florence because she doubled in the bookkeeping department and, when not on camera, wrote out the paychecks.

Norma was paid the maximum of forty dollars a week for her first leading role, after which Breta persuaded J. Stuart to add Norma to his stock company, where she drew the weekly minimum of twenty-five dollars and was put to use almost daily. Peg felt it was now expedient for her child to drop out of high school for good.

Even so, Norma's progress was blocked by stars who had the advantage of seniority. Peg found the situation further complicated because she happened to *like* the girls who were her daughter's rivals: Mabel Normand was a disarming zany; Lillian ("Dimples") Walker a harmless dumpling; Anita Stewart was conceded even by Peg to be the prettiest girl on the lot. In fact, it was frustrating that Anita was so sweet and unassuming because she provided Peg with no inspiration for wisecracks.

It took Peg more than two years to push Norma from a bit player into her second leading role, as the heroine of a propaganda film, *The Battle Cry of Peace*. This movie was designed to make World War I palatable to the masses and was produced at the behest of Teddy Roosevelt, with whom J. Stuart boasted friendship. Norma's performance won definite acclaim and J. Stuart raised her salary to $250 a week. But Peg was getting restive.

Meanwhile, Hollywood had begun to crystallize as the center of film activity. Every week Peg read the motion-picture trade publications that found their way into Breta's office. On one occasion she learned that the head of a new Hollywood film company had arrived at the Astor Hotel in New York on a scouting tour for talent. Norma's recent success had made her a natural for exploitation, so Peg had little difficulty in getting her a contract for four feature films at a munificent four hundred dollars a week, which to Peg seemed like an all-time release from penury. The company was committed to pay first-class railroad fare for Peg and Norma; Peg contrived to exchange this for four second-class tickets, with which they all got to Hollywood on the cuff.

The bright prospects and even brighter sunshine dazzled Peg, but not for long. She soon began to realize that the National Pictures Company lacked know-how; even more serious, it lacked sufficient backing. The settings were cheap, as were Norma's costumes, and for the title role in *Captivating Mary Carstairs* she was so badly lighted that Peg barged into the front office and complained. But there was no chance for retakes because the budget had run out, so Peg was brushed aside. The picture flopped, as did the company, and Peg suddenly found herself without a dime coming in.

Not only Peg, but her kids as well began to feel that the glamour of Hollywood was a hollow fake. On the other hand, Peg hated to be a quitter, and having learned through experience about fly-by-night concerns, she led both Norma *and* Dutch to the top producer of the entire industry, D.W.Griffith. And Peg found D.W. amenable to adding both her daughters to the rapidly increasing roster of actors he needed for the cast of *Intolerance.*

This time Dutch emerged into prominence ahead of Norma. D.W., who looked to real life for his inspiration, was amused by Dutch's offscreen clowning, and one day he plopped her into that Babylonian episode with her chariot and scallions.

Much to Peg's frustration, Norma, who had been a star in New York, was being overlooked. D.W. was absorbed in the filming of *Intolerance,* and the studio's other directors, engaged in turning out routine movies for ordinary release, felt obliged to copy the Master's faults as well as his virtues.

So they remained as unimpressed by Norma as D.W. was.

Soon Peg took to waylaying Griffith—even interrupting rehearsals with suggestions that he pay Norma a little heed. At that time I happened to be under salary to D.W. as the film industry's first resident scenarist. Among my chores in 1916 was a slapstick comedy called *The Matrimaniac*, in which Griffith had teamed Constance and the Broadway juvenile Douglas Fairbanks, who was as yet unknown in films. All I can remember of the plot is that Doug and Dutch spoke their marriage vows over the phone, because the groom, for some reason, happened to be trapped on top of a telephone pole.

Although *The Matrimaniac* was much less than a hit, D.W., worn down by Peg's hounding, sent for me and said, "I'd like you to write a film for the oldest Talmadge girl, one that could be directed by John Emerson. See what you can come up with."

The plot I came up with concerned a lady of wealth who, in need of a social secretary, turns Norma down because of the potential impact of so much girlish beauty on her impressionable son. So our heroine, in dire need, disguises herself as a homely girl and again applies for the job. This time she *is* hired . . . meets the son . . . and solely through her character as a noble young creature, wins his love. His mother, delighted by her boy's unusual interest in an ugly girl, fosters the romance. It ends in marriage, and on the first night of the honeymoon, the groom removes his bride's horn-rimmed spectacles, unleashing the full blast of her dazzling beauty. At which he utters the 1916 equivalent of "WOW." Happy ending!

The Social Secretary was a success and got rave reviews in the trade papers. And although I was unaware of it at the time, I'm sure that Peg put its author's name on a list of people who might come in handy on some future day.

Meanwhile, Peg began to realize that the Griffith Company was no place for either Norma or Dutch. They were not the

"Griffith type." D.W., deeply in love with Lillian Gish, was obsessed with *her* characteristics. His version of feminine allure was that of a timorous and helpless nubile creature, fleeing from sex to the extent of jumping over furniture to escape an embrace—a girl who, in extremity, would even faint dead away. And Norma, while in no way aggressive, had a flashy-eyed response to men that failed to turn D.W. on.

In the case of Dutch, Griffith was already supplied with a hoyden in Dorothy Gish, to whom he was committed out of his love and loyalty to her sister, Lillian. Peg realized that after the flop of *The Matrimaniac* and her one short scene in *Intolerance*, Dutch wouldn't be up for any further exploitation.

Peg was beginning to concede that she needed help . . . the kind of help that is engendered by s-e-x. She had raised her girls, through sheer force of derision, to be virgins. In the Talmadge family sex was treated like a joke, though not a very funny one. During the Vitagraph days Maurice Costello had cast eyes at Norma, telling her she'd never learn to act until she became a *woman*. Peg had learned that laughter was an invincible foe to sex, so when Norma reported Costello's argument to her mother, Peg said, "Ask the guy if he had to lose the Battle of Waterloo before he could play Napoleon." At this Norma giggled and found it no ordeal to remain chaste.

Norma had not been impervious to a certain Vitagraph star named James Morrison, with whom she was teamed in several films. But in those days sex, smothered by romantic overtones, manifested itself in the mildest form of dalliance. Besides, life at Vitagraph had been exciting enough without any sexual complications.

Nevertheless, Peg decided to take her kids away from the sort of timorous sex in vogue at the Griffith studio and to return East, where men were men. Norma didn't mind leaving Hollywood; one felt that she was indifferent to any surroundings. The only thing that Dutch regretted was leaving her clowning partner, Dorothy Gish. (As time went on the two would frequently be parted by work and gradually they drifted apart. There was little to keep the Talmadges and the Gishes very close in any event; much as Dorothy loved fun, she possessed the homespun qualities of her Ohio background, while Lillian, the serious one, would always seek out and idolize the intelligentsia.)

On their return East, Peg bypassed Brooklyn, where men, although sexy, were poor, and she settled for New York, taking up residence at a barely respectable hotel in the West Forties, from which she could attack the various Broadway agencies. Also, there were restaurants like Dinty Moore's and Reisenweber's that might serve as showcases for Norma. She was allowed to accept invitations from men in show biz, but always with strict instructions to be back at the hotel by midnight, when Peg would be lying in wait for a report.

Fortune lagged, however, and Peg had just about decided to take another trolley ride out to the friendly bustle of the Vitagraph Studio and to accept the penny-pinching tactics of J. Stuart. But one fateful night Norma came home to report on a party Peg had allowed her to attend with a harmless café society homosexual. The event had taken place at the Sixty Club, an institution founded by a group of glamorous Broadway stags: Flo Ziegfeld, Sam Harris, George M. Cohan, Billy Rose, Sam Goldwyn, and Joe Schenck. Those parties were held every two weeks in the ballroom of the Ritz Hotel on 54th and Madison, where a galaxy of crystal chandeliers shone down on the pick of the Broadway beauties. There the Follies girls were free from obligations to their sugar daddies and could disport themselves with their own kind. A few socialites were allowed in; one of them, Caleb Bragg, although tiresome, was endured because he was fostering the career of his secretary, a girl with a great voice named Ethel Merman (née Zimmermann).

Norma returned to Peg on the night in question and reported, "Mom, I've run into a problem."

"How come?" asked Peg.

"I met a guy at the party who owns the Palisades Amusement Park. He must be pretty rich because he's keeping Peggy Hopkins Joyce."

"*That* tramp?" said Peg, putting in her usual plug for chastity.

"While I was dancing with the guy he asked me to have dinner tomorrow at the Colony. But I'm sure he's going to make a pass. D'you want me to go out with him or not?"

"Go!" said Peg. "But *surprise* the guy! Don't even let him hold your hand!"

After Joe Schenck's years of easy success with the Broadway demimonde, Norma's surprise must have staggered him. And after the novelty of being held at arm's length, sex could offer Joe only one other new experience: marriage.

Joe was no Rudolph Valentino; his hearty appreciation of Jewish dishes was a constant hazard to his waistline. I think of Joe with the fondest memories, but they also bring forth the aroma of a special sort of smoked sturgeon that came from Barney Greengrass's delicatessen on West End Avenue. (Barney supplied all our favorite boyfriends, by parcel post if necessary, wherever they might be: Mike Todd, David and Myron Selznick, Billy Rose, and his equally appreciative bride, Fanny Brice.)

For all Norma's beauty, her sex appeal was not altogether superior to Joe's. Although he spent long sedentary weekends at poker regaled by large intakes of delicatessen, his trainer would appear on Monday mornings to take him jogging around the reservoir in Central Park. He was an outstanding example of the fascination that comes from power. Joe would have become a leader in any walk of life he chose. He had the casual self-assurance of one born to authority. It had first been put to use when he was a boy in the New York ghetto and delivered packages for a shady neighborhood drugstore. They contained drugs, and Joe's delivery route took him to the Broadway district and frequently to Park Avenue. Both Joe and his pal Irving Berlin made their first dimes as messengers for the underworld, where they spoke in the vocabulary of the gutter. But they both rose above their sordid backgrounds and became gentlemen. They were generous and good and, best of all, understanding.

Joe knew from experience the gritty undercurrents that lay beneath the surface of sex. He had an aggressive approach to it, which in his case was probably perfectly normal, but he realized that his sadistic inclinations would frighten a girl who was unschooled in the stranger necessities of sex. Deciding firmly to curb his violent impulses, Joe asked Norma to marry him.

There was no question of Norma's quitting her career. Joe would be so proud of the dazzling Mrs. Schenck that he would want to flaunt his conquest. As for Peg, she had come to look on the movies as a way of life, and she could see that Joe was part of that life. Also, along with her discovery of trust funds came a new version of her old theory "Why not grab while the grabbing is good?"

Joe and Norma were married only two months after their first meeting. He was nineteen years older than his bride, but it seemed possible that she was in love with him—many a Broadway baby had been. I could understand being in love with Joe, because I've always been a pushover for power that's governed by gentleness. I hoped that Norma would appreciate that rare combination and I waited with curiosity to find out.

Movie Making in Manhattan

Joe Schenck, motivated by love, set out to back Norma's career with all the wealth and influence at his command. He was well versed in show business; he and his brother Nick had run Palisades Amusement Park for years, with enormous profit. Joe now owned a piece of Nick's Marcus Loew chain of motion picture cathedrals, where movies were shown in a Gothic splendor that managed somehow to be cozy. Joe realized he had a lot to learn about the movies. Before meeting Norma, he had taken a flier in film production, having backed a couple of pictures starring a sweetheart named Josie Collins, who was a vaudeville headliner. But those films had failed because Miss Collins's main accomplishment was "coon shouting," and silent films couldn't reach the ears of her audiences. Furthermore, Joe was disturbed because most of the Griffith Studio's films for Norma had been unsuccessful; only *The Social Secretary* had been a hit.

Joe felt that he needed help. His pal Sam Goldwyn, with whom he played regular weekend poker, had produced several hit pictures. Sam knew the score, so Joe tried to entice him into partnership by offering him twenty-five percent of Norma's productions. Sam was not tempted. "Norma's got a pretty face," Sam admitted, "but faces don't mean nothing to a box office. I wouldn't touch Norma Talmadge with a pole-foot-ten."

"Okay," said Joe, "I'll go it alone." At which Sam might well have quipped, That's what *you* think! How are you going to lose Peg Talmadge?

At first Joe made no attempt to lose Peg. Recently she had been impressed by a turgid stage play, titled *Panthea*, in which Olga Petrova, an equally turgid Russian beauty, had starred with huge success on Broadway. So, at Peg's urging, Joe purchased the screen rights from its turgid English author, Monckton Hoffe.

The star role was that of a beautiful Russian exile who makes a bloodcurdling escape from Siberia and is shipwrecked on the coast of Britain. The moment Panthea's beauty is revealed to the male population of London, she is beset by further calamities. She falls in love with a handsome young musician but finds out that he is broke, and in order to finance a grand opera he has composed, Panthea must give herself to a rich old roué. But the composer, finding out about the affair, goes mad with jealousy, at which Panthea, in order to prove how she *really* feels about her seducer, shoots him dead.

"Oh, what have I done?" gasps Panthea, as she is once again forced to flee for her life. But bad judgment takes her back to Moscow, where she is arrested for her initial offense and sentenced to Siberia for life, indicating that she might just as well have stayed home in the first place.

But the dawn can rise again, even in Siberia. The lover for whom Panthea risked life, liberty, and the most elaborate collection of dresses ever to grace the silver screen tracks her down. There, in the frozen wastes of the Arctic Circle, the composer attains uninterrupted contact with his loved one. (And, let us hope, a piano.)

After Sam Goldwyn turned Norma down, Joe had made an affiliate of a very young director named Allan Dwan, who appreciated Norma to the extent of going into partnership with Joe. He directed *Panthea*, Joe's first starring vehicle for Norma, and always remained close to Joe through his long career as a director of important pictures. (Allan is in his nineties today, and he doesn't enjoy directing any longer, but he has his fun and still goes dancing with pretty girls.)

As Norma's leading man on that extraordinary sea of soapsuds, Joe chose the tall, blond and handsome Earle Foxe, who later had a real-life adventure that was much more dramatic than his pursuit of any Russian sexpot.

A year later, in World War I, Earle enlisted in the army and was sent to the French front, where he quickly rose to a lieutenancy. On one occasion Lieutenant Foxe found his unit trapped in an enemy gas attack. Remembering an obscure tactic to prevent asphyxiation, Earle quickly ordered his men to moisten their handkerchiefs and use them to screen their faces. Now the only source of liquid available to men on a battlefield is a rather indelicate one to mention, but the device worked; the entire battalion would have been wiped out, except for Earle's presence of mind. The young lieutenant was decorated and raised to a higher rank.

By the end of the war, Earle had become enamored with army life. Instead of going back into the movies, he opened a military academy for the youth of the film area. The Foxe Military Academy has educated three generations of sons of movie people. Chalk up at least one heroic ending for a real-life Hollywood story.

The success of *Panthea* was so enormous that every time Sam Goldwyn thought of having turned down twenty-five percent of Norma Talmadge he burst into tears. One might have thought Joe Schenck had nothing in the world to bother him. However, one day when I happened to be in New York, Joe sent for me. As I ventured into his elaborate office, Joe seemed harassed, and he didn't wait to launch into what was troubling him. "Look, Nita," said he, "I have to manage some way to get Peg Talmadge off my neck!"

"But why?" I asked. "Isn't she satisfied with *Panthea*?"

"It isn't *that*!" sighed Joe. "Now she's after me to make a star out of Dutch!" Joe wiped his brow as he continued. "And it's not only Peg. Every time I try to romance my own bride, she shoves me off and asks, 'When are you going to produce a film for Dutch?' " (Norma was already shoving Joe off. Oh dear!)

"I don't have any grand illusions about Dutch's talent," Joe continued, "but then neither does she. Dutch is slaphappy and she hates work." Joe then came to the crux of our meeting. "But now Peg has suggested that I get you and John Emerson to write and direct a film for Dutch, like *The Social Secretary,* the one you did for Norma. Would you be able to transfer your activities to New York?"

From early childhood my dream of earthly bliss had been to live in New York, but I was firmly entrenched in Hollywood, where I had been under contract to Doug Fairbanks, along with John Emerson, from the time Doug first organized his own producing company. I doubted we would be able to break our contracts, but I told Joe I'd take the matter up with John.

Over a long-distance phone call John reminded me that our association with Doug had changed from the old days when we were three movie musketeers, one for all and all for laughs. John had never objected that the plots he directed were penned by a ninety-pound authoress. But worldwide acclaim had made Doug touchy; his male chauvinism had been bruised when the *Ladies' Home Journal* published my picture with the caption "The little girl who made Doug Fairbanks famous." When John asked for a cancellation of our contracts, Doug was relieved to be rid of us. And we were free of Hollywood forever. . . . Hurray!

John Emerson had had a long, distinguished career as director in the New York theater before he ever went into the movies. We had first met when he directed Douglas Fairbanks in a movie I had written called *His Picture in the Papers*. But it turned out that John was a frustrated dramatist, who chose to look on my scenarios as a "collaboration." When time came to edit that movie, the eminent director said to me, "Look, my child, it's rather humiliating for a man of my experience to accept second billing in our collaboration. Do you mind if my name appears ahead of yours in the screen credits?" I agreed, only too thrilled that an unknown like me could grant a favor to such an important man. And from then on my scripts, in which John's main contribution was to correct the punctuation, were credited to JOHN EMERSON . . . and Anita Loos. (It was one of those situations that would one day inspire women's libbers to coin the phrase "male chauvinist pig." But no women's libber could understand my deep-seated bliss in giving my all to such a man.)

Peg used to chide me for years afterward about the authorship of Dutch's movies. "If that guy you torch for was a ditchdigger," said she, "you'd dig him the Panama Canal!" But it was easier to laugh off Peg's joke than to laugh off love. And I must admit that after I finished a script, John Emerson deserved full credit for its survival. Most scenarists complained that their work was ruined in the filming, but mine reached the screen intact. If a script happened to be entertaining, nothing was lost. When I wrote a dud, it was there for all to see. But even *that* was satisfaction of a sort, because it pinpointed the blame and taught me a lesson.

When our contracts with Joe went into effect, Joe gave us free rein to do anything we liked with Dutch. "If it works out, fine. But even if it doesn't, it'll get Peg off my neck and give me a chance to be a bridegroom for a little while!" (Oh dear, I thought. *Oh dear!*)

I then began to cudgel my brains for the best way to transfer Dutch's unique allure onto film. I felt I knew her as well as I had known Doug, whose personality I had dramatized for the first two years of his career. There had been no point in trying to make an actor out of Doug, nor would there be in trying to make an actress out of Dutch. But, to my mind, both of them were *better* than actors; they were in themselves enticing personalities. Dutch no more needed a plot than a kitten needs a dictionary.

I had dramatized Doug's screen characters from what he was in real life. Stunts and jokes came first with Doug, while sex had to be barely indicated. If I ever ventured into sentiment, Doug would send for me and say, "Dammit, I'm no actor. I can't play a love scene." So I'd cancel the sex activities and have Doug jump off an airplane. But with Dutch I couldn't dodge the sex issue, for she was a natural-born honeypot.

I had learned a lesson in script writing from another sexy lady, Marion Davies. I had shown men pursuing her for no other reason than that she looked adorable in close-ups. But those static shots bored everyone except W.R. Hearst, under whose orders I had included them. So I reasoned that no matter how pretty a heroine is, an audience is interested only if she has some insurmountable obstacle to overcome. Only when she *does* succeed has she proven the film worthy of its footage.

Our first movie for Dutch was adapted from *The Bachelor,* an old play by Clyde Fitch. (Fitch was acclaimed as "the American Oscar Wilde" in his time but today he is largely forgotten.) *The Bachelor* had flopped on Broadway, but John remembered it from his youth, when he had been stage manager for Fitch.

My archives mention another movie John and I filmed with Dutch in 1919, *A Temperamental Wife,* which I recall as an attempt to mix politics with sex. It concerned an unwordly young senator from Nevada whose flirtatious wife misunderstood her husband's association with his secretary. But everything worked out for the best when the senator's wife spied on his behavior and learned that his life was pretty dull during executive hours. The heroine was glad to scamper back to her Washington boudoir, where the action belonged.

But our following picture, *A Virtuous Vamp,* posed a more complicated problem. In order to make Dutch's romantic achievements seem difficult, I would have to show her in love with a man whose emotions were so atrophied that she would have a hard time bringing his libido to the surface. Okay. Our hero must be so entrenched in his own affairs that when he finally succumbs to Dutch's sex appeal, her triumph is noteworthy.

My script completed, John handed it to Joe, who approved it without giving it more than a glance, if that. When Joe passed it on to Peg, however, she called for an immediate conference in a tone that boded trouble.

Peg charged into Joe's office, shaking that script in my face. "How *dare* you do this to Dutch?" she screamed. "Dutch, who's been proposed to by every goddamn bachelor in the entire Racquet Club! And this character of yours chases after a man as if she looked like ZaSu Pitts!"

Joe did a little squirming but Peg didn't pause long enough to let him speak. "This script of Nita's treats Dutch as if she had smallpox, or a permanent case of Chinese rot!"

John kept silent, feeling there was no use going into the technicalities of plot construction with an ignoramus like Peg. But I resorted to argument. "I see your point," I told Peg, "but if our leading man pursues Dutch, it gives all the action to *him*!"

Joe now spoke up. "Why can't you trust Nita and John? They certainly did all right by Doug Fairbanks."

"Doug's an animated monkey!" Peg declared, which to her mind clinched the argument.

But now Joe, who was basically a true tycoon, made a stand. "Look Peg," said he, "I've set a deadline for this film that's going to be kept!" And turning to John he added, "Go ahead and meet your starting date!"

But Peg, still rejecting defeat, stopped on her way out to toss me one last barb. "If you want an audience to believe this trash, you'd better put in a subtitle that says Dutch has halitosis!"

As soon as filming began, Joe whisked Norma off to Atlantic City to try and recapture his honeymoon.

Our hard-to-get hero was played by Conway Tearle, whose British manners and good looks made up for my character's self-centered density. Dutch went through her paces in her usual carefree manner; I don't imagine she had even bothered to read the script. When Peg and I met, she glowered but nodded; she didn't even nod to John Emerson.

Our picture was almost finished before we decided on a title, but then Irving Berlin, taking a cue from his unrequited wooing of Dutch, sardonically came up with *A Virtuous Vamp*.

When we previewed the film in Newark, we watched an entire audience fall head over heels in love with Dutch. Her lack of vanity was so apparent that even the women in the audience viewed her charms without resentment. (In real life Dutch would frequently cause Nate's suitors to defect, to which Nate's invariable reaction was "I wouldn't respect a guy who *didn't* fall for Dutch. He wouldn't be a man at all! The hell with him.")

At the end of our preview *A Virtuous Vamp* was applauded,

an audience reaction that rarely occurred in early days. I wish I could see that movie again—watch Dutch make Conway Tearle lose his British cool and be swept into a savage passion that drove that Newark audience half wild with its own sublimated desire for Constance Talmadge.

Afterward came the reviews. One was by the poet Vachel Lindsay, the first writer of distinction who ever reviewed movies. His article appeared in that highbrow vehicle *The New Republic* and read: "Anita Loos has written a scenario in the purest tradition of Greek comedy—a gem. And Constance Talmadge is a new sweetheart for America; one who rises above the coy mannerisms of filmdom and attains a sharper sweetness all her own." On reading this Peg proclaimed, "That Lindsay guy is nuts! Furthermore, he's got a mash on Nita!" (The latter statement was quite true.)

Following the success of *A Virtuous Vamp,* Peg had the grace to show a sheepish regard for me; but I was out of sorts with her. She had put me through so much distress that I felt sure I'd never laugh at Peg again, no matter what the provocation.

Then, one afternoon at the studio, I was in the cutting room with the smart young expert who used to cut and title our films. He was so dedicated to his job that he had shown up for work on the very day his wife had given birth to their first baby, a boy—a pretty important event in the life of a young Orthodox Jewish couple.

Presently Peg stepped into the cutting room to congratulate the new daddy. "But why aren't you with the wife and baby?" asked Peg.

"Oh you know me, Peg," said he. "Nothing interferes with work."

"Yeah?" answered Peg. "Then when are you going to cut and title that son of yours?"

Morrie broke up laughing—and so did I. How could anyone hold out against a crack like that? My feud with Peg was over.

While World War I was in full swing, its repercussions for us were pretty trivial. The battlefields were far away and newspaper headlines were actually glamorized by French names like Cambrai, the Somme, the Marne, and Belleau Wood.

The Talmadge girls and I belonged to an exotic world in which few men were young enough to be drafted. We had all become the creatures of older men, most of whom had gotten rich in a booming wartime economy: Norma's husband was a self-made multimillionaire. Dutch had been discovered by the Racquet Club, to which the gilded males of the Social Register belonged. Nate had a wealthy suitor who was courting her from Chicago, where he was in the wholesale dairy trade. Peg dubbed him Nate's "butter-and-eggs man," a phrase that was quoted in the gossip columns and entered the vernacular of the twenties as describing any male who was rich and dull. In the area of charisma, I had the pick of the lot, and the four thousand a week that John Emerson made as Dutch's director made him even more of a catch.

It was the era of the gold digger, abounding with millionaires who kept their sweethearts in love nests that dotted Manhattan all the way from Murray Hill to Riverside Drive. It was a situation the girls of the permissive seventies can't understand. "Do you mean they got *paid* just for *that?*" they ask in amazement. They did indeed, and when I wrote *Gentlemen Prefer Blondes* one of them supplied me with a wealthy heroine. The era was of short duration, however, for when the stock market crashed in 1929, men could no longer afford those surrogate households. So the love nests disappeared and the gold digger was replaced in our sexual economy by the call girl, who operated on a short-term basis. She's still around New York in limited numbers, but mostly for the tourist trade. Today's native New Yorker can pick up a quicker collaboration al fresco, on the sidewalk, or in our numerous massage parlors.

The most opulent gold digger of them all was Peggy Hopkins Joyce, for whom Joe Schenck had picked up the tab briefly before he fell in love with Norma. Peggy had an Art Deco type of blondeness that may have inspired her sugar daddy to put up the Chrysler Building in her honor. It is one of the few Art Deco skyscrapers in the entire world and remains today a fitting monument to the twenties, when a high-rise office building could be unblushingly decorated with curlicues.

The job of entertaining a sugar daddy could be tedious, however, and Peggy's real lover was an adorable young reprobate who was Cole Porter's alter ego and the producer of his musical comedies. His name was E. Ray Goetz, and he supplied the title of Cole's show *Fifty Million Frenchmen*. E. Ray had been inspired by an aphorism then going around that "fifty million Frenchmen can't be wrong." And what did those Frenchmen do that was *right*? It was something about which Cole only ventured to hint in those fastidious twenties. Today we can watch the whole unsightly procedure acted out in X-rated movies, yet Cole's naughtiness seemed a lot more rewarding then than hardcore porn does today.

One of our few friends who was young enough to be drafted was Irving Berlin. He was in training at Camp Upton, where he was the idol of the camp because of his song "Oh! How I Hate to Get Up in the Morning." Although it was antiwar, Irving's protest was so humanitarian that it actually served to boost recruitments.

I sometimes used to sit beside Irving at his tiny piano and listen while he composed. He would go over and over a lyric until it seemed perfect to my ears. Then he'd scrap the whole thing and begin over again. When I asked Irving what was wrong, he invariably said, "It isn't *simple* enough," a self-criticism that illuminates the reason for Irving's greatness.

Irving followed the pattern of all young men and fell in love with Dutch. But she had become involved with a wealthy young Greek, an importer of tobacco. Joe Schenck, who had been a friend of Irving's since they were boys in the ghetto, rallied all of us to put some anti-Greek pressure on Dutch, a project in which even Peg sided with Joe. For Irving was already as rich as any tobacco broker, and his royalties promised to go on as long as folks would ever smoke cigarettes.

"I just can't understand Dutch," brooded Peg. "It isn't a question of choosing between little Irving and some gorgeous Greek god. But why pick a guy who looks like a Greek waiter?" Peg's criticism was false, for Dutch's young man was extremely handsome. At any rate, neither Peg nor Joe could swerve Dutch, who simply explained her preference by saying that John Pialogiou was "different." My feeling was that Dutch's choice may not have been the American ideal of rugged male beauty, but that John was certainly as personable and attractive as he was "different."

On one occasion when Irving prevailed on Dutch to visit him in training, she recruited us girls to trail along. The entrance into Camp Upton of four flappers wearing knee-high skirts boosted morale no end. We were escorted into a barracks where we crowded around a piano and listened to little Irving sing: "I scrub the dishes against my wishes, to make this world safe for democracy." Irving's feeble, quavery voice only added to the impudence of that lyric in which war was protested by jokes instead of the bombs that, in those days, fell only on trenches, while we at home were living it up at ease.

The more patriotic movie stars were touring the country to sell Liberty Bonds. But when our eager publicist, Beulah Livingstone, urged Peg to let Norma and Dutch join the project, Peg put her foot down. "The only bonds that interest us," she declared, "are Standard Oil and A.T.& T."

The War Department had organized a flamboyant joint tour for Mary Pickford, America's Sweetheart, and Douglas Fairbanks, who, not content to be merely a film idol, had become a symbol of moral rectitude to the youth of the nation. Doug, as an ardent disciple of Teddy Roosevelt, didn't smoke, never touched alcohol, and put T.R.'s "strenuous life" into daily practice. Doug never sat when he could stand or walked when he could run, and furniture was only there to be jumped over.

Doug had long been married to the sweetheart of his youth, as Teddy Roosevelt had been, and Doug followed T.R.'s precept of remaining forever faithful. He had recently written a book in which he strongly endorsed marital fidelity. It was selling like popcorn at a circus—its readers unaware that the author, while penning that ardent plug for monogamy, had stumbled pell-mell into a guilty romance with America's Sweetheart, who, like him, was, alas, married.

In the midst of that delicate situation, Doug and Mary arrived one night at a Chicago hotel, where they were scheduled to sell bonds at ten o'clock the next morning. After they were ceremoniously escorted to suites on separate floors, they were suddenly awakened at 6:00 a.m. by fans in the street below, screaming for the stars to show themselves on their balconies. Peering apprehensively down from Mary's window, the guilty sweethearts watched a mob blocking the early morning traffic. And then, to Doug's alarm, he realized that all those fans were waving aloft his endorsement of marital fidelity and clamoring for autographs.

A large part of Doug's charm lay in his sense of humor, for it was he who ultimately relayed that joke on himself and told of his anguished moments until that mob was finally dispersed by mounted police. After which Doug suffered the further humiliation of trying to sneak down the back stairs to his own bedroom, incognito.

Their romantic snarl was finally straightened out when Beth Fairbanks divorced Doug on the most ladylike terms, refusing to mention her rival's name. A little later Mary got a Reno divorce from her film star husband, Owen Moore. The king and queen of movieland were married, and Cupid chalked up a love affair that made history.

But Cupid took a beating, as he so frequently does in Hollywood and everywhere else. I had a private warning that the Fairbankses' honeymoon was over when, on leaving a Hollywood premiere one night, Doug anxiously got me aside to ask, "Do you think Mary got more applause than I did?"

The filming of our silent movies in New York was marked by nonchalance, not to say élan. Norma's troupe occupied the ground floor of a ramshackle New York studio that was as lively as a Keystone farce. One film I recall was *Poppy,* in which Norma played the role of a beautiful native of the South African veldt. The role of Poppy's suitor, a staid British aristocrat, was played by Eugene O'Brien, for whom Joe had raided Broadway, where Gene was a leading juvenile for such stage stars as Ethel Barrymore, Fritzi Scheff, and Elsie Janis. He was tall, blond, wavy-haired, and so excruciatingly handsome that Norma's fans fondly dreamed she was betraying her husband with him. But like so many actors who are endowed with great looks, Gene felt it the part of modesty to make a clown of himself. So he would emerge from the most tender love scenes to ham it up raucously with Norma. Joe's honor was not in jeopardy . . . yet.

Dutch's troupe held forth with equal ribaldry on the second floor. In those silent scripts dialogue was merely indicated, and the actors made up their own, which was sometimes funnier than intended. I recall a film in which Dutch, as Cleopatra, was heralded by a Nubian slave on ascending her throne. The slave was played by a dark brown muscleman fresh from Harlem who had been coached to proclaim, "Hail Cleopatra, daughter of Ptolemy!" But when the camera started grinding, our Nubian flubbed his lines and announced, "Hail Clara Patrick, daughter of Talmadges!"

Our Nubian broke us all up, but the sparkle of that contretemps seemed to enliven the scene. Today, should any film director worth his salt film such a shot, they'd send to the Nubian desert for their slave, costing their investors several thousand dollars for a scene that would be as heavy as lead.

The third floor of the studio was enlivened by Fatty Arbuckle and Buster Keaton, who were slapping out farces that abounded in pretty girls wearing corsets under form-fitting bathing suits, and sporting high-heeled beach sandals. A plethora of custard pies flew through the air.

Our top floor had been rented out for a wartime movie, *Old France,* in which a newly discovered young German actor named Erich von Stroheim was enjoying his first big movie break in the role of a Prussian officer. When not on camera, Von used to leave the studio to prowl Fifth Avenue in full make-up, flashing his monocle at every pretty woman who crossed his path. Such behavior mystified passersby, who wondered how a German officer had been allowed to invade the USA in the midst of war.

Peg used to warn Von not to wear that uniform on the street. "You're making yourself a target for rocks!" she'd say. Von would agree, with an enigmatic smile, but he went right on courting disaster.

It seemed obvious that Von harbored the "Prussian" trait of loving to be hated. Yet, on the other hand, we knew him to be as sensitive as a kitten. It now seems possible that surging through Von's mind were the first stirrings of a film masterpiece, *Foolish Wives*. Perhaps in those lonely strolls, he was bent on condemning women instead of seducing them. In matters of Art one never can tell, and we didn't dream in those days that films and Art had anything in common.

(Years later when Von, shamefully dismissed from Hollywood, was living as an exile in the village of Maurepas outside Paris, he was decorated by France with the Cross of the Legion of Honor. But because Von was ill and getting on in years, the presentation only reached him on his deathbed. Von is buried in the small cemetery at Maurepas, and when I visit there and stand beside an impressive black marble slab that covers his grave, I'm still apologetic about our ignorance of his genius when we were all young.)

During the war, Dutch and I had an exciting moment when the Prince of Wales visited New York briefly. One day we were swinging along Fifth Avenue, when suddenly an open car breezed by with that blond young prince in the front seat by the driver. His Highness was so pertly handsome and had such a "come hither" air that Dutch impulsively called out, "Hello, Eddy!" The prince turned, got one flash of Dutch's dazzling beauty, and stood up in the car to wave back at her. (Little could we have believed that years later in London Dutch would consider H.R.H. so tiresome that she'd yearn to be back at an eatery run by Dinty Moore, among the playboys of Broadway.)

My one wartime experience that was in any way serious took place at the Paramount office, where I was summoned by a group of executives who were trying to lure me away from Joe Schenck. During our discussion, a military band on the street below struck up the national anthem. None of us was even aware of it except a boy named Adolph Zukor, who stood up and remained rigidly at attention. After an embarrassed moment, the remainder of us sheepishly joined him until the music died away. (Ultimately Zukor became president of Paramount, which he guided for a life that lasted through his one hundred and second birthday.)

Dutch and I became a little more closely involved in the war one afternoon at a tea dance in the Sherry Netherland Hotel. We were introduced to a distinguished Belgian military attaché, a certain Colonel Osterreith, who was on a mission from King Albert, who had made that historic stand against the invasion of his country by the Huns. The colonel had been sent here to distribute some gold medals that had been struck in honor of American aid to Belgium and to bestow them on our President, his Cabinet, and other gentlemen of distinction.

Now the worthy colonel should have been getting down to Washington, instead of which he became enamored of our studio. He used to spend hours watching scenes being filmed. Dutch christened him "Stuffy" because his uniform looked as if it were stuffed. His Excellency took the nickname in good part, since Dutch sometimes accompanied it with a friendly pat on his midriff.

Stuffy found Norma an enormously worthy target for his monocle, but as a dedicated ladies' man, he was disturbed that Gene O'Brien wasted time joking with Norma instead of making love to her. He one day made so bold as to ask Peg, "Tell me, madam, is Monsieur O'Brien a homosexual?" At which Peg staunchly defended Gene by declaring, *"Not even!"*

Stuffy developed a rather professional attitude toward the cinema and soon began to venture helpful suggestions to anybody he could corner. One day he interrupted Fatty during a scene for a movie titled *Fatty at Coney Island* to declare excitedly, "I've just discovered a young creature you must put into this scene!" Then, forcing Fatty to accompany him upstairs, he revealed his "discovery." Fatty thanked the colonel for his tip but told him he'd already tried the actor out. "I had to fire him because he has no film potential, his emotional range is limited, he isn't photogenic, and he has sore feet." These faults were too technical for Stuffy's understanding, so he gave up trying to promote Charlie Chaplin.

Stuffy's dull life in diplomatic circles had caused him to look on our studio as heaven on earth. I'm sure he dreamed that just as soon as he got around to completing that mission for his king, he'd spend the remainder of his life on East Forty-eighth Street.

We all loved Stuffy and were disturbed when his visits suddenly ceased. We never saw him again and we never learned the reason, but I think he must have been a war casualty. For a day had come when his ebullience overflowed and Stuffy bestowed the king's medals on Dutch, Norma, Peg, Natalie, me—and even Norma's secretary, Anne, for her wartime achievement of being young, pretty, blonde, and accessible.

Those crude old silent films that Joe Schenck produced with so little effort and so much fun had a vitality missing from many a Hollywood superspectacle that costs time, energy, and zillions of dollars. And although we never knew it, Art was beginning to stick its nose through the chinks of Joe's ratty old studio, summoned by the youthful genius of Buster Keaton, Erich von Stroheim, and Greta Garbo.

Bubbles from a Tub of Glorified Soapsuds

My fond association with the Talmadges continued until 1925, involving several lively years that were embellished by my writing thirteen soap operas for Dutch and several for Norma while living through a real one of my own. Following *A Virtuous Vamp,* John resurrected another unsuccessful play, this time by a minor playwright, Antony Wharton. It was titled *At the Barn,* but cashing in on the vogue for Elinor Glyn's naughty novel *Three Weeks,* we condensed the sin and called our movie *Two Weeks.* Censorship required that marriage be the happy ending, so our heroine, unlike Elinor's, had to hold out for a marriage license.

John Emerson, a true devotee to the pleasures of leisure, devised a scheme whereby someone else would do the hard work while he lolled in a camp chair and supervised. He chose a young director who had mastered all the technicalities of his craft but had never learned to grant reality to human behavior. Had Sidney Franklin been ordered to direct *Romeo and Juliet,* he would probably have failed to include the balcony scene. But under John's supervision, the love scenes in *Two Weeks* were

CHAPTER FIVE

treated with expert know-how. And why not? During his career as a New York actor, John had seduced half the leading ladies of Broadway. Because John had begun to find our work together so time consuming, he had little opportunity for outside conquests, so as a sideline to teaching Sidney Franklin the tactics of seduction, he started to practice on his collaborator. I, who had tried to become a woman of the world to get John's attention, could now smile smugly at Peg, who had often said to me, "Will you stop hankering after that old boy? He's too cagey to be hooked by a kid your age!"

John's and my next collaboration for Dutch, *In Search of a Sinner,* was based on a magazine story by Charlotte Thompson. It concerned a young widow who had suffered extreme boredom with a husband who was a model of rectitude. As a widow, she falls in love at first sight with a handsome stranger. But on second sight, he proves to be even more righteous than her sainted husband was. The only course open to the young widow is to drag her loved one from his boring state of grace.

In those days the ladies' clubs of our country were self-appointed film censors and supposedly had great influence at the box office. Joe was worried that the club ladies would resent our heroine's trying to corrupt a good man. But when the hero started making passes at other girls, his fiancée began to yearn for his return to a life of probity. The theme that "love conquers all," including boredom, saved us from being blacklisted by the ladies' clubs.

In the cast were Rockliffe Fellowes, Gilda Gray, and Ned Sparks. Gilda had recently come to fame as the originator of a dance craze, the shimmy, and Ned would become one of Dutch's favorite clowning partners, on screen and off. The movie chalked up one more hit.

Our next film, *The Love Expert,* another "original," concerned a hero who was burdened with the upkeep of three virgin relatives and thus blocked from a marriage of his own. Our heroine, in order to liberate the man of her dreams, is forced to find husbands for three old maids, who were truly frightful. John cast Dutch's sister Natalie as one of our heroine's obstacles. But, instead of making good as an ugly girl, Nate merely made her dull, which ended her acting career and sent her back again to answering fan mail.

Looking about for an improvement on Sidney Franklin, John had re-engaged David Kirkland, a young director who had gotten his first kicks as a lieutenant during World War I and who had worked with John on *A Temperamental Wife* and *A Virtuous Vamp*. Kirkland proceeded to turn in a fine job on *In Search of a Sinner,* with so little trouble for John that he decided to take Dave on permanently. But by the time *The Love Expert* was completed, John began to have some second thoughts about Dave. For in my new status as woman of the world, I had become close friends with the young director, and John's carefree attitude toward my services was beset by apprehension. Suddenly he began to fear that our collaboration was being threatened by Kirkland, and in order to protect his standing as an author, he withdrew his longtime objection to marriage and asked me to be his wife. (The situation resembled an Emerson-Loos movie plot, showing how closely life can imitate soap opera—or perhaps how much involved we were with our work!) I couldn't wait to get to Peg and flaunt my triumph, but she simply observed, "Well, Buggie, Dave Kirkland would make a whale of a husband, but you'll be happier with some loafer who grabs your paychecks!"

Our marriage took place during a seventh collaboration on a film for Dutch, *The Perfect Woman.* Another "original," it told of a heroine who falls for a clod who hates girls and doesn't even prefer boys. Its cast is lost in the limbo of silent films, except that once again Ned Sparks filled Dutch's screen and private life with laughter. And Dave Kirkland, no longer a rival of John's, still hung in as director.

John's and my wedding was held at a lavish estate that Joe and Norma occupied in Bayside, Long Island. The ceremony was a perfect excuse for a typical Talmadge whoop-up. During the ceremony the groom's responses were so weak that Joe Schenck, as John's best man, had to come through with them. Henceforth, Joe used to make a joke of it and loved to repeat, "Nita's really married to *me*!" (If Joe's joke had only been true, it would have saved John, Joe, Norma, me, and even Peg a lot of grief.)

Since Dutch's career was now safely in orbit, Joe granted us newlyweds leave of absence for a honeymoon. Always happy to shake the movie stardust from our feet, we proceeded to Europe, while Dutch left for the tawdry shores of Miami to film *Good References*.

Good References was taken from a short story and it turned out to be the first disappointment of Dutch's career as a star. To begin with, there was little stimulation in its title, which tends to conjure up the dreary image of work. Its plot, about a good girl who sets out to reform a bad boy, was even worse. The scenarist, Dorothy Farnum, had completely missed the perversity of Dutch's charm.

I was swishing about Paris among the playful followers of Elsa Maxwell when a cable arrived from Peg! "Come back here quick. They've got the Dutchman playing a faithful wife!" Peg's plea was followed by one from Joe, who summoned us back to home base.

Art, like love, had a long and lumpy road to travel in those days and it got precious little help from the likes of Peg. In her attempt to find material for the girls' pictures, she took to reading the pulp magazines, and her choices as a rule were just what the public wanted. Joe lovingly placed each "literary" gem into an expensive setting and tried to perfect his knowledge of film production by trial and error. Peg's second selection for Norma, however, something called *The Law of Compensation*, brought complaints from fans that Norma's suffering lacked the exotic undercurrents of *Panthea*, and that her dresses reflected only the restrained taste of Park Avenue.

So for Norma's next film Joe took heed of an earlier success made by Mary Pickford, entitled *Tess of the Storm Country*, and he hired one of Mary's pet scenarists to cook up a sequel. It was called *The Secret of the Storm Country*, and for realism, the exteriors were filmed on the exotic snowfields of Ithaca in upstate New York. As an innovation, Joe switched Norma's leading man and substituted Niles Welch for Gene O'Brien. Alas, Niles's baby face lacked the menace that underlay Gene's sophistication. Fans and critics alike complained that in the love scenes Norma's virtue wasn't sufficiently at stake.

So in 1918, Joe again cast Gene O'Brien as Norma's leading man. The film, called *Ghosts of Yesterday*, was based on a play in which David Belasco had starred a red-haired socialite-turned-actress whom he snobbishly billed under her private name, Mrs. Leslie Carter.

The plot concerned a ravishing beauty married to an impoverished young artist so destitute that he is forced to use his wife as a model. While the two gorgeous specimens are thus unprofitably engaged, the wife dies of malnutrition. Her widower is burdened with guilt at never having gotten himself a paying job, but he continues to paint and is ultimately successful. He then meets a girl who is a ringer for his dead wife. (She was also played by Norma, but this time well nourished and dressed in gorgeous gowns by Mme. Frances.) The hero undertakes to paint a portrait of his dead love's look-alike, and in the process, confused by the resemblance and overcome by memories, he marries her.

Once again bad luck ensues. The new bride resents her husband's love for her predecessor. She leaves him, only to return on learning that he has gone blind. (Countless handkerchiefs were dampened by that movie, and it may even have inspired Mr. Lasker to promote Kleenex.) Tears aside, *Ghosts of Yesterday* established Norma and Gene as screen lovers, and Joe kept them together for the ten pictures that followed.

Next came *By Right of Purchase*, in which Joe presaged the advent of cinéma vérité, for the main scene was filmed in "Hero Land," a lavish charity bazaar conducted in the Plaza Hotel ballroom for the relief of war victims. The most prominent New York debutantes milled through the crowds, collecting donations in large cardboard cylinders of red, white, and blue. The bazaar's entrepreneuse was the famed international hostess Elsa Maxwell.

By Right of Purchase was about a feckless young socialite who flits from pillar to bedpost, working her way in and out of seductive gowns designed by Mme. Frances. In spite of her high spirits she wins the love of a worthy young millionaire, who succeeds in calming her down. Its hero, naturally, was Gene, and Norma wangled a bit part for a friend named Hedda, who had become the wife of veteran stage star DeWolf Hopper in a May-December marriage.

It turned out that "Hero Land" had harbored an enemy, who was caught making her getaway on a French liner with a quantity of red, white, and blue cylinders stuffed with green currency. The State Department barred the world's greatest party-giver from re-entering the USA for several years.

There was always plenty of time for fun in those days. As a writer of silent movies, I didn't have to bother with dialogue;

nor did Norma and Dutch have any lines to learn, while Nate's duties in the publicity department were negligible. Peg's gaiety made her just as much a girl as we were. It used to be a ritual to lunch at the Claridge Hotel, which was convenient for our girl friends in the Follies. On rehearsal days they could skip across Broadway to the New Amsterdam Theatre, where Fanny Brice held forth as a star, and show girls like Dolores and Nita Naldi won almost as much fame for merely stalking across the stage trailing a few yards of chiffon. Nita was also a wit who could match wisecracks with Peg, and at the same time retain her monumental beauty.

Most of the titles of Norma's films in those days were as provocative as her dresses from Mme. Frances and promised precious little of Park Avenue restraint: *The Branded Woman*, *The Isles of Conquest*, *The Passion Flower*, *Yes or No* (in which Natalie again played a small role, again convincing everyone, especially Peg, that she couldn't act).

Sometimes we all took lunch at Dinty Moore's, which resembled a vast yet cozy kitchen and was even further warmed by the sex appeal of its patrons, many of whom belonged to the sporting fraternity. But we went to Dinty's without Peg, who was uneasy among such stark virility. She may have been thinking of Mr. Talmadge when she'd proclaim, "Those crumb-bums never hand a girl anything but grief!" Just the same, we seldom had to pay a lunch tab at Dinty's; some Broadway gallant would always waylay it before it reached our table.

Dinty's was convenient to Tin Pan Alley, the stronghold of the song writers. One of them, John Golden, was a regular at Dinty's, and in addition to composing the popular song "Poor Butterfly," he was equally successful as a producer of Broadway shows. Johnny also pretended an interest in public affairs, which may only have been an excuse for his attentions to the neglected young wife of the rising politico Franklin D. Roosevelt.

There are those who pity Eleanor Roosevelt for having had no sex appeal, but I, for one, feel otherwise. It seems to me that the composer of "Poor Butterfly" was a much finer conquest than any gullible member of the Yalta Conference. People will forever be turned on by that torch song of Johnny's, and it was Eleanor Roosevelt who turned *him* on.

One day Dutch and I were witnesses to yet another conquest by Eleanor—none other than Dinty Moore himself. He was a tyrant, given to throwing patrons out of his place if he didn't approve of their taste. Should anyone order corned-beef hash *without* the onions, Dinty's screams would almost crack the ceiling. "Get outta here, you cream puff. I run this jernt strictly for conosewers!"

Eleanor's taste in food must have been formed by long attendance at political luncheons and Democratic banquets. One day when we were seated at an adjacent table, we overheard Eleanor's order: "You may bring me fruit cup, chicken croquettes, creamed peas, a chocolate sundae, and macaroons." We waited on tenterhooks for Dinty to give Eleanor the heave-ho, but it never took place. Her ladylike charm made Dinty restrain himself; he took down Eleanor's order without even wincing.

(Dinty's, like many of our hallowed landmarks, has disappeared. My last experiences there took place in the fifties during the rehearsals of *Gigi*, which I had dramatized from Colette's novel. The entire company used to troop into Dinty's at the lunch break, escorting Audrey Hepburn, who had just come over from London to play our title role. Audrey had suffered terrible privations during the Nazi occupation of Amsterdam, where she lived as a child. After the war Audrey's mother, the Belgian Baroness van Heemstra, fled to England with her child on the chance that they might find work there. But food was so expensive that the two were barely able to survive on the salary that Audrey earned in the chorus of *High Button Shoes*. When

Audrey reached New York to begin rehearsals in *Gigi*, she still regarded food as a breathtaking novelty. Dinty highly approved, but at the same time he was puzzled. "I just can't understand that kid," said he. "She acts as if she'd never had enough to eat." Dinty hadn't heard of the siege of Amsterdam, having been too busy hustling black-market beef.)

The Talmadge girls and I took frequent excursions into Harlem, which in those years was the gayest district in all New York. At night the population took to the sidewalks for its social life, which often included dancing. We never felt a hint of racial tension then. I got some insight into that question from my maid, who was about twenty-eight, statuesque and attractive, and who had a skin so pale that her bleached-blonde hair didn't seem incongruous. Because a light skin could command higher wages, some of Hazel's light-complexioned friends used to disguise the fact that they lived in Harlem. The owner of a dry cleaning establishment in Murray Hill allowed them to use his address and telephone number as a cover-up. One day I ventured to ask Hazel why she didn't "pass." "Why, I wouldn't be white for anything in the world," she explained. "You white folks let your big Cadillacs stand in front of the studio all the while, but if we colored folks owned an automobile like that, nothing could keep us from going on a picnic every day."

Hazel's attitude seemed so civilized that, by comparison, I suddenly felt like a clod.

Our shopping activities centered about such luxury spots as Bergdorf Goodman, Bendel's, Hattie Carnegie, Elizabeth Arden, Mme. Frances, and Patrick Herman Tappe, whose broad windows on West Fifty-seventh displayed what the well-dressed flapper would be wearing next.

Our choice of companions was typical of most show-biz females—we all went in heavily for hairdressers, milliners, and costume designers. Among the last-mentioned, Herman Tappe was unique, for he had a girl as a sweetheart, and when he married her, they went on a honeymoon to Niagara Falls, just like the most orthodox bride and groom. (They don't make dress designers like that today.)

But our very particular friend was a milliner named Nathan Gibson. We rarely went on a shopping tour that didn't wind up in Gibby's handsome white and gold salon, where he bustled among his clientele like a robust and warm-hearted aunty.

Gibby's patrons included many conservative Knickerbocker dowagers, for whom he designed a handsome type of hat inspired by Queen Mary of England. Gibby found the majestic type congenial, for he came from fine old colonial stock and owned property in upstate New York, where he could have lived as a member of the landed gentry. But Gibby's heart and soul belonged to millinery and the brouhaha that used to enliven the making of hats. Hats, believe it or not, once played a large part in the enticement of men. There's no mystery about today's hatless head, nor about a wig . . . unless it's the chilling contemplation of what must lie underneath it.

Although Gibby's prices were exorbitant, we never minded because his salon was such a hotbed of fun. One of his most risible clients (I'll call her Mrs. Duncan Peabody) was married to the governor of Massachusetts. But, affected by generations of New England culture, she had become delightfully dotty. She used to travel all the way from Boston to buy hats, but more specially to be mistreated by Gibby. For Mrs. Peabody was a dyed-in-the-wool masochist, yet so distinguished that nobody in Massachusetts dared bully her, while Gibby, in New York, provided her with the most exquisite malaise.

Masochism casts a more subtle spell than it is given credit for. A classic example is Greta Garbo, with whom friendly contact is almost impossible. But I know a certain young man who, while striding down Park Avenue, happened to pass Garbo going in the opposite direction. He gave her an impersonal glance, as a typical New Yorker might, and received no response. But about half an hour later, he happened to be trapped by traffic and suddenly realized he was standing a few feet from the great Garbo. This time *she* noticed *him* and glared him down. At which, being a typical New Yorker, he approached her and said in an accusing voice, "Miss Garbo, *are you following me?*"

There was a moment's shock and then suddenly she broke into a radiant smile. "*Yes!*" she replied. "Would you like to escort me to my doorway?" This he proceeded to do. And the pleasure was all hers.

So it was with Mrs. Peabody. People simply refused to belittle her . . . and it hurt.

There were times when Gibby used to call on us girls to give him a helping hand, and we would sit in the workroom merrily basting linings into hats, or inserting Paris labels into those Gibby himself had just tossed together in a matter of minutes.

One day when we were thus engaged, Gibby met the young creature to whom he would henceforth dedicate his life. A sporting friend sent Gibby a letter of introduction for a handsome young pugilist. The letter read, in effect, "This will introduce Ted, who is down on his luck. Could you suggest a way for him to get a little medium of exchange?" Big-hearted Gibby provided Ted with a stack of packaged stockings and a list of Park Avenue socialites to whom he might peddle them. The young man left, threadbare and forlorn, but when he reported to Gibby the next morning, he was driving his own red Stutz Bearcat, dressed exquisitely from the skin out by Brooks Brothers.

Another glorious shopping center we frequented was the dress salon of Mme. Frances. It occupied an entire brownstone in the East Fifties and was a rendezvous for the most expensively kept gold diggers in town. Frances herself was a sort of female Robin Hood; she would spot some poor, unknown cutie in the backwash of Broadway, send for the girl, and outfit her completely, from garter belts to *robes de style.* Then Frances would take the girl in tow and introduce her at the Stork Club. As soon as a romantic connection was made, Frances would present the gentleman with a bill for his sweetheart's finery. The process had the tempo of a dignified ritual and, as such, it made for permanence. Today there may be a few stately socialites on Park Avenue whose entire destiny was mapped in the salon of Mme. Frances.

The dresses worn by Norma and Dutch in films were paid for by the company, but for private consumption it was fun to shop for bargains. Our pal Fanny Brice, while starring in the Ziegfeld Follies with Will Rogers and W.C.Fields, had too much energy to expend on merely one career. So Fanny ran a dress shop at her apartment in the West Forties. "Come on up, kids, and look at my new collection," Fanny used to urge us. "I steal all my designs from Frances and the price is right."

Peg, while turning thumbs down on Dinty Moore's, never objected to us going there on our own. The one place she declared strictly out of bounds was the Algonquin Hotel. She had no patience with the exhibitionists of the Round Table, who had to ponder their wisecracks in advance and then cue each other in order to repeat them. It happened that two of its members were really smart, but when they cast sheep's eyes at Dutch, Peg warned her, "Stay away from Charlie MacArthur and that Hecht boy. Their foolishness will always keep them from getting anywhere," a prophecy that proved how wrong Peg *could* be.

And yet in later years, I remember that Peg thought quite highly of our foolhardy young mayor. For Jimmy Walker was surrounded by racketeers to whom graft was flowing in golden streams. Our mayor's female contingent reeked with sex appeal, for which reason it seldom included the mayoress. It's possible that she had been attractive as a bride, but years of a marriage that was flavored by martinis had widened her, and Jimmy's affections had been taken over by a chorus girl named Betty Connors. Jimmy, however, remained true to type, for Betty was just a younger version of his noisy wife. Indistinguishable from hundreds of her ilk, Betty might have been a Music Hall Rockette, and not even the prettiest girl in the line. But she had the right chemistry to turn our suave, sophisticated mayor into a City Hall dropout.

I remember one occasion when a large hegira took place from Broadway to Philadelphia for the premiere of a new musical. We all put up at the elegant old Ritz Hotel, which was noted for the length of its corridors. In the still hours following an opening-night party, Betty Connors noisily thrust Jimmy out of their suite without benefit of clothing. Simultaneously the doors along those endless corridors burst open as in a Feydeau farce. It seems to me that our mayor in the buff was a lot more appealing than the politicos of a later day in Washington when Fanne Fox and Elizabeth Ray were wooed by their respective congressmen.

Home Would Never Be Like Hollywood

Time rolled on in this merry way until finally Joe Schenck was tempted to give in to the lure of Hollywood. The California sunlight was free, while the klieg lights in our midtown studio were very expensive to operate. Although it had been a convenience to cast pictures with players from Broadway, a great many of them were moving West and joining a colony of utility actors, which simplified casting enormously: A marvelous organization called Central Casting had developed, with types helpfully listed under such headings as "rustics," "sophisticates," "beards," "midgets," "gigolos," "cockneys," and so forth. And, when it came to outfitting them, the huge Western Costume Company saved both time and money. One could film the glittering ball on the eve of Waterloo or the retreat from a burning Atlanta with very little preparation.

And so, on one blustery day in 1921 when New York was crashing into one more winter, Joe moved his troupe to California. It meant saying good-bye to the beloved old rattletrap studio, to the fascinating shops of Manhattan and their colorful shopkeepers, to Herman Tappe, Gibby, Mme. Frances, Fanny

Brice, our mayor, the glamour of the Sixty Club, and the sparkle of our girl friends in the Follies.

Joe would never cease to be homesick for New York, nor would my husband and I; the idea of returning to Hollywood made us determined to start up a truly international existence. Whenever possible we would take off for the capitals of Europe, only returning to Hollywood when it became financially expedient to do so.

The transfer of our studio from Manhattan's East Forty-eighth Street to Sunset Boulevard was an enormous project. Joe entrained our company as a group on the Twentieth Century Limited, from which we changed to the westbound Santa Fe in Chicago. I pity folks who never knew the railroads of our youth! Today a cross-country trip consists in processing human bodies from one teeming airport to another. The degradation starts with being frisked for firearms like common mafiosi, after which we are herded into places like mammoth capsules, identically fitted out with chromium and vinyl of cheap gaudy colors.

Those old Pullman cars, however, were palaces on wheels, in which we became part of a royal procession. The cars sparkled with polished mahogany, mirrors, brass, crystal, and hand-crocheted doilies. The trip to California took five days, during which we were served by porters chosen for their black charisma. They brought breakfast to our compartments, and we lolled in bed, savoring excellent coffee and gazing out on winter prairies where farmhands warmed their icy fingers with breath that rose like steam. There's no more exquisite joy than one that's based on sadism.

Once we arrived in Hollywood, our troupe took refuge in a sprawling old wooden structure—the Hollywood Hotel. And we immediately went to work at an outdoor studio, lighted by the sun. The lives we led in New York had encompassed as many different forms as there were social groups. But Hollywood was all of a piece. Its social life centered about the Thursday night dances in the lobby of the Hollywood Hotel, and they were a hangover from a time when Hollywood was a resort for middle-aged tourists who came to bask in the winter sun on the hotel's wide verandas. Its proprietress, Miss Hershey, was an ancient lady who tried to control the movie crowd that invaded her premises like a swarm of chimpanzees. Miss Hershey's austerity program forbade any hanky-panky on her dance floor; she was given to shoving amorous couples apart with the admonition, "Watch your manners, young people."

All of this was a far cry from the Ritz in New York and the glamour of the Sixty Club. Our main diversion was to bribe Miss Hershey's string orchestra to substitute for "Over the Waves" and "The Millions of Harlequin" with a sensuous number called "My Melancholy Baby."

There was but one example of escape from that hollow glamour. Theda Bara, who had made a fortune wrecking men's lives on film, had retired and, in the very shadow of her licentious movie image, forged her way into Los Angeles society. She was an earnest young woman who had found an objective more precious than her movie career. She wanted to be in society. Theda had paved her way by a series of romantic lies about her lowly past. She described her parents as being royalty in a tribe of Egyptian nomads and she even concocted an accent to prove it. She and her husband were listed in The Los Angeles Blue Book as Mr. and Mrs. Charles Brabin, and their parties made a gallant stab at culture. (Ethel Barrymore defined a "cultured" Angelino as anyone who hadn't been kicked out of grammar school.)

While she was on tour with a play, Ethel Barrymore spent some time studying the film community. She was the most classically beautiful actress of her day, and Norma stood in awe of her, but the feeling was not mutual. Senior by quite a few years, Ethel was apparently jealous of Norma's youth. One evening when the two stars met at a ball, Ethel exclaimed, "What a charming creature you are, my dear!" At which she effected a phony caress that smeared Norma's lipstick onto her nose.

Lacking communication with Ethel, Theda, or their kind, we remained mavericks even at the studio. It turned out to be a collection of yes-men of both sexes, among whom the acerbic Talmadge viewpoint wasn't appreciated. One day when Peg and her girls were entering the front gate, I overheard a comment: "Here comes the Leviathan and her three Dreadnoughts."

Before long we moved from the Hollywood Hotel into rented homes furnished in Hispano-Mexican fakery complete to the pepper and salt shakers. I spent my time cooking up plots for Dutch, going as far as possible in that age of restraint, sneaking in just enough sensuality to spark twitters in the audience. Once in a while Joe called me to his aid on some film of Norma's. She had completed a tearjerker called *Way of a Woman*, which had all the earmarks of a flop. Joe asked me to run it in the projection room and see if a few racy subtitles might help the situation. On watching the film, it struck me that the characters of Norma's husband and her lover might be switched; that if the lover behaved like a husband and vice versa, the audience might mistake the film for comedy and laugh.

Joe was skeptical about such a major switch in the story line, but he told me to go ahead, and the idea worked. Although never a good movie, *Way of a Woman* was saved from disaster. (Any motion picture cutter with imagination can conjure up a passable movie from scraps off a cutting-room floor, but a film editor of genius can dramatize even a hodgepodge of news clips into a masterpiece—which is probably where the first documentary came from.)

The love life of the three Talmadge girls was a fairly minor issue during this Hollywood phase. Norma's and Dutch's were largely confined to fan letters, numberless but not very stimulating. "I just seen your last picture and you was wonderful." Of course Joe's adoration of Norma never deviated, but she was beginning to get restless and to look around, not so much at other men as at the loot collected by her peers.

William Randolph Hearst was spending more on Marion Davies than Louis XIV had lavished on Madame de Maintenon. Actually, jewels meant so little to Marion that her most valuable accessory could have been a safety pin, but Norma was different. One day I overheard her tell Joe with blunt cruelty, "You'd be giving me bigger diamonds if I had never married you!" For in spite of Joe's adulation, he was never fatuous. He gave his wife the jewels he could afford as a simple millionaire; he would have considered himself uxorious and less than a man had he spent more than he had to satisfy the whims of his wife . . . or any other woman, for that matter.

Another excuse for Norma's rebellion at this time might have involved Joe's sexual habits, which tended toward violence as a show of affection. This undoubtedly produced a mass of tangled emotions—love, hate, ecstasy, and revulsion. I don't know, but I do know that the one thing that kept their relationship alive was the absence of indifference.

Peg was still searching the horizon to find a better mate for Natalie than Buster Keaton, but there weren't even any gigolos around to take up the slack.

And I feel that this may be an opportunity to hand a bouquet of poison ivy to the Southern Californian male of that day. In most cases he was a migrant who, having failed to make good in his native locale, had traveled to the West, where a sparse population reduced competition. But he always retained a gnawing lack of self-confidence that made for sexual timidity. There was little aggression even in the ranks of movie stars—none of the graceful give-and-take of courtship. A studio Casanova would express glandular urgency in a sudden lunge, but if it failed, he was inclined to let the matter drop.

Nevertheless, Dutch's sex appeal was so potent that even Hollywood's most confirmed bachelor was obsessed by her. Irving Thalberg, at the age of twenty-one, was the studio manager of Universal Pictures but so deeply in love that he even neglected work . . . a little. Every night Irving used to hide in the shadows across from the Talmadge residence in Beverly Hills and wait, just to watch Dutch return at dawn with the slaphappy young comedy star Bill Haines and his boyfriend. In one sense Irving couldn't be jealous, because Bill and his friend were as gay as jaybirds. But it was true that Dutch preferred laughing it up with them to making love with Irving.

I would like to take issue here with an opinion expressed by F. Scott Fitzgerald, who described Irving in *The Last Tycoon* as being coolly invincible to emotion. Dutch caused Irving to flounder in despair. Peg was quite content at Dutch's lack of enthusiasm for Thalberg. She had seen too much fly-by-night success and overnight disaster in the movie business to be impressed by such premature achievements as the young Thalberg's.

To Peg, movies per se would always be a risk. For some men, making movies was a kind of aphrodisiac, but how much longer would a man like Hearst be able to endure the enormous losses he was taking on Marion Davies? Or that Boston billionaire who was backing Gloria Swanson? Even though Joe Schenck did make money on both Norma and Dutch, he was backed by other assets that were far more solid. Peg fully appreciated the ample salaries of her daughters and the securities they allowed her to purchase, but she was anxious to get her girls back to the lustier manhood and sturdier affluence of New York City.

Eventually Joe Schenck came to Peg's rescue, as usual. Hollywood was headed into another searing hot December when Joe, homesick for the poker games of Broadway, decided to film some movies that called for Eastern backgrounds. Our excitement over going to New York for Christmas was unbounded. The stirring heat of Southern California couldn't help but inspire in us all a yearning for a snowy Christmas. True, the chamber of commerce did its best to fake one by turning Hollywood Boulevard into "Santa Claus Lane," complete with street signs dripping plastic icicles. Decorations everywhere blazed with poinsettias, which only reminded us of tropical Mexico and made us all the more homesick for holly, mistletoe, and the aroma of pine.

During the two weeks before Christmas Day, the chamber of commerce would arrange a parade, led by Santa in a red sports car camouflaged as a sleigh. Santa might be personified by Jean Hersholt, who was the epitome of clean, hearty fun, but in typical fashion Hollywood injected a sexy motif by giving Santa a sweetheart, who might be Clara Bow or even Baby Peggy. And on the couple's progress through Santa Claus Lane, they were caressed by a snow flurry of cornflakes blown about by an electric fan.

When Dutch was approached to play the role of Santa's sweetheart, Peg nixed the idea. She was holding out for a New York Santa, the kind who was listed by Dun and Bradstreet and belonged to the Racquet Club. The Christmas spirit that elevated the hearts of Hollywood failed to turn Peg on.

As a social arbiter, Hollywood had a substitute for Elsa Maxwell in Ouida Rathbone, wife of the rangy British movie star Basil, whom Peg called "Rassel Bathbone." He was a darling; we all loved him and wished his wife would stop giving parties that cost even more than Basil's enormous salary could provide.

During one Christmas season, Ouida swathed the entire Rathbone estate on Fairfax Boulevard in cotton batting to simulate snow, and hired a group of carolers from Central Casting. But on the day of the party the climate fouled Ouida up, for the sky opened and a steaming tropical rain poured down, reducing the cotton batting to a gray goo and making the carolers under their tiers of capes and woolly mufflers sweat miserably.

An annual Christmas party was given by our queen of gossip columnists, Louella Parsons. There has always been a misconception that Louella was an ogress who wielded a poisonous pen and chortled while she ruined people's careers. But when she wasn't scouting down scandal, Lolly Parsons was as flighty and soft as a puffball. She was always in love—not with film actors, but with solid citizens who had "manly" careers. At the time I first knew Lolly, she was in the midst of a flirtatious sort of marriage with Dr. Harry Martin, a lusty lover of sports and a member of the State Boxing Commission. After the doctor died, Cupid replaced him with that romantic Irish-American troubadour, Jimmy McHugh, who composed "I Can't Give You Anything But Love, Baby." And make no mistake; Lolly's tender sentiments were returned in full measure. Her practical, down-to-earth daughter, Harriet, was always on the qui vive lest one of Mama's flirtations end in an elopement. Men found Lolly irresistible. It was always a strain for those Hollywood males to make casual conversation. Louella supplied a thrilling alternative. She could turn any encounter into a flirtation that instantly caused sparks to fly. And it was this utter sincerity concerning matters of the heart that brought the movies to life for her millions of readers. Every Christmas Eve would find the greatest of the movie greats sitting on the Aubusson rug in Louella's pink and gold parlor, watching her unwrap an avalanche of gifts. Two secretaries used to stand with notebooks to keep score so that Louella could remember the next day who had sent what.

It used to be a cliché to describe Louella's Christmas loot as breathtaking. But in a sense it was. I recall one tribute, a silver-plated copy of the Eiffel Tower that doubled as a pepper grinder. I also remember an Early American spinning wheel that did duty as a floor lamp. There were bronze bookends in the guise of Paolo and Francesca, who were thus separated by books instead of being brought together by them. Replicas of the "Mona Lisa" used to show up in all sorts of materials—ceramics, alabaster, wood—or printed on sofa cushions. There would be dolls of Meissen china with brocade skirts designed to hide Lolly's many telephones, over which came scoops of nerve-shattering scandal.

The unveiling of each present was greeted with applause, but one had a feeling that by Easter those treasures would be pitched into a bin for the goodwill charities. Just the same, Christmas was an occasion to thank Louella for past favors and favors yet to come, such as the life-saving reprieve of a cover-up in the event of future scandal. For in that innocent age we all thought that waywardness could ruin a star's career. It had indeed done so in the case of poor, bumbling Fatty Arbuckle, who was accused of having caused a play-girl's death in an accident during a wild party. Although he was acquitted by a jury, the publicity that ensued caused Fatty's downfall, from which he never recovered. Louella, as an advocate of true romance, had gone out of her way to blast his behavior.

Of course the Talmadge girls could never be open to attack, but one morning Peg had a foretaste of disaster when Louella phoned to ask about Dutch's presence during a ruckus in a gay bar down in the slums of Los Angeles. It so happened that Dutch *had* been there, with Bill Haines and his boyfriend, but just as the police entered, they had escaped through a back door. Peg assured Louella that her child would never dream of setting foot in such a low dive, to which Louella's crisp reply was, "Don't give *me* that, Peg! *This* is *Louella*!" And she banged down the receiver. Peg broke into a cold sweat and waited for the dread item to appear that would end Dutch's salary forever.

But apparently Louella had smellier fish to fry and she dropped the matter. She wasn't inherently a bitch; it was only that she highly honored the readers to whom her column had become scripture. She could not love movie stars so much, loved she not gossip more.

Just the same, it was Louella's reportage on the behavior of Bill Haines that later helped to do him in. Bill was one of MGM's top stars—the idol of bobby-soxers—an endearingly wholesome boy-next-door. But his personal life was beginning to get out of hand, and vague hints of misdeameanor were cropping up in Lolly's column. So one day Bill was summoned by Louis B. Mayer and issued an ultimatum. "I'm going to give you a choice," said L.B. "You're either to give up that boyfriend of yours, or I'll cancel your contract!" Without even a hesitation, Bill opted for love and told L.B. to tear up his contract.

(As an aside, let me note that Bill went on from being a yokel in films to become an international arbiter of taste—an interior decorator among whose achievements was the decor of the American Embassy in London. Bill and Frank remained sweethearts until Bill died at an advanced age. Frank could no longer face the future without Bill, and he committed suicide. As a love-and-success story, Bill's legend was far more thrilling than any he ever filmed for L.B.Mayer.)

Norma represented the exotic, as turned out by New York's most expensive couturier, Mme. Frances, who specialized in dressing the gold diggers in an era when gentlemen clamored to pay their sweethearts' upkeep. Madame created this chiffon evening gown in poppy tones, and Norma, the perfectionist, demanded a special set of topaz jewelry from Cartier to match. (The Museum of Modern Art/Film Stills Archive)

In the category of looks, the pick of husbands was my own John Emerson. (Photo by E. F. Foley)

During Joe Schenck's summers in Bayside, Long Island, he gave massive barbecues (above left). He is here seated center front, backed up by family and friends. Standing, third from the left, is Archie Selwyn, the Broadway theatrical producer; next to him is Irving Berlin; then Alma Reubens, the silent-film star; next to Alma stands John Emerson. To John's left is Sam Harris, who in partnership with George M. Cohan produced the smash hits that George M. wrote and starred in. In front of Sam is A. Loos, with Norma to her left. Between Sam and Norma stands Beulah Livingstone, who handled public relations and did her best to make Norma and Dutch behave like film stars. Dutch looms up seventh from right, with Peg behind her, and the pretty creature just behind Peg is Hedda Hopper, then a minor film actress.

Sometimes Beulah Livingstone's most inspired publicity went for naught. During World War I a group of Allied dignitaries visited the studio, and Beulah ordered a photographer to record the occasion (left). But those dignitaries had had too much champagne for lunch and posed for a picture that could have given comfort to the enemy had it fallen into the wrong hands!

Natalie Talmadge married Buster Keaton in a flower-decked ceremony in the Schenck mansion in Bayside. At the extreme left Anita Loos is straining to see over Peg's shoulder. Next to Peg is Norma; then Buster, the bridegroom, and his bride. Constance, as matron of honor, is flanked by her own bridegroom, John Pialogiou. Behind them Joe Schenck can be spotted as Buster's best man. Joe, seemingly lost in the shuffle, was really the best man of them all. (Courtesy of Beulah Livingstone)

Script writers always seemed to feature Norma (left) in the throes of running away. And her most romantic, dramatic escapes were made without a suitcase. (Courtesy of Lester Glassner)

In their silent films Gene O'Brien kissed Norma's hand to express his feelings. But a day would soon arrive when Jimmy Cagney, reaching across a breakfast table, pushed half a grapefruit into Mae Clarke's ravishing face, an act that must have caused many a girl to wish that time marched backwards. (Courtesy of Lester Glassner)

There was no rule that a movie writer had to be dowdy (right). Mme. Frances chose beige silk in a sort of nude tone for me, added a touch of emerald green for dash, and topped it all off with willow plumes on a Merry Widow hat.

Below: A study in contrasts at the entrance to Marion Davies's bungalow on the MGM lot. Norma's outfits were invariably chic, while Marion preferred the Hollywood look. (The Museum of Modern Art/Film Stills Archive)

This photograph shows Constance in an unnatural pose, for she seldom glanced at a mirror. Her reaction to this silly garment with its tight bodice and floating sleeves was to get out of it as soon as possible. (The Museum of Modern Art/Film Stills Archive)

Escape from Sex and Mammon

By early December we had completed every detail for our long-awaited Christmas in New York. None of us trusted the local California stores; we had a theory that the moment something began to look chic it was a sure sign that a girl had "gone Hollywood." So we ordered presents by mail from the Christmas catalogs of favorite New York shops, Bendel's, Cartier's, and Hattie Carnegie, specifying that everything was to be gift-wrapped and delivered to our New York hotel well in advance of our arrival.

Dutch was to finish her film in time for us to reach New York on December 19th, allowing five days for last-minute preparations. Because Joe had to attend a business meeting in Atlantic City, he took Norma east ahead of us. But delays began to accumulate in Hollywood. Dutch was detained for retakes, which went on infuriatingly so that it became impossible for us to reach New York until the 24th. This meant a drastic cutting of corners, but since our train would get in at 8:00 a.m., there was no need for despair. We would still have one entire day to acquire a tree, which we could spend Christmas

Eve decorating. By Christmas morning everything would be back on schedule for the arrival of Norma and Joe from Atlantic City.

In Los Angeles, Peg, Dutch, Nate and I boarded the Santa Fe in the Southern California sunshine. But with New York as our goal, no Western heat wave could wilt our spirits. Those trips between the East and West coasts were an enormously cozy experience. In the constant ebb and flow of show business, one always found friends among the passengers; it was like a commuter train to New Haven, except that the trip was long enough to make new friends or to elicit lengthy confidences from old ones.

We were thrilled to discover that the entire staff of *Photoplay* magazine was in our car. Its attractive editor in chief, Julian Johnson, was of special interest to me. So we all settled in for a pleasantly flirtatious trip East.

As our train pulled into Albuquerque, the desert heat swept in like a gust from hell. In those days air conditioning was provided by electric fans, which were pretty inadequate, so we used to travel with ice bags to wear on our heads during the hot, gritty stretches of the Mojave Desert. We were already adjusting our ice bags when suddenly a harbinger out of the east appeared: our conductor handed Peg a telegram from Norma in Atlantic City: "Hurry and get to New York while it's still snowing." *This was going to be the white Christmas of all our dreams!*

Our friends from *Photoplay* left us in Chicago, where their magazine was published, while we changed stations to board the Twentieth Century for that last, long pull into Manhattan. On our way across Chicago we were greeted by a flurry of beautiful snowflakes as big as silver dollars, but then, just outside the city, the train was slowed down by snow drifts. A late arrival in New York would sabotage our plans for Christmas; we tried to push the Twentieth Century ahead mentally by force of will, only to be stalled for hours on Christmas Eve just outside Poughkeepsie.

When the train finally slid into Grand Central Station, it was long after midnight. All the shops were closed; our Christmas would be treeless! Frustrated and worn out from tension, we were led through the terminal by a corps of porters. On reaching Vanderbilt Avenue, Dutch stopped and called out, "Look!" She gestured toward a row of pine trees lined up for sale along the curb, wafting their perfume on the crisp night air. "Christmas trees!" exclaimed Dutch. *"Real, genuine Christmas trees!"*

Dutch flagged the vendor just as he was about to quit for the night and promptly bought the bushiest specimen of a pretty scrumpy lot. Peg grumbled bitterly that there was nothing very glamorous about a naked tree, but Dutch protested: "Never mind! It *smells* like Christmas!"

At the hotel the night clerk ordered our luggage to be taken to our rooms, adding that he would send someone up in the morning to install our tree.

"You needn't bother!" snapped Peg with an accusing eye on Dutch. "Just pitch it out!"

"No, don't!" cried Dutch. Then, turning to the clerk, she ventured, "Would you know where we could get some decorations for it?"

"Not on the holiday," he answered. "Sorry!"

It was at this juncture that Nate emerged from a sleepy stupor to recall that when we crossed Grand Central she had noticed a shop with a sign that read "We never close."

The clerk told her that the shop was merely a drugstore, but Dutch insisted we explore it for goodies.

"For Chrissake, let's go to bed," scolded Peg. "We can face Christmas when it gets here."

"But it's already here!" argued Dutch. *"Let's go!"*

Peg was escorted upstairs to our suite, leaving three girls all aglow with Christmas spirit to barge out into the night.

Park Avenue was deserted and as safe as a Quaker kindergarten. (New York doesn't have muggerless nights like it used to.) It was only a short walk around the corner to Grand Central Station. It, too, appeared rather comatose, but when we reached the drugstore there was a jumble of oddments in the window and we could see some red and green lights blinking inside. We entered and unearthed a drowsy clerk; he was young, unusually attractive, and moreover he recognized Dutch. "If it isn't Constance Talmadge!" he gasped. "Now I *know* there's a Santa Claus!"

When Dutch explained our purpose, however, the young man's spirits sagged. "Gee, I'd love to help you out, but Christmas tree ornaments are just about the *only* things we don't stock!"

There seemed nothing to do but return to the hotel and face Peg's derision and our barren Christmas tree. Dutch was never one to give up easily, so she asked, "Haven't you got *anything* that's wrapped in tinfoil and gives out glitter?"

"Not in *this* store!" was the forlorn reply. And we were on our way out when the clerk, seeing romance about to disappear from his life forever, called, "Oh, Miss Talmadge! *Come on back!*"

He proceeded to unearth a box of small objects wrapped in silver foil, which glistened in the light. When Nate asked what they were, he said evasively, "What does it matter? They look like icicles, don't they?"

Dutch agreed eagerly and purchased all he had of them. The young man now ventured further. "Could you use some . . . balloons?"

"Terrific!" Nate piped up. At which our benefactor produced

a package of small deflated balloons, which he explained could be blown up and secured with dental floss. Dutch cornered the market on *both* items. After which our young friend bethought himself of surgical cotton to serve as snow. Then, in a parting gesture, he presented Dutch with the two strings of colored lights that were blinking above the cash register.

"Thanks and *Merry Christmas!*" exclaimed Dutch, devastating the young man with her smile. And then, in a hurry to put our treasures to use, we started to leave.

But the warmth of Dutch's handclasp had encouraged her conquest. "Just give me time to lock up the store," said he, "and I'll carry the packages to the hotel for you." So on that night the shop that never closed was shut down tight.

We found the tree in the parlor of our suite, propped against a wall and giving out its Christmasy perfume. Warned by Dutch not to rouse her mother, our new friend noiselessly propped up the tree using luggage racks, after which, in silence, we went about the job of decorating it. By the time we finished the job and turned on the lights, nobody could have guessed that those makeshift ornaments had any destiny other than to glorify the spirit of Christmas.

"Let's wake Peg up to see it!" dared Nate. And it was agreed to risk Peg's fury. When she entered wearing her nightie and sleepy-eyed, we waited breathlessly for her reaction.

"Why," she exclaimed, "it's *absolutely gorgeous!*"

Dutch's suitor now felt safe enough to introduce himself to the mother-in-law of his dreams. "Mrs. Talmadge," said he, "my name is Lester Noonan and I'm honored to make your acquaintance."

As Peg blinked at him, Dutch placed a caressing hand on his arm. "Lester dug up all the ornaments for our tree!" she announced.

But she spoke a little too fondly, for Peg immediately began to assess the young man's attractions. As if he were not even present, she asked, "And where did you dig *him* up?"

"At that all-night drugstore!"

"*Drugstore!*" Peg repeated in a tone that placed all drugstores in a category with cesspools. Suspiciously, she turned to remove one of the icicles from the tree, examined it, and then in smoldering fury she addressed Lester.

"*Why you sonofabitch!*"

"Peg!" we all remonstrated.

"Do you *know* what this thing *is?*"

"What?" asked Dutch.

"*It's a suppository!*"

Lester blanched and looked flat enough to creep under the wall-to-wall carpet.

"What's a suppository?" inquired Nate.

"That's right! Show your ignorance!"

Now Peg yanked one of the small balloons from the tree. "And d'you know what *this* object is?" she thundered.

Lester's color changed from white to red. "Oh, please, Mrs. Talmadge," he begged.

"It's a goddamn contraceptive!"

"What's a contraceptive?" asked Dutch.

"It's only due to my upbringing that you don't know!" Again Peg turned on Lester. "*It's scum like you who give movie stars a filthy name!*"

"How can you *say* that," Lester asked in deep distress, "when my feelings for your daughter are"—he paused for the proper word, and then he said it—"*sacred!*" (Many a scabrous Hollywood episode could be alibied with the saying "Honi soit qui mal y pense.")

Lester's declaration of love may have softened Peg a trace, but she nonetheless issued an ultimatum. "Take that nasty thing apart before Walter Winchell gets wind of it! Or 'Town

Topics'! Or, God help us, *Louella Parsons!*"

We removed the unholy objects from our tree and Lester found a trash bin in the back hall where he could bury them.

We had scarcely finished when Norma and Joe descended on us from Atlantic City, Norma flashing some pre-Christmas diamonds Joe had bought at a jeweler's on the Boardwalk.

"Merry Christmas!" exclaimed Norma. But then, spotting the tree with its unlit bulbs and gobs of cotton snow, she gasped, *"What is that thing?"*

Norma took no comfort in our explanation that we had reached town after all the shops were closed. But at that point Joe was already coming to the rescue. He picked up the phone, called the hotel management, and commandeered the enormous Christmas tree that decorated the downstairs lobby.

By that time the bells of St. Bartholomew's were chiming "O Come, All Ye Faithful" and through the windows we saw snow-flakes drifting like a benediction. There is nothing in the whole world that can warm the human heart like a snowy Christmas in New York. And as Lester forlornly approached Dutch to say, "Well, Miss Talmadge . . . good-bye," Peg, in an upsurge of Christian spirit, invited him to join the family party. In reaction, Dutch's gaze took on the nearest thing to love light I had heretofore encountered.

In short, that Christmas party paid off for all those events at Louella's, where every guest arrived with fish to fry or a rusty ax to grind.

A hotel staff, under the ebullient direction of Lester Noonan, installed the tree and stacked a landslide of Christmas gifts under it. Beside family gifts, there were presents for everyone who might show up unexpectedly: Shalimar perfume (king size) for the ladies and, for men, expensive scarf-and-necktie sets from Charvet.

Festivities were to start with brunch, and by noon guests

were already arriving; most were from the upper registers of Broadway, the movies, and Tammany Hall. There were no cameramen to record them, for Madison Avenue hadn't yet become a ghetto for the public relations industry.

Joe had arranged for his favorite Hungarian orchestra to cater to the ethnic in his soul. Their uniforms were red and gold; their melodies were hot and fast; the scraping of their violins was frantic. Through all the brouhaha champagne never ceased to flow, leaving in my memory a phantasmagoria of unrelated incidents.

Jimmy Quirk had come on from Chicago "for business reasons," to report the party for *Photoplay*. Hand in hand, he and I wandered among the merrymakers, feeling a little superior at times because we were intellectuals.

Among the early arrivals was William Randolph Hearst, with Marion Davies clinging to his arm. He had just arrived from San Simeon on newspaper business, and they were in residence at the townhouse on Riverside Drive that was Marion's pied-à-terre in New York. Marion, who took no interest in fashion, dressed to please her beau, with results that were as dazzling as his yellow journalism. W.R.'s enormous frame must have posed a problem to his tailor, but the great man never looked less than imperial. He moved with the stately swing of a circus elephant and yet was so light on his feet that his Charleston was better than pint-sized Stan Laurel's.

But his fits of Olympian gaiety never weakened the awe that W.R. inspired in everyone—except his sweetheart, for Marion took a mischievous delight in ribbing the great man. I think W.R. knew that behind his back she called him Droopy Drawers. But surrounded by an army of sycophants, W.R. took delight in an impishness that only served to highlight Marion's devotion.

At a time when the great Hearst empire stood in danger of

bankruptcy Marion offered her sizable fortune to help save W.R., asking him in her stutter, "Why do I n-n-need diamond brooches when I have p-p-plenty of safety pins?"

Luckily W.R. was rescued by a brilliant legal adviser, and Marion's sacrifice wasn't required. So she remained one of the most powerful forces in American journalism until W.R.'s fatal illness.

I once had evidence that the great man could even laugh about his situation as a lover. It happened following a dinner party at Marion's town house, where all the male guests were prominent and the girls frivolous. And I, as Marion's chum, had been placed next to W.R. at table. It so happened that the very next evening, thanks to *Gentlemen Prefer Blondes*, which had turned me into a "literary" figure, I was invited to dine by Mrs. Hearst at the apartment where she held forth as the great man's wife. And when I took my place beside W.R. at his wife's table, he observed, with a naughty twinkle, "Well, young lady, we seem to be sitting next to each other in rather diverse locations, don't we?" (Millicent Hearst and Marion were so much alike that one could understand W.R.'s being fond of them both, as he was. The two women displayed the same soft femininity, the same lighthearted natures. And they both stuttered.)

In my recollections of that merriest of Christmases, I recall Norma pulling Marion aside to ask, "What was your Christmas haul from W.R.?"

It appeared that Mr. Hearst's main gift was the Ritz Tower Apartment building on Park Avenue. "B-b-but," Marion added, "for a stocking present he g-g-gave me a cute little painting of a b-b-bull."

"*No bull?*" Nate piped up in one of her lousy puns. (Actually that painting was a masterpiece by the great Dutch painter Paulus Potter. We were often in its presence at Marion's New

York dining room. One wonders in what priceless collection it hangs today.)

I recall Mabel Normand arriving at the party rather disheveled, with a big hole in her stocking and minus her permanent escort, Sam Goldwyn. Mabel explained that en route to the party she had ditched Sam, not to get rid of him, but on a sudden impulse to pop into St. Patrick's Cathedral and say a prayer in his behalf. Blocked by a mob of people Mabel had to pray on the stone steps outside, where she got roughed up.

My journalist beau asked Mabel if he might print her prayer. "Why not?" Mabel asked. "A thousand people on Fifth Avenue heard it. I prayed to Saint Anthony for Sam to get a nose operation that would make him look more like a goy." (Because Sam was a big advertiser in *Photoplay* magazine, Jimmy killed the item and Sam's nose remained status quo.)

By the time Dutch fetched Mabel a pair of stockings, Lester had had enough champagne to release all his pent-up manhood, and seizing the gallant opportunity, he helped Mabel change her stockings. While doing so, his ardent gaze remained on Dutch and he dared to boast, "If you were lucky, Miss Talmadge, I'd be putting these on *you!*"

"I was *born* lucky," said Dutch, "so I can wait!"

To the accompaniment of a rhapsody by Liszt, sex further invaded the milieu. But it was the type of sex that prevailed in the twenties, when a kiss was still a kiss, instead of being a preliminary to a grapple; a sigh was still a sigh; and there was always a delicious prelude before that fundamental thing would finally apply.

At that time the sex goddess and toast of Broadway was blonde little Marilyn Miller, star of the Ziegfeld Follies. (It was she who introduced the name of "Marilyn" into American usage, causing a rash of infant Marilyns from coast to coast.

And, in due course, she inspired the most famous of all Marilyns to become her namesake.)

Marilyn arrived at the party late, having been required by her Prussian father to take her daily ballet lesson. Marilyn had then sneaked away from the family flat on West End Avenue, but that only postponed the beating she'd get from her father when she returned. Peg sympathetically asked, "Does Ziegfeld know about those beatings?"

"How could he? Papa always hits me where the marks don't show."

"Then why don't you *tell* Ziggy?" demanded Peg.

Marilyn shuddered in distaste. "And give him an excuse to *look* for the scars?"

At that point Love in the person of Jack Pickford rescued Marilyn and conquered all. As Jack led Marilyn into the mainstream of festivities, Peg remarked, "That young man can make the kid forget a whole acre of black-and-blue marks!"

It went without saying that Dutch deserted all her other aspirants to concentrate on Lester Noonan. For one unforgettable night he was the successful rival of the dashing mayor of New York, of the only millionaire tunesmith in Tin Pan Alley, and of a number of swells from the Racquet Club who, to quote Peg, were "panting after the Dutchman's virginity like wolfhounds at a dog race!"

Lester's triumph was made a little more palatable to Peg because of Freddy Rhinelander, who came in proudly swinging a half-pound box of candy, for which he'd spent one dollar of his half a billion, as a Christmas tribute to Dutch. "I've dreamed of the Dutchman hooking a heavy spender," said Peg. "But I'm learning some bitter facts about the rich."

When Joe, as Santa Claus, distributed the presents, one of his gifts to Peg was a white satin ball gown from Mme. Frances's, for which Peg chided him, "I haven't been to a ball since the sprouts' father took me to an Elks convention!"

"Don't worry, Peg," said Dutch. "We'll *give* you a ball on the Pope's birthday!"

But Peg's other gifts from the girls (paid for, incidentally, by Joe) were not to be joked about—a diamond and ruby clip the size of an ashtray (from Cartier) with earrings to match; and a floor-length coat that was a glorious resurrection for a thousand hapless little minks.

Peg's swag was still far from ended. A message was phoned from downstairs that threw her three girls into fresh excitement. We all followed them down to the street, where a Cadillac limousine was parked. On the door in gold enamel was the dedication, "With love to Peg." There was a chauffeur in uniform, who announced that his name was MacDonald. But when Peg asked, "Do you mind answering to 'Mack'?" he replied, "Anything you wish, modom." "That 'modom' is a give-away," said Peg. "Your real name is probably Moe," so that's what Peg christened him.

The clock had gone full circle before the orchestra switched from the wild melodies of Hungary and brought the party to a close with the sweet strains of "Auf Wiedersehn." The last stragglers left noisily, one of them wearing a Charvet necktie dangling from his ear. After the excitement had simmered down, Peg's girls gathered around her in a way that brought to my mind a family scene out of the past: the one in which the "Little Women" of Louisa May Alcott gather about their beloved "Marmee" to assess their blessings, chief of which, as they all agree, is "We've got each other!"

Peg, sitting there surrounded by masses of loot, presently began to chuckle.

"What's funny, Peg?" asked Dutch.

"I was just thinking what a joke it would have been on me if

I'd gotten rid of you brats before you were born!"

"Did you try, Peg?" asked Dutch.

"Oh sure! I went every day to Coney Island and rode that Bump-the-Bumps from dawn to midnight."

"Which goes to show," said Norma, giving Peg a hug, "that sometimes it's a blessing for a girl to get knocked up!"

Soaring Salaries and Movie Moguls

In 1921 John Emerson and I sailed to Europe on the *Paris* with all the Talmadges and Joe Schenck in tow. I remember the boat train approaching the city of Paris, slowly making its way through the tawdry suburbs on the wrong side of the tracks. With our noses glued to the windows, we saw numberless little girls on the sidewalks, and I remarked that we must be in the vicinity of a school. But it seemed an unusual hour for school to be out. Finally it dawned on us that those "children" were actually grown women wearing the first knee-revealing skirts in the history of fashion. We were actually looking on at the beginning of a clothes revolution that was going to affect women all over the world, changing the rhythm, culture, and even the moral tone of every generation up to now.

Those short skirts worn by hoi polloi in the Paris slums had exploded overnight from the creative genius of a gamine named Coco Chanel, whose name as yet we hadn't heard.

Milling about among the fashionably dressed clientele of the Hotel Crillon, we felt that our ankle-length skirts were very dowdy indeed. Peg and her girls felt that they could endure the situation until they had a chance to buy some Paris dresses. I couldn't. My first act on reaching our suite was to call a valet and order a good three inches to be whacked off my skirts. The result was so instantly rejuvenating that, having looked all of sixteen on my arrival, I might now have passed for twelve. The effect was heightened by a new hair style devised just before I left New York. I had taken scissors and thinned my pageboy bob into tousled locks that appeared windblown.

On our first morning in Paris we girls ventured forth to inspect the dress collection at Lanvin's. Although Mme. Frances's dress establishment in New York had occupied a mansion, the house of Lanvin had once been a palace, and its entrance was so chastely regal as to overawe us. We were further disturbed when a directrice on guard at the door wanted to know who had invited us. Dutch announced that we had merely stumbled in from the street, and the woman, smiling icily, led us across a slippery oriental rug to some gilt chairs that were so uncomfortably small as to chill our spirits even more thoroughly. The few clients who happened to be there were French and obviously felt entirely at home. They paid us no attention, in spite of Norma's and Dutch's sparkling beauty. We looked on, spellbound, as mannequins started to show the dresses, but we had no idea how to go about making a purchase. Our insecurity was presently increased when a vendeuse approached to address *me* and said, "I beg your pardon, mademoiselle, but Mme. Lanvin wishes to know if you would step into her office."

Convinced that we were to be ordered to leave the premises, I bolstered my courage to swish my short skirt into Madame's office. She was seated behind her desk, a motherly type in a black dress that made no pretensions to chic. She graciously asked my name, which of course meant nothing to her, and then said, "Mademoiselle, would you permit my designer to make a sketch of your coiffure so that one of my mannequins can copy it for modeling the show?" I was almost dumb with amazement over the request, and at the same time no end relieved that we weren't going to be thrown out. I eagerly agreed to pose, whereat Madame sent for a young man, who sketched me then and there. When I returned to the girls and reported what had happened, they were as astounded as I was. But at the same time, my adventure made us bold enough to summon a vendeuse, try on dresses, and purchase a whole slew of them.

(The pay-off for that adventure came a little later, when at Diaghilev's presentation of Nijinsky in *Afternoon of a Faun*, a significant number of the chic Parisiennes in the audience were flaunting my hairdo, which they had seen on Lanvin's mannequin.)

In that same year, back in Hollywood, Dutch came through in a big way with *Dangerous Business*, which was adapted, from the prizewinner of a scenario contest run by some film magazine, by Madeline Buckley and Roy William Neill.

In *Dangerous Business* the heroine becomes engaged to a stupid oaf in order to cover up her affair with a fascinating libertine, only to find that the oaf's "stupidity" is itself a cover-up for an overly active libido. Finding this out, our heroine switches her preference, making for a delectable ending. Actually, if the truth be told, all of Dutch's films had an undercurrent of pornography. But it was the delicate porno of the twenties, softened by pretty camera angles, with no hairy nakedness to distract the audience.

Once more back on the job, John and I adapted a play by Rachel Butler entitled *Mama's Affair*. It dealt with the victim of a possessive mother, one who suffers a "heart attack" every time a suitor tries to date her child. As a result, the daughter finagles her mother into hiring a heart specialist who is a bachelor with sex appeal, and Dutch then elopes with him before Mama finds out that she's been had.

In the cast of *Mama's Affair* were Effie Shannon, a brilliant character comedienne from the Broadway theater, and Kenneth Harland as leading man. (Today Ken's first wife and I live in the same New York apartment building. Hello, neighbor!)

To direct *Mama's Affair,* John chose a newcomer, Victor Fleming, who only recently had been a taxi driver. Vic had stationed his cab just outside the MGM studio in Culver City, with the intention of crashing its gates. Eventually he did so as a movie extra. I respected Vic's enterprise and was intrigued by the interest he took in things outside the movies. I recall one night when Vic was bringing me home from a party and we stopped to watch a fleet of fireflies skimming about Beverly Hills. "Those small insects have mastered a problem that's never been solved by science," Vic informed me. "They can produce *light* without *heat!*" Vic's active mind ultimately brought him fame as director of *Treasure Island*, *The Wizard of Oz*, and many other film masterpieces.

During those years with Dutch, we were getting rich. John, as a parlor socialist, used to regard the movies as the first major American industry in which employees were granted a large piece of the "take." Our combined weekly salaries came to several thousand dollars, which John multiplied in the soaring stock market before the crash of '29.

On one momentous day, I was summoned by Joe Schenck, who said, "Nita, when I put Dutch into your hands it was only to pacify Peg. I never expected to make money on the deal. But the pictures have turned out to be gold mines, so I'd like to give you a little bonus." And he handed us a check for fifty thousand dollars. Our mounting prosperity only granted John a fresh chance to do nothing. And breaking with Joe, he again took leave, during which we fooled around London, Paris, Vienna, and Budapest. Joe replaced me with a sterling scenarist, Grant Carpenter, and a soon-to-be famous director, Chet

Withey. And among the acting talent was the recently discovered Flora Finch. (Remember Flora? As a precursor of Barbra Streisand she proved the fascination that lies in sheer lack of comeliness.)

Dutch's next film after our departure was *Wedding Bells*, from a play by Salisbury Field. Its heroine was a rattle-brained flapper who, in defiance of her husband, bobs her hair. He promptly leaves her, at which point she goes to Reno for a divorce. But Fate brings the husband to Reno, and his child-wife triumphs by winning him back *with her hair bobbed.*

Wedding Bells had a cast of nonentities, with the exception of a new leading man, Harrison Ford, who, as every film buff knows, went on to a reputable career. But the title of *Wedding Bells* smacked too much of conformity to be "box office" and it suffered from the lack of John's supervision.

Again Joe Schenck dragged John and me back to Hollywood, and again Dutch came into her own with *A Woman's Place.* Another of our "originals," it concerned a liberated woman who runs for the office of mayor in her town, confident of winning because its women voters far outnumber the men. But our candidate learns about women's disloyalty to women by losing the election. She achieves her female domination, however, by marrying the elected mayor. (Once again the director was Vic Fleming.)

Following *A Woman's Place* came *Polly of the Follies*, which was also filmed in Hollywood. I shared authorship with John, but we were forced to collaborate by long-distance phone, because he had gone to New York, where he had become a leader in the Broadway actors' strike. It was then that John first allowed my name to *precede* his on the screen; the story was credited to Anita Loos *and John Emerson.*

Polly of the Follies was true to the lives of Follies girls I knew. Most came from small towns and, if sexy, had no trouble land-ing jobs with Ziegfeld. Flo required a girl to audition without benefit of make-up or peroxide, dressed in the simple gingham she had worn at home. For Flo claimed that the true gauge of sex appeal lay in the images that little boys carried of the little girls whose books they had toted home from school. But, once Flo hired those homespun beauties, he turned them over to Ben Ali Haggan, an artist who designed costumes of the most exotic whimsy.

There was no dearth of lovelies in Hollywood to cast as Follies girls. The loveliest of all was Billie Dove. Billie was a neighbor of ours in Santa Monica, and we frequented the same beauty salon at Henshy's department store. Its hairdresser was the only male I ever heard deride Billie. "I wish that Dove girl would get someone else to do her hair," said Mr. Peavey. "These Santa Monica housewives all want to look like her, and when they don't, they put the blame on *me!*" Sniffing derisively into his walrus mustache, he added, "I wish I'd never seen hide nor hair of Billie Dove!"

Billie earned more substantial respect from the billionaire Howard Hughes, although it was his practice to place a number of pretty girls under contract, with no other duty than to be in their own apartments every afternoon at five. Promptly on the dot, a phone call would come through to inform each girl whether or not she'd be Howard's date for that evening. If not, they were supposedly free to do as they wished, although in fact they were always trailed by sleuths.

Howard Hughes had tried to toss his net over both Norma and Dutch, but Peg turned thumbs down. "Heaven protect my kids from any guy who can't make up his mind!" said she. Just the same, Howard's list included such future stars as Jane Russell and Jean Harlow.

I had an indirect connection with Hughes, by way of friendship with his uncle Rupert, the popular novelist and historian.

He wrote a biography of George Washington that backed up my own suspicions that there were a few skeletons in George's closet at Mount Vernon. One day when Rupert's nephew was piloting his plane, it crashed and burst into flames. A youthful bystander pulled him away from death, but Howard never bothered to reward or even thank his rescuer. On hearing this Peg prophesied, "That ungrateful son-of-a-bitch is going to come to no good end!"

After *Polly of the Follies,* I rejoined John in New York and my pal the screenwriter Frances Marion stepped into my place, with complete expertise. Her first film, *Her Primitive Lover*, revealed Dutch as a woman who is bored by a scholarly husband, but who falls in love with his unscholarly violence when she walks out on him.

In *East Is West*, Frances tackled a racist theme. Dutch, a beauty of San Francisco's Chinatown, is loved by a Caucasian and encounters resistance from his aristocratic Nob Hill family. At the end, Frances proved that Dutch, far from being a Yellow Peril, was as white as the snows of Mount Shasta.

Joe tried to hold Frances under contract, but she happened to be prettier and sexier than most of the stars she wrote for. When Frances left her job to keep a love tryst of some sort, Joe called John and me back to write the screenplay of *Dulcy.* (In these days when almost everyone yearns to write movies, it's refreshing to recall a time when we were striving to get away from them.)

Dulcy was from a Broadway hit by two members of the Algonquin Round Table, George Kaufman and Marc Connelly. Dutch played the title role, a daffy young bride whose stupidity drives her husband up the parlor wall at the same time that her enchantment tempts him back into the boudoir. *Dulcy* proved that Dutch was capable of high comedy. The role had been created on stage by a brilliant young English comedienne, Lynn Fontanne.

Dulcy was followed by a pedestrian historical subject by one of Hollywood's stalwarts, G. Gardner Sullivan. In *The Dangerous Maid,* Dutch played a frolicsome damsel of eighteenth-century England who finds herself in a jam and enlists Conway Tearle to get her out of it. The movie was successful and Joe kept G. Gardner on for Dutch's next film.

The Goldfish concerned a marriage that was avant garde for those days. The young couple agrees that if either of them gets fed up, the discontented one needs merely to present the other with a goldfish. Its direction was credited to one Jerome Storm, who immediately disappeared, never again to surface. The reception of that film was only so-so, and Dutch's lack of interest in work was making her increasingly restless.

At this point Joe Schenck went out on a limb with a farce titled *In Hollywood with Potash and Perlmutter.* It concerned two zany characters who aspire to be movie moguls, just as in the recent Mel Brooks film *Silent Movie.* It, too, had an all-star cast in which Norma and Dutch played themselves and made fun of their personal traits—Norma the sob sister and Dutch the feather-brained vamp. But fans didn't want the movies to kid themselves, and that movie went the way of most film satires.

Joe produced another disaster in 1924, *Her Night of Romance,* by Hans Kraly, in which Dutch, a multimillionairess, poses as a penniless old maid who falls in love with Ronald Colman, a playboy-aristocrat posing as a hard-working doctor.

For the last time Joe called John and me to the rescue. It was accomplished by *Learning to Love,* in which I stepped back to second place in the credits, John having by that time successfully steered the Broadway actors through their strike. In that opus, Dutch played a flirt who leaves a long trail of broken hearts but is brought to her senses by a man smart enough to pretend indifference.

I would have been content to go on with the Talmadges, but it was now 1925, the year that *Gentlemen Prefer Blondes* came out. (My book caused Robert Sherwood, the playwright and critic on *Life* magazine, to observe that although a number of successful novelists had invaded the movies, A. Loos was the only *movie* writer to succeed as a novelist.)

I had written the book to occupy my leisure and, incidentally, to poke fun at a witless blonde who was taking up too much time with the idol of my cerebral dreams, H. L. Mencken. But, much more seriously, the book proved to be a nemesis to my husband, one against which he had no defense. It revealed in the clear, bold type of sixteen different languages that he had not been a very active "collaborator."

It now seemed pointless for John to go on pretending he was an author. So on his decision, we retired.

After we quit Dutch for good, she was placed in a film that made history of a sort. It was called *Her Sister from Paris*. Its author was Ludwig Fulda, a Hungarian (the middle-European invasion of Hollywood was on in full force with Ernst Lubitsch, Ernest Vajda, and all). Dutch played twin sisters whose psyches are so unlike that one is a humble Paris housewife while her twin leads the life of a gadfly buzzing about Montparnasse. I was in London when I received a report from Peg. "Sidney Franklin is directing Dutch as if she were born, bred, and educated in Paris, Kentucky."

Although *Her Sister from Paris* was a failure, it so tempted the star ego to play *two* roles that Constance Bennett refilmed it in 1934 as *Moulin Rouge*. Then, in 1941, it came to a monumental destiny by wrecking the career of Greta Garbo. Under the title

Two-Faced Woman, it felled Garbo with one single blow. She has never acted again.

Dutch frisked through three more movies—*The Duchess of Buffalo, Breakfast at Sunrise,* and *Venus,* which was filmed on the French Riviera. But in 1929 Dutch quit for good, to be followed by Norma in 1930. Norma's fans consisted mostly of housewives and the gay community, but Dutch, without any effort or intention, was the true object of desire of every full-blooded male who saw her. Better than beautiful, she was pretty, which is less forbidding and a far greater joy to handle. With Dutch, a sense of *fun* took the place of a sense of humor and, being more spontaneous, relaxing, and feminine, it was downright sexy.

Today there are a few creatures like Dutch hovering about the entertainment field, but they are devoted to men of charm and wealth who keep them for their own private consumption. The wives of Frank Sinatra, Walter Matthau, and Bob Evans and the current sweetheart of Joe Namath not only resemble Dutch but follow her formula—they are funny, sunny, and uncalculating.

But along with her many delights, Dutch harbored a cool remoteness that frustrated predators, filling them with overwhelming jealousy, impotence, and rage. I contend that Dutch, given the proper time slot and circumstances, could have brought about the Trojan War . . . and done it with a giggle.

Only in
Hollywood...

CHAPTER NINE

As the silent films were drawing to their close, our lives began to take off in different directions. Norma and Dutch replaced their careers with marriages that were more or less temporary. Nate divorced Buster Keaton, and having dissipated all her energies on being a shrewish wife, spent her remaining years as a sulky divorcée. She called herself Mrs. Talmadge and legalized that name for the two sons she had by Buster.

Where are they now, those scions of a famous clown and heirs of Norma, Constance, Natalie, and Peg? After the "Talmadge" boys were grown, I heard that they worked in one of the technical departments at Joe Schenck's studio. But recently when I tried to track them down, I found that nobody in the Hollywood area knew where they were; a great many didn't even know of their existence.

Then came a glimmer of light; I happened to appear on a television talk show with the comedian Georgie Jessel, who had been Norma's second husband for a few years. Georgie told me that the last he heard of Buster's sons they were operating a ranch together on the outskirts of Reno, Nevada, trying to cope with the tribulations of ranch life without the gags of their inspired father.

After Norma and Dutch quit the movies, Joe Schenck joined with Darryl Zanuck, and for years the two presided over the vast empire of Twentieth Century-Fox. Joe made John and me an offer to remain in his employ, which would have pleased me, but my husband was bent on retirement. Having flirted with Communism for several years, he was anxious to give more time to the Cause.

John's motive, as in many cases, was a disarming one, because it was rooted in guilt over the enormous salary he accepted for "work" that was largely fun and games. Any card-carrying Communist felt he held a passport to self-esteem; it was an absolution to thumb your nose at the very Establishment that was pampering you. But, like many a movie martyr, John nevertheless enjoyed his undeserved loot, so he proceeded to damn the rich from the vantage point of a Palm Beach villa and a Rolls-Royce convertible.

I was bored by such nonsense and went my own way, looking for better entertainment, from the profundity of Aldous Huxley and H.G. Wells to the raucous iconoclasm of Edmund Wilson and H.L. Mencken. I also idolized the show-biz wiz Mike Todd, who once broke a contract with me but won my heart by declaring, "Baby, I've been on the level with you just as far as any Broadway hustler can!"

There were two long periods, during World War I and World War II, when Europe was out of bounds for normal living, so the wealthy, the cultured, and the fashionable were enticed to Hollywood. Great artists like Stravinsky, Huxley, and Auden and social figures like Lady Charles Mendel moved west into the sunshine. Eventually most of them "went Hollywood."

I think that a miasma of psychic foolishness hovers above the area, mixes with the smog, and infiltrates everybody. Charlie

Chaplin gave princely banquets in a mansion while playing footsie with Communism. Doug and Mary acted their off-screen love scenes so incessantly that they ended by throwing dishes at each other. The Stravinskys, the Huxleys, and the Artur Rubinsteins kept themselves aloof, but even darling Aldous went a little kinky experimenting with LSD.

I used to fear falling under the cultural blight of Hollywood . . . my only warning came when I went shopping and began to think that the dresses looked chic.

But much as I preferred other places to Hollywood, there was a sort of gentility about its early culture. Film stars tried to conceal their infidelities like ladies and gentlemen of the old school. Illicit affairs were generally sweetened by the worthy goal of marriage, no matter how rowdy it might turn out to be. I cite the marriage of Mary Pickford's sister Lottie to a bootlegger, who decorously posed as a mortician in order to deliver his contraband in a hearse. Drugs were a relative novelty, to be used in private, not passed about on platters as they now are.

In the matter of art, a portrait of Clara Bow by Howard Chandler Christy might be placed beside *The Night Watch* by Rembrandt. Most furniture was imitation Spanish and spanking new but had been polychromed to make it look antique. And no time was wasted on cut flowers when plastic was flashier and needed dusting only once a week.

One couldn't blame the Hollywood males for insisting on their weekly poker games, for after a long day in the studio there was little diversion except for the chitchat of the girls, who dominated the conversation generally with horrendous tales of the misbehavior of domestic servants. The only alternative was to run a movie, which at least cued the guests into talking back at the picture in wisecracks that were sometimes funny.

But on Thursday evenings the boys had it all to themselves. They would meet in Joe's rumpus room; the sessions ran until dawn and the stakes were colossal, sometimes running into six figures. The aroma of imported delicatessen and Cuban cigars filtered up from the rumpus room and never disappeared completely, even though Norma used to attack it the next day by squirting Shalimar perfume from her crystal atomizer.

Social life was rather homespun. The most elaborate banquet at the San Simeon castle of Hearst and Marion Davies might boast solid-gold service plates, but there were paper napkins, and the centerpiece was an arrangement of catsup, pickles, and condiments with their commonplace labels (which, by the way, matched the quality of the table talk). The worst faux pas I recall from the early Hearst era was when Marion's nephew, Charlie Lederer, while horsing about in the picture gallery, thrust his foot through a Goya. Evening parties generally ended by eleven, at which hour Mr. Hearst would escort Marion upstairs as solemnly as if she were Queen Victoria on the princely arm of Albert.

Close friendships were few in Hollywood, but I was witness to one so unusual that I'm tempted to go back to its beginning and treat it in depth.

In 1918 the Talmadge group was in Hollywood, where Norma was filming a sophisticated movie titled *Her Only Way*. In its cast was a statuesque young redhead from New York named Jobyna Howland.

Jobey's career started when she was a showgirl in the Ziegfeld Follies. As such, she became a favorite model for Charles Dana Gibson, whose "Gibson Girl" glorified American beauty. But contrary to the opulent impression Jobey created, she was practical to an extreme.

We first met when Jobey, still in the Follies, occupied a Manhattan lovenest by courtesy of a well-heeled Wall Street broker. One day when showing Peg and me around the apartment, Jobyna gestured toward her Louis XVI bed and declared,

"It was auctioned at Parke-Bernet for ten thousand dollars! But I've never let the old boy plant his fanny on that mattress!"

Peg may have muttered, "Sez she!" but time would prove Peg wrong, for that sexy-looking creature turned out to be Hollywood's most ardent virgin.

Jobyna was one half of a team of notable girl friends of which the other half was the distinguished playwright Zoe Akins. Although the two were inseparable, their characters were widely different. While Jobey dismissed sex with a snort of disdain, Zoe's heart was set on an all-out love life. She was a short brunette and her dark eyes were rather slanty, giving her face a touch of Oriental charm. But she was, alas, roly-poly beyond any control. When Zoe walked she teetered.

Zoe had won fame on Broadway in 1919 with a tragicomedy in which Ethel Barrymore enjoyed one of her longest runs. It was titled *Déclassée* and concerned a British lady of title who had fallen so low on the social scale that she was associating with vaudeville performers.

In its most poignant scene, Zoe's heroine predicted her own imminent death and made the declaration, "I've never believed in doctors; I've never believed in lawyers, but I've always believed in fortune-tellers!" That statement, delivered in Ethel's deep-throated tone, gave full scope to her heartbreaking charm. And the fact that the speech was easily burlesqued by female impersonators only increased the prestige of its author.

Like all girl friends, Jobey and Zoe had their squabbles. Zoe, as a poetic but frustrated fatty, brought forth all of Jobey's derision. "You ought to stop your mooning and go on a crash diet," Jobey used to advise. But such gibes actually held the key to their devotion. How seldom in life does someone who meekly craves to get slapped have the luck to find instant, slam-bang response? Theirs was an antagonism made in heaven.

When the glamour of New York show biz shifted westward,

Zoe and Jobyna joined the exodus to Hollywood, Zoe as a high-salaried script writer, and Jobey to begin her movie career in Norma's picture. The two soon took places as leaders in the elite of the film colony. Jobey settled in a strictly functional bungalow at a crossroad in Beverly Hills. Designed by Frank Lloyd Wright, it had "open-heart" plumbing (insofar as one could look through glass panels and admire the pure utility of the pipes) and its walls were six feet thick. (Mr. Wright never explained why a bungalow need be fashioned like a fortress.) There Jobey held forth, aided by a Navajo houseboy named Hernando. He was an excellent servant, but being homosexual, he used to steal Jobey's lipsticks, and sometimes she found his fingerprints in her face powder. This resulted in fisticuffs, but Jobey was sportsmanlike, and since she was heftier than the Navajo, she pulled her punches.

Zoe's life-style was completely different. She considered the film colony vulgar and could only breathe the rarefied air of Pasadena, that elegant suburb built in the eighties by retired tycoons and still so snobbish that it looked down on movie stars. Zoe purchased an Edwardian mansion, furnished it with opulence, and engaged a staff of British servants.

There Zoe presided with such prestige that Peg used to complain, "I'm always afraid she'll order everyone to leave the room except dukes and duchesses." This was not strictly fair. Although the tourist colony abounded in titles, both real and phony, many movie personalities were sufficiently beautiful and sophisticated to meet Zoe's requirements.

Lilyan Tashman wore dresses imported from Mainbocher in Paris; the Talmadge girls sported the more flashy styles of "Lucille," who, to Zoe's delight, was actually *Lady* Duff Gordon. Her Ladyship's sister was Elinor Glyn, who wrote *Three Weeks*, the sizzling novel of low behavior among the upper classes. Elinor was also famous for presenting Clara Bow as the "It" girl. (Clara and other riffraff such as Mabel Normand and Viola Dana never got invited to Zoe's.)

The gentlemen on Zoe's guest list included Lionel and Jack Barrymore, Adolphe Menjou, Edmund Lowe, and Lowell Sherman, all of whom were models of London tailoring from Savile Row.

When coffee was served at Zoe's dinner parties, she used to summon her butler, who was an amateur virtuoso on the flute, to divert the guests with a snatch or two of Mozart. Now a Mozart solo was a pretty mild amusement, even for Pasadena. But Jobey might relieve the tedium by calling out, "For God's sake, stop that mumbling music and let us talk!"

On one such occasion, an embarrassed Zoe placed a finger to her lips and whispered, "Shush!" At which Jobey jumped up from the table to declare, "Don't you shush *me*! *I'm speaking for every music lover in this room.*"

A smattering of tipsy applause rose from Jack Barrymore, causing the butler to fluff an adagio, and again Zoe whispered "Shush!"

Jobey then picked up a Meissen bowl filled with hothouse strawberries and heaved them at Zoe, just missing her expansive décolletage. We all helped the butler pick strawberries off the Aubusson rug, during which activity Jack Barrymore pinched a couple of tempting ankles and the occasion turned into a very lively get-together, which Zoe, with a sort of abashed sportsmanship, was forced to join.

By this time Hollywood was drawing attractive fortune hunters from all over the world, so it was in the cards that Zoe's quest for romance would ultimately succeed. Her hero, Hugo Rumbold, was a British aristocrat, and the fact that Zoe was earning $2,500 a week at MGM made him all the more authentic.

Hugo was then in his early forties, handsome and witty, and

his old-world manners gave spice to a very masculine charm. Zoe's beau was also talented in many ways; he could have been a successful painter, photographer, or costume designer—careers from which he may have been blocked by a certain mild affliction in the form of a stutter. But Hugo's main handicap was his all-out devotion to fun.

When the English go in for being outlandish, they can rise above every other nationality. (As examples, I cite *Alice in Wonderland*, the operettas of Gilbert and Sullivan, and the comedy antics of Bea Lillie and Danny La Rue.) One of Hugo's minor diversions was to dress up in women's clothes, not as a beauty but as a hag. He once fooled everybody at an Elsa Maxwell party, claiming to be the wife of the German consul general to New York City. Shapeless and ungainly, wearing baggy cotton stockings, sporting a distinct mustache, and speaking a hilarious fractured English, the Frau Generalkonsul was a sensation, even before she was identified as Elsa's pal Hugo.

Hugo sometimes had a practical motive for this behavior. As a young blade, he had once taken a trip to Venice with his beautiful English mistress *and her husband.* Disguised as the lady's frowsy Italian maid, he enjoyed an entire week of undiscovered dalliance.

And his eccentricity was now responsible for Hugo's presence in Hollywood. Just before going there, he had been a houseguest at a mansion on the Lake Shore of Chicago, having faked a letter of introduction as a dowager British duchess.

Now it so happened that a niece of Hugo's hostess unexpectedly popped in from finishing school, and because all the guest rooms were occupied, the "duchess" was asked if she'd mind sharing her twin beds with the young lady. Actually the girl was a horsey type and stood in no moral danger. But one morning she barged in on the "duchess" taking a shower, discovered Hugo's gender, and told Aunty. Hugo was ordered out of Chicago in disgrace, and as any footloose adventurer might, he headed for Hollywood.

Soon after Hugo became one of Zoe's favorite dinner guests, disaster caught up with him. A member of the Chicago elite on a visit to California told of Hugo's being thrown out of Chicago. And Zoe, believing he must have made an attempt on the virtue of a debutante, was alarmed that such a bounder had invaded her chaste household. So to clear the atmosphere, she sent for Hugo and demanded an explanation. "How did you come to commit such a breach of etiquette?" asked Zoe. It was only then that Hugo told the motive for his aberrant behavior.

As a child, Hugo's speech had been perfectly normal. But one night when his nanny left him alone in the family castle, the little boy was visited by a ghost. She carried her head under one arm, and dangling about her severed throat like a necklace was a bloody crown. The sight so terrified little Hugo that a stutter invaded his speech—one that endless years of therapy had failed to cure.

While still a boy, Hugo developed a penchant for those bawdy entertainers so dear to the British music hall. And once, while imitating a scraggy old variety star, he suddenly realized that his stutter had departed, only to return after he finished his imitation. The ruse of pretending to be somebody else instantly freed him of the hated affliction. Hugo could have found equal surcease in an attractive disguise, but he enjoyed the impudence of being female and a frump.

For Zoe, that moment of truth was particularly touching . . . an ancient British castle, a ghost who might have been that of Mary, Queen of Scots, a mysterious and hopeless affliction. It could have been a story by Lord Byron, with His Lordship himself as the hero. And Zoe's emotional forgiveness led directly to their betrothal.

Just the same, Hugo's lack of sterling qualities had always bothered Jobyna. Zoe's heart was set on a romantic wedding under the bower in her rose garden. But, to quote Jobyna, "A groom like Hugo could louse the whole thing up." So on the wedding morning Jobey drove to Pasadena, barged into Zoe's boudoir, and issued an ultimatum. "Push that lazy gigolo out of bed, so he can arrive at his wedding *respectably*, through the front gate!"

While Hollywood marriages were failing all around us, theirs seemed likely to endure a lifetime (which it did). Many ladies of fashion, beauty, and wealth superior to Zoe's had tried in vain to land Hugo. But possibly he was fascinated by a character as feckless as his own. Hugo was much more cultured than his bride, which led to browbeating that delighted her masochistic heart even more than those petty squabbles with Jobyna. The honeymoon might have gone on indefinitely but, alas, Hugo suddenly came down with hepatitis and died.

When the Talmadge girls and I arrived at Zoe's estate for the funeral, Jobyna met us in the baronial hall. But grief had softened Jobey and her face was streaked with mascara over the loss of a man she had so often defied. Her tears now gave evidence of a sneaky, underlying fondness. "Come into the parlor and see Hugo!" Jobyna sobbed softly. "He looks so distinguished, the goddamn pimp!"

Jobey had not exaggerated Hugo's distinction, for Zoe had gone to the MGM prop department and borrowed an assortment of medals with which to deck him out in a manner appropriate to his heritage. Before the obsequies could begin, however, there was an awkward pause while the medals were retrieved so they could be returned the next day to the prop department. Then the bier was wheeled into the garden, for a ceremony beneath the same rose-covered bower under which Hugo and Zoe had so romantically exchanged their wedding vows.

The eulogy was deeply touching, for Zoe had supplied the clergyman with a quote from the lovely poem by Rupert Brooke which assures any wandering Englishman a resting place "that is for ever England."

We were just starting to accompany Hugo to his last resting place, when the burial was suddenly canceled. It was explained in whispers that Zoe, in her grief and confusion, had purchased a gravesite in a lowly suburb outside the chic enclave of Pasadena. It would require time for Zoe to find a proper place in the "right" cemetery.

We all dispersed in silence, but Hugo had been spared from resting forever between a dealer in used cars and a humble Altadena dentist.

In looking back, I begin to realize that my most endearing memories of Hollywood are of those who made us laugh. For it was no small trick to inject smiles into the funeral of someone we cherished as much as we all cherished Hugo Rumbold. In pulling that trick off, both Zoe and Jobyna disdained trying to be other than their own true, outlandish selves, let the laughs fall where they might. And if Hugo's spirit was present, we knew he would be laughing more heartily than anyone else.

As a widow, Zoe visited England to meet Hugo's aristocratic family. There she was presented with a number of crude drawings Hugo had made as a little boy. When Zoe brought them through the customs in New York, she declared them as works of art of such value that the inspector was puzzled. "They sure look like hen scratches to me!" he remarked. But, insisting that they were masterpieces, Zoe paid that self-imposed duty and went broke.

In those palmy days the most poignant love affairs could take place off screen, without benefit of Gable or Garbo. Nor did one have to be a film star to "go Hollywood." So we were all aware that Zoe couldn't forever go on paying the high cost of her quixotic self-indulgence.

On that fateful day, when Peg and I had left Hugo's canceled burial, Peg nudged me. "Well, Buggie, the next affair we'll be asked to here will be the auction!" In due time the Universal Finance Company pulled that auction off, just as predicted. And it became one more instance strengthening Peg's lack of trust in the galloping gold of the movies.

The Other Side of Cinderella

The films of Norma and Constance paid off extremely well in cash, but Peg looked on them as showcases for the wares she had to sell. In spite of her persistence, however, her three Brooklyn Cinderellas, between them, chalked up eight rather unsatisfactory princes.

Joe Schenck had every male attraction except good looks. He always had to fight overweight, his hair was getting sparse, and a slight cast in one eye was disturbing to look at until you got used to it. It is probably not too surprising then that Norma decided she was in love with her handsome Mexican leading man. Peg did her best to separate the sweethearts but was defeated by the fact that they were in the midst of filming a picture, while Joe was even more chagrined at having chosen the actor who would be his rival. But he counted on Gilbert's good looks losing their novelty and thought that perhaps his allure depended on the love story he and Norma happened to be acting out. Joe was right, for eventually Norma lost the urge to marry Gilbert.

But by that time divorce proceedings were under way, and

when Joe made no move to stop them, Norma could only admire the calm dignity with which Joe walked out on the humiliations of being married to a film star. He left a void in Norma's life that no other man would ever fill.

During the climax of Norma's affair with Gilbert Roland, a rumor went the rounds that Joe had called on the gangster element of his entourage to kidnap Roland, hide him in one of those Hollywood canyons where so many dark deeds take place, and emasculate him. But that rumor simply couldn't be true. In the first place Joe always accepted his losses stoically, like the born gambler he was. And, a few years later, Roland married Constance Bennett, who would never have considered any suitor who didn't rate an Academy Award for competence.

Although Peg was vastly relieved when Norma weeded a film star out of her life, she feared an impending loss of her solvent son-in-law. However, when Norma first married Joe, she had nicknamed him "daddy," and after their parting Joe continued to be the same ideal father figure—not only to Norma, but also to Dutch and Nate.

It takes a true ladies' man to be as faithful a husband as Joe was, and on becoming a pseudobachelor he enjoyed affairs with a number of movie beauties, among them Marilyn Monroe. But he remained well outside the Hollywood marriage market, and having occupied a series of cheerful homes with Norma, he never tried to establish another. I recall Jack Warner once advising Joe, "You ought to buy a gorgeous place in Beverly Hills, where you can entertain your friends."

"Who needs the kind of friends that have to be entertained?" asked Joe.

One day I discovered that Joe *had* manufactured a family life of sorts for himself. Sometimes when I spent the summer abroad, Joe borrowed my beach house in Santa Monica. Once, on returning home for Christmas, I ran into him leaving the house with his arms full of toys. Joe explained that they were for his butler's little girl. I found out later that he had formed a close friendship with the seven-year-old child, a relationship none of his associates ever knew about. (I hope that when little Barbara grew up she shared my devotion to Joe Schenck.)

Norma, spoiled, petulant, and bored with the sort of attraction she had found in Gilbert Roland, started to search for more lively diversions. She found them in one of "daddy's" own poker-playing chums, the prominent stand-up comedian George Jessel. Joe benevolently coached his successor on the best way to handle their skittish loved one, and eventually Norma married Georgie. Because the talkies had ended her film career by then, she had nothing to do but be amused by Georgie's jokes.

To Peg, Norma's second marriage would have smacked of degradation. Georgie would always be assured the salary of a top vaudevillian, while Norma, thanks to Joe, was rich, with all of her assets in her own name. But after a few years Georgie began to detect signs of boredom in his lovely wife. Hopeful of a cure, he induced Norma to join him in a vaudeville act. She could save face by citing the example of the great Sarah Bernhardt, who had toured the USA in a theatrical company.

But Norma was no Bernhardt; neither could she match her husband as a stand-up entertainer. Worst of all, Georgie's jokes had ceased to entertain his bride at home. (Possibly it's a fault of stand-up comedians that they persist in standing up when they should lie down.) And so it came about that, during the same period when Constance was fighting off the doldrums with alcohol, Norma fell afoul of drugs. It may have been Norma's addiction that led directly to her third and final marriage, for she chose a physician, who she thought could guarantee her a steady supply of drugs.

In time Norma developed a crippling arthritis, which is so

often the aftermath of taking drugs, and she spent long years bedridden and in pain. Frequently immobilized by ill health and dependent on a doctor-husband, Norma took what comfort she could in relations with gay men, as do many retired sexpots. But she was through with love affairs and she knew it.

Though Norma's marriages were anything but comic, Dutch's tended to be farces, although her four husbands might not have agreed with that description. Dutch's first, John Pialogiou, was a dignified and sensitive man who had been enticed far out of his element into the mixture of lightweights that surrounded Dutch.

When Pialogiou met Dutch, she had been the cause of numberless heartbreaks: Irving Thalberg, Irving Berlin, Richard Barthelmess, and several other international swells. Pialogiou was Greek; his family dealt in the importation of tobacco, and he lived at the St. Regis Hotel, which at that time was a center of Manhattan chic and luxury.

Their marriage was the outcome of a "dare" on an occasion when Dutch and her chum Dorothy Gish (otherwise known as "Doates") were on a weekend jaunt with two suitors, Dorothy's being the movie actor James Rennie. "I'll go through with it if you will!" said Doates, and Dutch assented. I believe the deed took place somewhere in Connecticut, after which the two virgin brides insisted on going directly home to summon enough courage to tell their families.

Mother Gish and sister Lillian, although shocked, were lenient. They didn't disapprove of Rennie, although Lillian could not—and can't to this day—look on a man as an adjunct to any film star's career.

Peg was more or less philosophical about Dutch's marriage. After all, Pialogiou was rich and Peg was fed up with her child's refusal to accept either of two promising Irvings (Thalberg or Berlin). But the marriages of both Dutch and Doates, like most spur-of-the-moment affairs, broke records for their speedy endings.

John Pialogiou, who had been flabbergasted by his good luck in winning Dutch, was so bewildered on losing her that he never got over it. He couldn't understand that his devotion bored her. It is a man's greatest stupidity to marry a sexpot and then expect her to turn overnight into Whistler's Mother. John never married again.

Joe Schenck activated a divorce for Dutch, and not long afterward she met Captain Allaster MacIntosh at a posh cocktail party. The captain held a commission in His Majesty's Horse Guards and had a charisma that equaled Dutch's own, so their romance seemed a foregone conclusion. The only one to hold out against it was Peg, who had heard that a guardsman's income barely paid for horse feed. On the other hand, Captain MacIntosh was a favorite playmate of the Prince of Wales, a connection that seemed rather exciting, even to Peg. After all, Dutch's earnings had made her independently rich.

No sooner was the marriage consummated than Peg had to pay for her lapse into snobbery. For, like the young in every walk of life, Allie yearned to get into the moving picture racket, and Dutch's husband took a mercenary tack.

Joe Schenck came to the rescue as usual, and provided the young husband with an executive job in his New York office. But the bridegroom soon found that a movie job entailed work, and he began to absent himself from dull discussions of movie franchises to play polo at Southampton with Tommy Hitchcock, or enter tennis tournaments—two diversions in which his bride had little interest.

Meanwhile Allie was being urged by the Prince of Wales to join him in London. Dutch was footloose and Peg, fed up with trying to be polite to her son-in-law, consented to the honeymooners' departure for the Court of St. James's.

On Dutch's first encounter with the Prince of Wales, she had watched him from a sidewalk as he sped down Fifth Avenue in an open roadster, his blond locks rumpled by the breeze and his face wreathed in a provocative smile. But after she was ensconced in a royal suite at Claridge's, the dashing Mrs. MacIntosh began to form a different impression of H.R.H. There was an insidious rumor afloat that he was emotionally involved with the young American star Glen Hunter, a man whom all London idolized in a stage play, *Merton of the Movies*. And, although the Prince was supposedly paying court to Mrs. Jean Nash, the predecessor of Wallis Simpson, H.R.H occupied a front row seat at *Merton of the Movies* whenever he could sneak out on royal chores.

Actually, I believe that His Highness was identifying himself with a young star who closely resembled him, that in watching Glen Hunter he was seeing himself as he would have preferred to be . . . a movie actor. At any rate, Dutch felt that the Prince's feet, if not of clay, were of rather brittle crockery.

Dutch was ardently pursued by that fabled set of young aristocrats who were known as London's Bright Young People. Among the diversions they invented was a "treasure hunt," in which they spent night and day digging for hidden loot in unlikely places and making nuisances of themselves to the London bobbies. Dutch felt that those amusements were contrived, and like H.R.H.'s defunct grandma, she was not amused.

The Talmadge girls and I exchanged occasional postcards while traveling, but once in a while our paths actually crossed, and on one of my annual visits to London, I ran into Dutch. I was viewing the London season from a different angle from hers. I had a beau who, although one of King George's gentlemen-in-waiting, chose his friends among such dissidents as Margot Asquith, Lady Cunard, Willie Maugham, and H.G. Wells.

Dutch once said to me, "Those highbrows you trail with scare the heart out of me. Every time I open my mouth, something silly comes out." She was wrong; her "silliness" was a spontaneous and disarming gaiety. But let's face it, Dutch saw no point in wit that was contaminated by wisdom.

One day while lunching at Claridge's, Dutch flagged me on my way out. "Come to my suite at five," said she. "I can't wait to ask what's going on at home."

When we were alone that afternoon, Dutch's first question was "Buggie, do you ever see *Martin Herman?*" From her eagerness you would have guessed that Martin was an ex-sweetheart. He was anything but. Martin was the half brother of Albert H. Woods (who produced such Broadway hits as *Up in Mabel's Room* and *Getting Gertie's Garter*), but was somewhat less erudite than his brother. He was in his mid-forties, with the rugged looks of a Humphrey Bogart. He wore his brown derby at such an angle that it almost touched the stogies he smoked, and his vocabulary, while ingenious, was strictly from Brooklyn.

Yet Dutch, surrounded by the bright ambience of her British drawing room, was yearning for Martin Herman. With tears streaming down her Botticelli angel face, she said, "Oh, Buggie, I'd trade in the best of these royal geegans for just one hour with Marty Herman!"

There came a respite in Dutch's boredom that season when New York's Mayor Jimmy Walker, on a ceremonial visit, was feted by the dashing American hostess Mrs. Gilbert Miller at her town house in Mayfair. All the Bright Young People were there. But His Honor got tight, as he so often did, and on meeting Dutch declared, "Let's give the brush to these show-offs." Jimmy pulled Dutch into a hall closet to indulge in a little private necking, but the situation exploded when Allie whammed the door open; Royal Favor came to grips with Tammany Hall and Tammany lost.

Not long after that debacle, Dutch phoned Joe Schenck in New York and begged him to set things right. And Joe, tactful as always, arranged a divorce, which I presume was sweetened by that institution imported from France and termed a *"cadeau de rupture."* It is a cash gift, generally accorded to a deserted female, but in Dutch's case the payoff went to the male member of that faulted romance.

Escorted by Peg, Dutch returned to Manhattan. But for all her ebullience, Dutch was the helpless type who needed a man. And it stood to reason that she'd look for comedy relief in her next husband. She found it in Townsend Netcher, scion of department store tycoons in Chicago. His brother was married to one of the glittering Dolly Twins from Hungary, who starred as a sister act in the Folies Bergère, the Ziegfeld Follies, and other international show spots.

That ambience provided Dutch with the sort of easygoing vulgarity that made for domestic zest. Their lives revolved about New York night clubs, and they were sustained by alcohol, which led, perforce, to an increase in their intake.

Let it be said for Dutch, however, that she got tight the way she did everything else, delectably and with nothing more raucous than a giggle. Her pretty face and youthful figure remained intact. This, however, was not true of Netcher. Dutch at length got fed up with her third mate's grossness, but by then she herself was well into a drinking problem.

Dutch's fourth was Walter Giblin, a Wall Street broker who had long been hovering around Dutch's periphery. I was impressed on first meeting Walter and complimented Dutch on her choice. But she, who couldn't bear to be serious on *any* subject, replied, "Thanks, Buggie—but *you* take him!" Just the same she was grateful for Walter's qualities as a gentle human being, and she didn't mind his dullness.

Dutch, worn out by the repetitious fun of night clubs, was now content to do her drinking in the peace and quiet of their suite at the Drake Hotel. When Walter was on Wall Street she was spared isolation by the company of a cute girl friend, "China" Harris, the young widow of Sam H. Harris, the Broadway producer. The two girls shared a love for martinis, laughter, and gossip among that group of deluxe guys and dolls who frequent the 21 Club.

But Giblin suddenly died in 1964, and Dutch was left, without warning, to join her pal China in widowhood. Still girlishly pretty, Dutch was frequently wooed, but she never married again. However, she never lost a disarming fondness for the male sex and she never forgot the men in her past.

There sticks in my mind the memory of a certain supper to which Dutch invited her three ex-husbands and included her successors in their lives (a wife, a fiancée, and a sweetheart). But the party broke up with the ladies in high frustration over their mates' obvious nostalgia for that blonde, fun-loving widow.

The last time I saw Dutch was at a cocktail party given by Leonard Sillman, the New York theatrical producer. Walter Giblin had only recently died, and Leonard took it on himself to drag Dutch back into the New York scene. But her situation was pitiful. "Oh Buggie," she said to me, "I was never cut out to be a widow. I don't know how to go it alone. I've never even had to call a taxicab or learned how to write a check. I just sit and wait. But there's nothing to wait for!"

At that time Dutch was being urged by Sillman and other Broadway producers to go on the stage, to which she replied, "Are you kidding? Why, I couldn't act even when I was a movie star."

Not long after Giblin's death, his family began to unleash a resentment they'd always felt about Dutch's honesty, candor, and—more forgivably perhaps—her drinking habits. Finally Sillman learned that Dutch was about to be declared incompetent to handle the fortune left by her husband, and Dutch, in order to escape persecution, ran away to California. Dutch found an obscure hiding place in a nondescript beach cottage occupied by Nate and her two kids. And at length Giblin's kin gave up hounding his widow and she was left in peace.

By that time Dutch and I were widely separated, she living in retirement and I very active in the superficial affairs of London, Paris, and New York. Dutch was not a letter writer so we didn't correspond. It was several weeks after Nate's death before I even heard about it. At any rate, Nate had been put out of circulation by arthritis, and apparently she was taken off by sheer lack of zest for living.

Alone of all the Talmadge misadventures, the marriage of Natalie to Buster Keaton reached a climax of unmitigated tragedy. Their romance had developed rather gradually—which should have made it all the more enduring. Throughout their early friendship, Buster had had an affair with a boisterous young movie star, Viola Dana. But she flashed in and out of his life, leaving no repercussions.

Natalie, having failed as star material, was quietly holding down a secretarial job at the studio, in the course of which she and Buster frequently ran into each other. Their encounters had begun to verge on romance when World War I intervened. Buster was called into the infantry and sent overseas. By the end of the war, Peg had come to grips with the fact that Nate might just as well marry a movie star. Joe Schenck came to their aid as Cupid, and ultimately he granted Buster a company to make his own comedies.

But Joe's generosity was solely a matter of nepotism. He had no understanding of the depths that lay beneath Buster's antics; he was never to learn that those films he financed would go down in movie history as works of art. Not only did Buster's creative talent, of which he himself was scarcely aware, suffer neglect at the studio, but he was also made miserable at home by Nate's lack of interest in his work.

As Mrs. Buster Keaton, Nate could feel important only by indulging the pretentiousness her two famous sisters lacked. She "went Hollywood" with a vengeance. Buster, who had been brought up in small-time vaudeville and had spent his early years in shoddy theatrical hotels, had dreamed all his life of owning a bungalow with a garden in California. But married to Nate, he was pulled into a succession of showy homes which were burlesques of Hollywood bad taste.

The fifth and final of Mrs. Buster Keaton's silly homes was an "Italian villa" in Beverly Hills. It was of the type that should have been approached through a long alley of formally clipped yews. But because acreage in Beverly Hills was at a premium, the villa occupied a rather narrow lot, which brought all its hideous curlicues into bold relief.

I've never forgotten a certain afternoon when I happened to be inspecting Nate's rather scanty garden. I ran into Buster, who was digging a tiny ditch in which the water trickled aimlessly. Buster was as intent as if he were constructing the Panama Canal. When I asked what he was doing, he replied, "Just having fun! I can make my little ditch go anywhere I choose . . . to the right . . . or left or straight ahead." He paused to sigh in satisfaction. *"I sure have authority over my little creek!"*

That was the only authority Buster ever knew as a member of the Talmadge clan. Henpecked by a wife who considered any male an automatic enemy, poor Buster remained an uncomplaining husband as long as Natalie would have him.

During Buster's lengthy ordeal, Nate gave birth to two boys, who might have cemented the union if they hadn't been taken over by Peg and spoiled by their aunties Norma and Dutch, who indulged the infants with disturbing gifts such as automobiles, when they would have been more comfortable with a set of building blocks or a jack-in-the-box.

Buster Keaton ultimately found an anodyne for the neglect he suffered at home; he took to rather heavy drinking, at which the entire Talmadge clan, led by his wife, ganged up on him. After Nate divorced Buster he went further into alcoholism and inactivity, but he was rescued by an intelligent and appreciative second wife and eventually won the acclaim of critics, who would compare his movies to the farces of the French master Feydeau, or going further back in time, to Molière. But recognition came late, in 1959, with a special Academy Award. Buster died in 1966.

In Peg's mind, too, a husband was an enemy. Fred Talmadge, however, had enough spirit to rebel and, after fathering three infants, he ran out on the whole lot. Following his disappearance, Peg seemed not to think of Fred. When she did, it was easy to visualize him in his normal boozy state groveling in some low dive far from Brooklyn where he would never bump into Peg or their offspring.

Peg had done a rather thorough job of weeding sentiment from her kids' experiences, so they scarcely thought of Daddy at all. During the years when Norma and Dutch were reaching the peak of their beauty, fame, and wealth, it appeared that their father must be lost forever in some neglected cemetery. Why else would he have failed to show up and demand a slice of that fabulous pie?

There had always been a vague rumor that Norma and Natalie were true daughters of Fred Talmadge, but that the youngest, Constance, had been fathered by the Viennese waiter who was a tenant in Peg's Brooklyn house. This I have never believed; Norma, Natalie and Constance bore a marked resemblance to one another, except that Dutch's brown eyes had a brighter sparkle.

One dramatic incident convinced me that Dutch had a flesh-and-blood tie with Fred Talmadge. Peg and the girls were out for a spin through New York City in Peg's famous Cadillac with her golden logo painted on the door. They were dripping in mink, for it was midwinter and, as Peg put it, "colder than a penguin's behind." The farthest thing from all their minds was that long-lost father.

As they cruised along Riverside Drive, Peg glanced ahead and noticed a tramp huddled on an icy bench. She gave a start but made no comment until they'd passed him, when Peg ordered the chauffeur to stop. Then, gesturing toward the shivering derelict on the bench, Peg remarked, "Will you girls take a look at that bum back there?" As they turned to look, Peg added casually, "He's your father." During their unified gasp, Peg addressed the driver: "Just buzz off before that barfly spots us."

Norma and Nate were too startled to utter a word, but Dutch took charge. "Just a moment!" she ordered the chauffeur. "Back up to the gentleman on that bench."

Peg rolled down the window and in her most offhand manner called out, "Hello, Fred."

The tramp peered at her blearily and answered in a tone as casual as Peg's, "Hello, Peg."

"Where've you been these last fifteen years?" Peg asked.

"Around," he ventured, with the infuriating vagueness of a child.

As Peg hesitated, searching for words, Dutch hopped to the sidewalk, gestured toward the car and said, "Get in here, Pop!"

Fred squinted at Dutch and then, paraphrasing Stanley's question to Livingstone in darkest Africa, he ventured, "Constance, I presume?"

"That's right," said Dutch. "Will you get in out of the cold?"

Fred shivered and then, more in politeness than enthusiasm, replied, "Don't mind if I do." Fred stumbled onto a jump seat, adding the aroma of stale beer to the perfume of damp mink and the Jasmine of Houbigant, which the girls then affected.

Peg's car sped on, and there was little further conversation between her and her spouse. Why talk about a situation that had bored Peg long ago? Just the same, Fred had behaved in a manner Peg approved. There was no nonsense, no description of experiences which were self-evident in Fred's stubbly chin and watery red eyes. Later on Peg was even to compliment Fred on his behavior. "I'll say one thing in the bum's favor," she observed. "In all those years he never showed up to put the bite on us for money!"

However, Peg was not going to give Fred a loophole for taking advantage. She and Dutch cased Third Avenue for a semirespectable hotel, and Fred was esconced there after they paid a week's rent in advance. Then the two took Fred off to Bloomingdale's to be outfitted. Peg then ordered Fred to show up at the studio the next morning, which, rather to her surprise, he actually did.

Peg introduced Fred to Eddie Mannix, the studio's manager and head bouncer. "This is the sprouts' father, Ed. Will you dig up some kind of job for him?"

"Oh sure!" said Eddie, never refusing an odd request of Peg's.

Fred was introduced to the prop department, and his first assignment was to tie artificial leaves on the bare branches of a prop tree. He made no complaint other than to indicate his shaky hands and observe, "This is one hell of a job for a drinking man!"

As time went on, Fred became less and less of a nuisance. He chose a few drinking companions in the Irish saloons along Third Avenue, where he tippled on beer that was relatively harmless. Peg and the girls were too busy to accord Pop much attention. But when they happened to meet him on the set, he was agreeable company—right up to the time of his demise.

That event took place during one of the company's Hollywood phases. Fred's social life had switched from the cozy drinking spots of Third Avenue to their equivalents on Hollywood's Sunset Strip. But his constitution, long a storage tank for excess alcohol, finally gave in to the strain, and Fred was no more.

I was not with the family at that time, but Peg wrote me the following belated confession of tenderness: "The funeral was held last week in Beverly Hills. It seemed as if every florist out here had orders. Hundreds of set pieces and a Hawaiian orchestra played "Aloha" during the services. Fred looked about thirty; such a change! Joe said he was glad when it was all over, because the sprouts and I barged over to the funeral parlor to look at Fred three or four times a day."

Peg's letter concluded, "We were wrecks! Specially the Dutchman. She and her father were a lot alike."

From the vantage point of that letter, I began to sense that Peg's antagonism to her husband may have been a cover-up for much milder feelings. I recalled that her earnings had been confiscated by Fred whenever feasible, but that Peg had never barred him from her bed on his sporadic visits home. She had even passed up that safe marriage to a wage-earning waiter.

Possibly more revealing was her reaction to Fred's neglect. Her attitude had always been flavored by jokes and never by the fury that such behavior merited. For in Fred's veins flowed the blood of a pimp, a type that lives by sheer charisma and whose disregard may seem even more tender than a love pat.

Dutch had always been Peg's favorite, and it's possible that, born at the climax of a long period of irresponsibility on Fred's part, Dutch may have been truly a love child.

Loot, Life, Love, and Sex— in That Order

Personalities were about all that interested Peg and her girls; events, no matter how important, escaped their notice unless they were mentioned in Walter Winchell's gossip column. To read a book, one had to be sick in bed and the book had to be *Three Weeks* or *Forever Amber*.

Norma and Dutch spent long, repititious hours on the set. Other than that, there were outside duties (such as dialogue to learn), and once the cameras ceased to grind, the girls were free to enter into the luxurious life-style of upper-class Bohemia. Shopping took high priority, and enormous interest could be lavished on such activities as trying on hats, in those days when everybody wore one, and patronizing beauty salons, at a time when wrinkles—for the girls—were far in the future. Peg, who would have benefited greatly from a few facial treatments, couldn't be bothered with them.

The most tiresome element in their jobs was provided by the studio's press agent, Beulah Livingstone, who was deadly serious about a profession that was just coming into being. (Camouflaged by the label of "public relations," that profession was soon to dominate the lives of many Americans.) Beulah would arrange interviews for Norma and Dutch, whom she would try to instruct in the art of talking like a movie star, and then she would monitor the girls to be sure they kept appointments.

On the surface the girls' lives seemed to meet with Peg's approval; she joined in all their fun with gusto and one could have assumed that Peg had safely attained her version of Utopia. But on one occasion she launched into one of the few serious conversations we ever had. I found that underlying Peg's satisfaction over the girls' fame, wealth, and glitter was the chilling fear that everything achieved might disappear as quickly as it had come, engulfing them in the poverty they had suffered long ago in Brooklyn.

During our talk that day I learned that they had scarcely reached stardom before Peg began to formulate some terrible anxieties. "You know it isn't my habit to be gloomy," Peg confided to me, "but when I'm alone with my thoughts, Buggie, I take a close look at my kids and I get disturbed."

In order to explain her fears Peg brought up the dire fate of little Jewel Carmen. "A couple of years ago Jewel was the hottest bet in Hollywood. She could have stashed away one year's salary in tax-free bonds and been independent for life. But through sheer lack of will power, Jewel started giving in to every man on the lot. And then, because she was under the legal age of consent, the entire company was forced to cross the border into Mexico to keep several higher-ups from being sent to jail. For Jewel, that was only the beginning. One day when they were filming on the streets of Tijuana, Jewel spotted a Mexican bullfighter and walked right out of her million-dollar contract. She's still down there, hustling at bargain rates and being paid off in pesos!

"Then there's gorgeous Alma Reubens," Peg continued.

"She's still a star but in her advanced state of drug addiction, it can't be for long.

"On the other hand," Peg went on, "I look around at the film stars who are foolproof. How come Theda Bara, with a face like a smudge and a body that hasn't had an outline in years, has retired, a millionairess in her own right and a society leader with her name in the Los Angeles Blue Book?

"And take that older Gish kid . . . she's moved away from her mother and sister into her own apartment, just to have peace and quiet to study those scripts D.W. dreams up for her. Folks like to wisecrack that she wants a place of her own to entertain Norman Kerry, but I know better. I bet the movie ham will never be born who can take Lillian's mind off her salary check."

I tried to argue that Lillian's interest was in art, not money. "Then she'd better change," snapped Peg, "or she'll end up in Springfield, Ohio, where she came from, taking in lodgers.

"But nothing short of the apocalypse is going to stop that Crawford kid from getting ahead. And when Gloria Swanson gives her all, it's to a Boston billionaire.

"So there's got to be some difference between kids like Jewel and Alma and my kids. It can't be a matter of talent, because any clod can be trained to make faces at a camera. I'm telling you that a movie star is in as dangerous a spot as a baby who's been set down in traffic on Forty-second and Broadway. Her looks open up bigger areas to make mistakes than any ugly girl ever runs into. She attracts a larger assortment of freeloaders, pimps, agents, husbands—worst of all the kind who try to handle all four rackets wrapped up in one.

"It would be dangerous enough if Norma and Dutch were wild over sex. But they aren't. In Norma's case it's practically the reverse. She backs away from Joe like he was a swamp. But it begins to look now as if she's getting a crush on that sex-sufficient hambone Joe hired to play opposite her. Joe is a big-hearted schmo, but just the same I can't imagine him giving those two his blessing. And much as I hate to face the fact, I realize that Norma is lacking in forethought.

"Seeing that Natalie didn't develop along sexy lines, the fact that her brains rattle isn't too dangerous. It's Dutch I'm most scared about—scared that laughs are always going to mean more to her than security. Mind you, I understand her feelings about movie fans who grab, squeeze, and even go so far as to make free. I wouldn't want Dutch to take herself seriously and get a swelled head, but there's a limit to foolery.

"D'you know what happened last week?" Peg asked. "Well, I dropped by the publicity department, where Nate was autographing Dutch's fan pictures. Now Beulah Livingstone had had one of those asinine brain waves she gets paid good money for, and she thought up a new slogan for Nate to write on Dutch's pictures; it was 'Merrily yours, Constance Talmadge.'

"Well . . . what did I find? I find that Dutch had objected to Beulah putting a coy word like 'merrily' into her vocabulary, so she ordered Nate to write 'Screw you!' on those pictures and sign them Constance Talmadge! If I hadn't torn up a whole stack of those photos, Dutch would have lost a hundred paying customers!"

Such were the nightmares that kept invading Peg's dreams of security.

In due time our personal relationships began to lead us in different directions. But the separation was so gradual that at first I scarcely noticed it. During one of several holidays we took, *en famille*, in Paris, my attitude toward that city began to take on dimensions that conflicted with Peg's ideas.

Our first split came about through Mme. Gerbel, the manicurist at our hotel. She enjoyed an outside clientele of aristocratic Parisians, and feeling that an American flapper with a bent for writing movies should be recognized, Mme. Gerbel asked her client the Comtesse Greffulhe to invite me to one of her regular Thursday afternoon salons.

Trembling with apprehension, I heard my name announced by a butler in livery, and I was ushered into a series of drawing rooms, one opening into another, each decorated in a different color: red, orange, yellow, green, blue, indigo, and violet.

I was the youngest guest by at least two decades. But they all spoke English, more or less, and were extremely hospitable. (The old Comte Greffulhe granted me the *politesse* of a quick pinch on the *derrière*.)

In those days it was chic to be American. Our own Josephine Baker dominated the Folies Bergère, while her fellow American Bricktop entertained in Montmartre and sang the songs of Cole Porter (who was born in Peru, Indiana). Everybody who was "in" danced the Charleston. Mainbocher, the dress designer from Chicago, was calling the shots for the best-dressed Parisiennes. Irene Castle set the vogue for ballroom dancing, along with Florence Walton, Clifton Webb, and Barbara Bennett, the kid sister of movie starlets Constance and Joan.

Gertrude Stein from San Francisco was in full charge of Parisian culture. In their town house, she and her friend Alice Toklas were entertaining the intelligentsia, the highlights of whom were also Americans—Ernest Hemingway, Scott Fitzgerald, and Sherwood Anderson. And Janet Flanner, who came from the American Midwest, was writing weekly letters to *The New Yorker* from her attic room at the Hotel Continental overlooking the Tuileries, and under the pseudonym "Genêt" was becoming the historian of that glorious epoch.

(As a sidelight on the unique glamour of the twenties, I recall a day many years later when Paulette Goddard and I visited New York's Museum of Modern Art for an exhibit in which all the items had been collected by Gertrude Stein. There were masterpieces of Cézanne, Matisse, and all the great Impressionists, dominated by the superb portrait of Gertrude by Picasso. When we were making our way out through the crowd, I noticed that Paulette was depressed and asked the reason. "I was just thinking about Gertrude," Paulette mused. "She was ugly, fat, and a lesbian, but she collected more loot than all the jewels of Liz Taylor, Marlene, and mine rolled together." Paulette had just learned the same lesson that had once puzzled Peg Talmadge: In a contest between brains and beauty, it's possible for brains to win.)

When I returned to the hotel from my visit to the Greffulhe mansion I was glowing with excitement over my adventure. But Peg soon let me down by asking, "Why waste time with those geegans when you could have gone shopping with us and let Joe pick up the tabs?"

I could have talked to Peg for an hour and never explained what it meant to me to tread on the Aubusson rugs in drawing rooms where Marcel Proust had found inspiration, or to meet the Comtesse Greffulhe, who was said to be the original of his Duchesse de Guermantes in *A la recherche du temps perdu.*

If moments of truth sometimes pop up in our lives, there must also be moments for lies. The only way I could make Peg understand my ecstasy over that day's adventure was to announce, "Guess who I spent the afternoon with? *Bugsy Siegel!*" Bugsy, who was handsome enough for a career in the movies, chose to be Hollywood's local representative of the Mafia. And as such, he was finally murdered in true gangster style. Meantime, he had helped me restore my status with Peg by the mere mention of his name. But just the same it was evident that Peg and I were beginning to operate on different wavelengths.

As we drew apart, Peg tried to bridge the gap between us by writing letters. Peg was lonely—let's face it. The girls no longer needed her; to their husbands or lovers she had become a nuisance. True, she was funny, but not quite funny enough. So Peg was grounded. She could have taken to tippling, but that would have been a waste of money. She didn't even know that Norma's surcease from boredom lay in drugs. Peg's education had ended with grammar school, but somewhere in her ancestry there must have been a Mme. de Sévigné, for she was a natural-born letter writer. I here quote a few of Peg's written comments on life, liberty, and the pursuit of happiness, which, in her case, was dominated by a particular medium of exchange.

Dear Buggie,   *Beverly Hills*
These days the kids and I meet only for breakfast. A flock of popular brats leaves much to be desired. But I ought not to blame them. They might as well enjoy life before they put the bridgework in a glass of water by the bedside.

                                                New York
Elsie and Brad were married here yesterday. Willie Stewart and Dutch were best man and matron of . . . *honor* (?) They had a hell of a time swinging it. The bride demanded a church and a preacher, and when you think that she was the private property of the Racquet Club, to all points East & West, not even slighting North & South, it may give you something to unravel in your idle moments.

Buggie dear,   *Hollywood*
These days a popular target for jokes is the marriage of big-chested, big-hearted Bill Hart, known far and wide as the idol of the Westerns and also for the tenacity of his grip on a nickel. Well—we were all agog when we went on our first visit to his honeymoon rancho. From the time you hit the front door till you leave, Navajo rugs jump at you, costing all the way from twenty-five cents to a dollar. And as a crowning insult there is

one on the bed where Bill hopes to cheat the government into a yearly allowance of $200 for every infant he can produce. The rumor is that Bill's bedroom habits run amok all over the ranch. When in the corral in full view of the cattle, Bill will slip his hand up the lady's front and down her back, claw her legs, and when she tries to push him away, Bill says, "You're my bride and I can do what I want." Then he prowls around for a new clawing spot. That boy sure knows how to take advantage of a bargain.

Beverly Hills
Nate is beginning to look like a small popover and methinks it's a boy. If so, out it goes hot or cold. [N.B. In later years, Peg would have led a parade of women's libbers.]

Dearest Bugs—   *January 15, 1922*
Well Lottie Pickford got married this week. On our way into the church Dutch asked her brother Jack if he was going to give the bride away and he said, "No, and if anybody else does, she'll start a hell of a riot."

Mary Pickford reached the church early, in full curl, but the one and only Doug delayed his entrance so as to cash in on publicity, and when he bounded to his front-row pew the entire assemblage stood up and gave him a standing ovation. Doug bowed right and left before he finally took the count and joined his mate.

Dear Buggie,   *Hollywood*
Sorry we weren't in N.Y. for the big parade. I mean Valentino's funeral—I'm still wondering about Pola! That four-flushing dame—some publicity hound—they were kidding about her to Walter Wanger and he said, "She fainted all the way from Hollywood to Kansas City and then laid down on the job—but promised her press agent to come through with some

really big swoons in Chicago and carry it right through to
Rudy's bier in New York.

At the end of every letter, Peg begged me for a reply, but I
have forgotten what gossip I wrote in return . . . certainly not
about a cerebral flirtation I was having with H.L.Mencken, or
one with the Irish essayist Ernest Boyd, or with the novelist Joe
Hergesheimer, or with New York theatrical critic George Jean
Nathan. Peg looked down on my highbrow boy friends with
something like embarrassment—as if I were up to shameful or
even illegal activities.

It is a mistake to pretend that anyone can live without some
sort of enchantment. The public, like children, has to have its
toys, and among the most fascinating, for a while, were Norma
and Constance Talmadge . . . toys manufactured by Peg.
Today catalysts like Peg are scarce, and in times of dearth those
toys have to be manufactured by the public relations industry,
which can always provide makeshifts, and thus we have Farrah
Fawcett-Majors and Bianca Jagger.

But Norma and Constance were no products of a publicity
department. Their enchantment registered on the screen with a
sort of endearing innocence that was for real.

The raw nudity in today's films may be offensive, the gaudy
spangles of yesteryear, never! But fascinating as Norma's moodi-
ness and Dutch's razzle-dazzle were, their movies sometimes
failed to hit the mark. On the other hand, Peg, homely, fat,
and beset by honest greed, provided unfailing entertainment for
everyone who knew her.

A few weeks before Peg died of cancer in 1934, I had an opportunity to visit her in a Hollywood hotel room. Sitting at her
bedside, I remembered the fears she used to harbor about her
daughters' futures, but I now realized her mind was at rest. For

Joe Schenck had survived Norma's betrayal and was standing faithfully by to watch after all the girls' investments. Peg's last days were untroubled, thanks to her loyal son-in-law.

Of all Hollywood's heroes, on screen and off, my favorite is Joe Schenck. There once came a time when a certain partner of Joe's was threatened with jail over a tax evasion; Joe stepped forward and took the rap, his argument being that he had no children who would suffer from the disgrace, whereas his partner was a family man. Joe was sentenced to two years. He wrote me from prison to say, "Don't worry about me. I'm working in the library and doing fine."

Two words out of our movie lingo have invaded the everyday vocabulary of the nation. The terms "scenario" and "dialogue" emerged during the Watergate trials. Our President would urge his co-conspirators to trump up a "scenario" that would provide an alibi for his evil deeds, or invent some "dialogue" for the same purpose.

I would like to borrow another word from our movie jargon, viz., "continuity." We never used to refer to a script as a "screenplay"; the term we used was "continuity." (A producer might stop me as I was trying to sneak out of the studio to join cronies and say, "Don't let me catch you in that saloon with Buster Keaton until you've turned in your continuity.")

Although far from the movies today, I like to look on life as a continuity. The term can be used as a synonym for Fate, but it is much less forbidding, grandiose, or definitive.

Scanning the continuity of Norma's and Dutch's lives, I realize that a certain major sequence is missing: a truly satisfying sex episode. Even in the steamy ambience of Hollywood, they missed out on that adult experience, for reasons that were widely disparate but could at the same time be traced to Peg. She had trained her girls to look only for faults in the male sex and to bypass any possible virtues. Joe Schenck's devotion to Norma was one of a kind, especially in the film world, but he lacked the physical beauty of Gilbert Roland, for whom she deserted Joe. When she later married Georgie Jessel, she learned that, for all his witty dialogue, he lacked Joe's fond absorption in her as a woman. For Norma to have found all her requirements in a single male was out of the question, particularly in Hollywood.

Constance, the definitive sex symbol for an entire generation, had been raised by Peg to be turned on by nothing but cash. But even when married to a man of wealth, Dutch could never emulate Peg's love affair with money. She simply wasn't geared to complete her services to any husband. In Dutch's case the sexual act was a cause for giggles that could only wound a husband's ego. None of her husbands was man enough to rise above the challenge of a snicker.

In writing scenes for the girls to play with sexy leading men, I too had to fight off an attitude that sex was ridiculous. H. L. Mencken used to chide me by saying, "Do you realize, my child, that you're the first American writer to make fun of sex?"

It's true that from the time I was a girl I had crushes on men of genius. (In early youth I fell in love with the mind of the New England philosopher George Santayana. But I would never have dared write him a fan letter, as was the custom of my friend Zoe Akins, who once received a flirtatious hand-written acknowledgment from Bernard Shaw.) But, just lately, while reading the biography of Edith Wharton, I ran across an item that staggered me. Mrs. Wharton quoted her friend *George Santayana* as saying that years ago he had found a kindred soul in . . . Anita Loos! Santayana has long been dead, but now I can imagine how the missing sequence in the continuity of my own life might have been supplied: In some downy New England four-poster I might have experienced that climactic, earth-shaking, unforgettable, indescribable clutch that even a ribald authoress like me could not laugh off. As a matter of fact, all of us girls may have outsmarted ourselves.

I search history to find some character who might help me describe the ineffable charm of Constance Talmadge. The nearest to her is Augusta Leigh, Lord Byron's happy-go-lucky half-sister and sweetheart. Like Augusta, Dutch looked on sex as an unfortunate happenstance. But Dutch had certain instincts of a lady; she never hoarded jewels, as Norma did. Her only extravagance was fur, for Dutch cuddled into mink and ermine like a baby. Completely without ambition, forethought, or interest in the more serious experiences that life might have held for her, she only valued the superficial *fun* of living.

Countless film actresses as pretty as Dutch had much more talent, but they failed, while Dutch succeeded with neither effort nor intent. It was as if the inner joy she took just in living emerged from a silent screen and brought delight to untold millions through the magic of ESP.

As a widow Dutch settled permanently in southern California, where Peg and Nate lived, and where Dutch was joined by her favorite pal, China Harris. But the drinking habits of the two young widows began to pose a problem to those who loved them. And at one point Dutch and China were taken in hand by Fanny Brice, who pressured them to go for a drying-out cure at a nearby health spa. The treatment consisted of spending two weeks on a regime of raw fruit, vegetables, and uncooked grains.

But as the girls' ordeal drew near they began to dread it, so Dutch borrowed a suitcase from W.C.Fields that he had fitted up as a bar for fending off drought.

On arrival at the spa, however, luggage was examined by the directress, who confiscated the portable bar. Dutch put up a valiant attempt to salvage its contents, declaring that she herself was a vegetarian and that the suitcase contained nothing but her own vegetarian diet *in liquid form*; that a jug of applejack included all the natural ingredients of its source; that the nutrients contained in a potato were all present in 100-proof vodka; that grains were just as pure and more palatable in bourbon; that uncooked hops were prone to scratch the throat, whereas, when converted into beer, hops caused much less danger.

Dutch didn't actually think that her arguments would convert the directress, which they didn't. She advised the girls to remove their diet to one of the nearby speakeasy motels and continue their cure from there, which they did.

It wasn't long before tragedies started to beset the Talmadge family. Peg had been felled by cancer. On Christmas Eve of 1957 Norma died, a victim to arthritis aggravated by drugs. A decade later Nate followed, through a sheer disinterest in living, and at last Dutch was left alone as only an ex–movie star can be. She withdrew into a suite at the Beverly Wilshire Hotel, where only a chosen member of the hotel bar staff ever saw her.

Sometimes I tried to phone Dutch from New York, always to be told she was "unavailable." I recognized the rebuffs and finally gave up. But not long after Dutch died in 1973 I visited California and learned from the Beverly Wilshire's barman why Dutch had broken off all contact with the outside world. Although she had never been the least bit vain, Dutch considered it unseemly to have gotten fat.

I was able to conjure up an image of Dutch as she may have looked toward the end. It comes from a description of the heroine of Tolstoy's *War and Peace*, as she appeared in middle age: "Her face no longer had that ever-glowing fire of eagerness which had once constituted her chief charm, but she was more attractive, with her handsome, fully-developed figure, than she had ever been in the past."

I have even found a reference in the Bible to someone much like Dutch. It occurs in Genesis, chapter 21, verse 6: "And Sarah said, God hath made me to laugh, so that all that hear will laugh with me."

At a typical Hollywood banquet (opposite), *all the girls were pretty and the VIPs (with the exception of Irving Thalberg at the far right) were not. Standing at the far left is Louis B. Mayer, the mighty mogul of MGM; seated next to him is the dazzling Anita Stewart, behind whom is another dazzler, Marion Davies. Towering above Norma stands the gorgeous British redhead Elinor Glyn, whose naughty novel* Three Weeks *was conditioning readers for the even naughtier Jacqueline Susann of a later day. Norma obviously regards Irving Thalberg's adoration of Dutch with fond approval, for Irving, the boy genius who headed Universal Studios, was already on his way to fame and fortune.* (Photo by Susan Edwards Harvith)

Norma's fans were seldom stingy. Hiram Abrams, president of United Artists, expressed his devotion (below) *in a tribute that was publicized as boasting seven varieties of imported orchids.* (The Museum of Modern Art/Film Stills Archive)

Louella Parsons's gossip column revealed secrets so damaging that they could wreck a star's career. But Lolly's heart was warm and always in a delicate state of flutter.

Constance (above) *is following her natural bent, clowning with comedian George Bancroft during a kiddy party at the beach in Santa Monica. George's expression seems to nullify the contention of Dutch's mama that a girl can escape the snares of sex by laughing.* (The Museum of Modern Art/Film Stills Archive)

At a time when the whole world was at Constance Talmadge's feet, her favorite companion (opposite, above) *was a Pomeranian named Dinkey.* (The Museum of Modern Art/Film Stills Archive)

A major attempt was made by Lady Charles Mendel, who was better known as Elsie de Woolfe, the high priestess of interior decoration, to establish an outpost of old-world culture in Hollywood. Her Ladyship took up residence in a bungalow which she poetically called "After All" (opposite, below). *Whatever Elsie did, the world of fashion imitated. But Her Ladyship's disciples preferred the life-style of the movies, and before long she too deserted decorum and went completely Hollywood.* (Elsie de Woolfe)

AFTER ALL
BEVERLY HILLS,
CALIFORNIA

By the late twenties, Hollywood was a
gathering place for international fashion,
thrills, and beauty. More colorful than any
movie star was a great British gentleman,
Hugo Rumbold. It amused Hugo to assume
this pose of an eighteenth-century fop,
reflected in the mirror at the right.

After John Pialogiou, Dutch's Greek connection, came the dashing Captain Alastair MacIntosh (above) *of His Majesty's Horse Guards (The Museum of Modern Art/Film Stills Archive)*

After Captain MacIntosh's British chic palled, Dutch bounced over to Chicago and married department-store tycoon and playboy Townsend Netcher (opposite). *(The Museum of Modern Art/Film Stills Archive)*

The loving scene above of the Keaton family in Hollywood could only have been contrived by our never-discouraged press agent, Beulah Livingstone.

Constance Talmadge (right) *fulfilled everybody's need for beauty in the 1920s. But times have changed (far right)! (The Museum of Modern Art/Film Stills Archive)*

In Tender Is the Night, *Scott Fitzgerald spoke of Norma Talmadge* (above left) *as the epitome of the glamour of the 1920s. Scott never met Norma but he wrote that "she must be a fine, noble woman beyond her loveliness." In the 1970s a rather different taste in femininity* (above right) *has taken over. (The Museum of Modern Art/Film Stills Archive)*

> WE DEEPLY APPRECIATE YOUR KIND
>
> EXPRESSION OF SYMPATHY FOR
>
> "OUR PEG."
>
> NORMA, NATALIE AND CONSTANCE

At long last, the instigator of all that beauty, charm, and prosperity was at rest.

Constance Talmadge (below) *in one of the memorable scenes from* A Virtuous Vamp. (*The Museum of Modern Art/Film Stills Archive*)

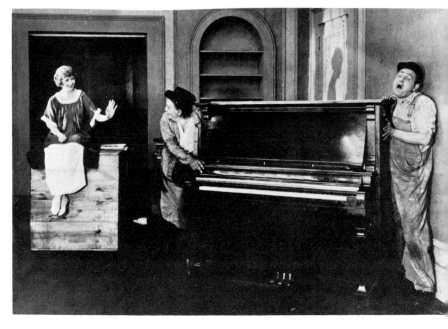

APPENDIX: A VIRTUOUS VAMP

TITLE   IF YOU WILL LOOK THROUGH THE HISTORIES OF
        THE FAMOUS VAMPS OF THE WORLD YOU WILL
        FIND THAT THEY ALL HAD A PRETTY ROUGH TIME
        AND THAT VAMPING ISN'T SO EASY AS IT IS SUP-
        POSED TO BE.

TITLE   OUR HEROINE, A CONGENITAL VAMP, WAS BORN
        IN SAN FRANCISCO, A DESCENDANT OF AN EN-
        GLISH ARISTOCRAT WHO DRIFTED OUT TO CALI-
        FORNIA IN '49 AND LIKED IT AND GOT RICH.

TITLE   (Illustrated with yap wagon and man with megaphone)
        LADIES AND GENTLEMEN, ON YOUR RIGHT YOU
        WILL SEE THE MAGNIFICENT HOME OF THE LATE
        MORTIMER CHOLMONDELAY ARMITAGE ON THE
        MORNING OF THE 16th OF APRIL, 1906. (The day fol-
        lowing the big earthquake)

1. LONG SHOT—The ruins of the Armitage house. The house is on
the side of a hill and is completely destroyed, perhaps an arch or two
standing, and behind on the edge of the hill are other ruined build-
ings and smoke is rising from them.

FADE IN—LONG SHOT—MRS. ARMITAGE is walking about distracted
and calling "Gwen!" and near her trudges her little son, also calling
for his sister.

TITLE   MRS. MORTIMER CHOLMONDELAY ARMITAGE,
        WIDOW OF THE LATE MORTIMER CHOLMONDELAY
        ARMITAGE, AN ACKNOWLEDGED LEADER OF SAN
        FRANCISCO'S SMARTEST SET.

CLOSE-UP—MRS. ARMITAGE. She is a woman of about thirty, very
smart, stately looking, but at this time her face is covered with dirt,
her hair is disheveled. She is wearing a petticoat, a man's vest, a big
picture hat, and bedroom slippers, and is carrying a bicycle wheel in

one hand and a garbage can in the other, with "garbage" written on it. She is looking around in all directions, calling:

SP.   "GWEN, GWEN, GWENDOLYN!"

TITLE   MASTER EDWARD CECIL ARMITAGE, HEIR TO THE ARMITAGE POSSESSIONS AND MONARCH OF ALL HE SURVEYS.

CLOSE-UP—EDDIE, a four-year-old kid, wearing absolutely nothing but a butler's long tailed coat, with the tails dragging on the ground. He is walking about, looking among the debris, crying, and saying:

SP.   "I WANT GWEN, I WANT GWEN."

LONG SHOT—The mother and son looking distractedly about for the girl. A fireman enters and tells Mrs. Armitage she must leave the neighborhood and go to the park for safety. Mrs. Armitage tells him about her little girl who is lost, and he starts to hunt for her, climbing into the ruins of the house.

TITLE   GWEN ARMITAGE, KNOWN IN *BURKE'S PEERAGE* AS THE HONORABLE GWENDOLYN DIANA BEAU-FORT-BEAUFORT —— —— ARMITAGE, A CONGEN-ITAL VAMPIRE AND THE HEROINE OF OUR STORY.

CLOSE-UP—The foot of a little girl sticking up out of the debris and kicking like mad. On her foot is a man's shoe.

SEMI–CLOSE-UP—The fireman approaches the kicking leg, realizes it is the little girl's, and starts to dig her out. (She has nothing on but a night gown and pair of pants.) He pushes a lot of the stuff off from the girl and gradually pulls her out. She grips in one hand a little framed mirror and in the other her best Sunday hat. The fireman then grabs the little girl and takes her out to where her mother is. The mother drops the garbage can and bicycle wheel and clasps the little girl in her arms and kisses her.

Then the fireman tells the mother they must leave at once. She ab-sent-mindedly picks up the garbage can and bicycle wheel, calls the little boy, who is picking up a framed coat of arms and looking at it; and the mother starts off followed by the boy, who perhaps drags the coat of arms along by the picture wire.

Then the little girl looks up at the fireman, adjusts her hat, looks at herself in the mirror, smiles at him, asks if he would mind taking her by the hand. He doesn't want to do it but he does, and she then stops him, smiles up at him, and asks if he would mind carrying her. She finally wins him over by her smile and he picks her up and carries her off.   FADE OUT.

INSERT—EXCERPT FROM NEWSPAPER:

SOCIETY NOTE. THE MORTIMER CHOLMONDELAY ARMITAGES HAVE MOVED FROM THEIR MANSION ON KNOB HILL AND TAKEN UP RESIDENCE BACK OF THE MUSEUM IN GOLDEN GATE PARK.

2. GOLDEN GATE PARK. (FADE IN) LONG SHOT—In the background are twenty-five or thirty refugees dressed in all sorts and conditions of clothes and carrying all sorts of things with them. They have a number of baby carriages and boys' carts loaded with household effects, etc., etc.

Mrs. Armitage, carrying her garbage can and bicycle wheel, enters. She is followed by Eddie with his crest under his arm and the fireman carrying Gwen. Mrs. Armitage and the boy are worn to a frazzle and sit down exhausted but Gwen is quite fresh and chipper. The fireman sets her down beside her mother and wipes the perspiration from his face. Gwen pulls him down to her and kisses him. He is quite pleased with this, pats her on the head, tells her that they will be all right there, and goes back.

Gwen goes over to her mother and says:

SP.   "MOTHER, YOU ARE A SIGHT!"

She holds up the mirror to her. Mother looks at Gwen and says: "Trust you to save a mirror!" Gwen then looks at the things her mother has brought and asks her why she brought them.

The mother finally comes to and realizes what she has been carrying all the while, looks at the bicycle wheel and the garbage can and then at Gwen and says:

SP. "HAVE I BEEN CARRYING THESE THINGS ALL THE WAY FROM THE HOUSE?"

Gwen says yes, evidently she has. Mrs. Armitage shakes her head in despair, looks up at Gwen and says, "Whatever will become of us?" and begins to weep. Gwen puts her arms about her and comforts her. The mother then looks up at Gwen and says:

SP. "DO YOU REALIZE, CHILD, THAT ALL WE HAVE IN THE WORLD IS A BICYCLE WHEEL AND A GARBAGE CAN?"

Gwen then holds out her mirror and says, "But we have a mirror," and then looks at Eddie who enters with his contribution, saying, "Look what I got." The mother takes it and looks at it.

INSERT—CREST.

The mother looks at it, shakes her head, and says:

SP. "YOUR FATHER'S FAMILY CREST! THAT WILL HELP A LOT."

She takes the crest, lifts the garbage can lid, and drops it in. The kid, resenting this, goes around and fishes it out. The mother turns to Gwen, shakes her head and says:

SP. "WHY COULDN'T ONE OF US HAVE SAVED A CAN OF SOUP?"

Gwen says yes, this would have been a good thing, takes her mirror, sits down, and begins to primp before the mirror. The brother meanwhile is fishing the crest out of the garbage can and the mother sits dolefully looking about at the people around them and sighing. Gwen goes on looking in mirror.   FADE OUT.

LONG TITLE TO THE EFFECT THAT ENOUGH WAS SAVED FROM THE WRECK OF THE FAMILY FORTUNE TO ENABLE THE ARMITAGES TO EKE OUT AN EXISTENCE AND PUT GWEN THROUGH SCHOOL AND BUSINESS COLLEGE. BUT GWEN, ARRIVING AT MATURITY, REQUIRED MORE FRILLS AND FURBELOWS THAN THE FAMILY FORTUNE COULD SUPPLY, AND FOR THE SAKE OF LARGER OPPORTUNITIES FOR HER AND THE BOY, THE MOTHER BROUGHT THEM TO N.Y.

3. ARMITAGE FLAT IN NEW YORK. In the foreground is a dining room with double doors leading to a sitting room and behind that a door leading to an outside hall. (FADE IN)

In the foreground is Mrs. Armitage unpacking a box and on the other side of the room is Eddie, now 17, unpacking another. Gwen in background—other room—sitting on box ordering men about. Mrs. Armitage comes to something heavy, turns, and says:

SP.   "COME HERE, EDDIE, AND HELP ME."

He leaves what he is doing, comes to his mother, and helps lift this object out of the box. The mother then fishes in, pulls out the coat of arms, unwraps it, and says:

SP.   "IF YOU WANT THAT THING, KEEP IT IN YOUR OWN ROOM."

He takes it, looks at it rather proudly. Then the mother says:

SP.   "WHAT'S GWEN DOING?"

Eddie looks around toward the other room, then turns to his mother and says:

SP.   "SHE IS IN THERE VAMPING THE EXPRESS MEN."

The mother smiles quizzically, raises her eyes, shakes her head.

THEN CUT to a CLOSE-UP of GWEN sitting on a packing box, smiling, and directing the furniture men.

LONG SHOT of this room showing Gwen directing the furniture men and them putting the various things where she tells them. (This room is about half furnished.)

They place an upright piano in one part of room. Gwen smiles at them, looks up, and then says:

SP.   "LET'S TRY IT OVER THERE."

The men look a little sore but Gwen smiles again so they struggle to lift the piano to the other place. Gwen then tells them to push it in a little closer. One of the men looks at her smiling at him, gives it a good push, and crushes the other fellow up against the wall. She is very sorry at this but the man says it is all right, it didn't hurt him very much. Gwen then looks at it critically and says:

SP.   "OH, I THINK I LIKED IT BETTER WHERE IT WAS."

The men give her a dirty look. She smiles at them, flatters them, and they finally soften and they pick up the piano and put it back where it was first.

CLOSE-UP—GWEN smiling at them in approval of what they have done.   FADE OUT.

TITLE   ON GRAMERCY SQUARE, NEW YORK, LIVE
          THE CROWNINSHIELD SISTERS, WHO ARE
          THOROUGHLY ON THEIR FEET IN NEW YORK
          SOCIETY BUT A LITTLE WOBBLY WHEN IT COMES
          TO LONDON, NEVER HAVING BEEN QUITE ABLE TO
          MAKE THE MUCH-DESIRED BRITISH HURDLE.

4. GRAMERCY PARK. LONG SHOT—DISSOLVE IN—DISSOLVE OUT.

4-a EXTERIOR OF CROWNINSHIELD HOUSE—DISSOLVE IN—DISSOLVE OUT.

5. DRAWING ROOM (DISSOLVE IN) Room of the Crowninshield home, an English-looking room, in which are two very aristocratic-looking women, Minerva and Flora Crowninshield.

They are seated, one at the desk and the other perhaps at the fireplace, the latter reading a British magazine, the former opening and reading letters. At length the one reading the letters comes to a letter which interests her very much and she calls the other one to her and they both read the letter.

INSERT—THE LETTER:

San Francisco, 1919.

My dear friends:

I know you will be interested to learn that I am sending to your brother James a young friend of mine who, were she in England, would be known as the Honorable Gwendolyn Diana Beaufort-Beaufort —— —— Armitage, direct connection of the Armitages of Warwickshire. Of course her social position is assured anyplace in the world, but she is a charmingly original child, and insists on working as a stenographer in order to augment the family fortunes, which were devastated by the San Francisco fire.

Her grandfather was —— Armitage, second son of —— Armitage, who came to California in '49, etc., etc.

The two sisters are immensely excited by this letter and jabber about this marvelous girl. They immediately get down a copy of *Burke's Peerage* from their books.

INSERT—BURKE'S PEERAGE.

They look through it and find the Armitage crest (same as in scene 2) and discover that this girl is a direct descendant of the old boy. In the seventh heaven of delight, one says to the other:

SP.   "CAN YOU IMAGINE WHAT A HELP IT WOULD BE TO US IN LONDON IF WE COULD CLAIM HER AS A FRIEND?"

The other agrees it would be a very wonderful thing but says:

SP.   "WE CAN'T ALLOW HER TO ACT AS STENOGRA-
        PHER FOR BROTHER JAMES. WE MUST HAVE HER
        IN THE HOUSE WITH US AS SECRETARY-COM-
        PANION."

The other agrees to this and they decide they will go see brother
James about the matter.

One of the sisters then looks at the clock or her watch and says:

SP.   "JAMES WILL BE HOME NOW. LET US GO AT
        ONCE."

And they get ready to depart hurriedly.   FADE OUT.

TITLE   THE SUMMER HOME OF JAMES CROWNINSHIELD,
        UPON WHOM FATE AND A LETTER OF INTRODUC-
        TION ARE ABOUT TO WISH OUR GWEN.

6. CROWNINSHIELD'S SUMMER HOME, a very beautiful and attractive
place.

FADE IN.

The sisters' car drives in and the two sisters get out and go into the
house.   DISSOLVE OUT.

7. TENNIS COURT AT CROWNINSHIELD'S HOME (DISSOLVE IN)

LONG SHOT—CROWNINSHIELD and KIRBY are playing a game of
tennis.

TITLE   JAMES CROWNINSHIELD.

CLOSE-UP—CROWNINSHIELD just picking up a ball, standing on the
back line, calling out the score, and delivering the service.

LONG SHOT—CROWNINSHIELD serves the ball, Kirby returns it, and
the play continues until the point is won. Kirby then places himself
for the next play.

TITLE   HIS LAWYER AND FRIEND, BOB KIRBY.

CLOSE-UP—KIRBY taking his position and setting himself for the next play.

CLOSE-UP—CROWNINSHIELD just getting ready to serve again. A Japanese servant enters and tells him his two sisters have called. Crowninshield is rather bored at this information, but says to Kirby:

SP.   "MINERVA AND FLORA ARE HERE. DO YOU WANT TO SEE THEM?"

CLOSE-UP—KIRBY politely but firmly declines the invitation, says no, he will wait until he gets back.

LONG SHOT—CROWNINSHIELD goes off, followed by the servant. Kirby sits down on the grass or a bench somewhere to wait, perhaps lights a cigarette.

8. PORCH OF CROWNINSHIELD'S COUNTRY HOUSE. (It is as picturesque as possible.) He comes in and greets his sisters, rather formally. They each kiss him on the cheek. Then he sits down, asks them what is the idea, what can he do for them. One immediately gets out the letter and shows it to him as though it were a matter of great importance. He reads it.

INSERT—LETTER:

San Francisco, 1919.
My dear friends:
    I know you will be interested to learn that I am sending to your brother James a young friend of mine who, were she in England, would be known as the Honorable Gwendolyn Diana Beaufort-Beaufort —— —— Armitage, direct connection of the Armitages of Warwickshire. Of course her social position is assured anyplace in the world, but she is a charmingly original child, and insists on working as a stenographer in order to augment the family fortunes, which were devastated by the San Francisco fire.

> Her grandfather was —— Armitage, second son of
> —— Armitage, who came to California in '49, etc., etc.

Crowninshield is evidently displeased at this letter. He doesn't quite know what to say to his sisters, not wishing to be unkind. He scratches his head a moment as he finishes reading it, and then turns to them and says:

SP.   "YOU KNOW HOW I HATE MIXING UP THESE
        SOCIAL AFFAIRS WITH BUSINESS."

Then they assure him they don't want him to take her into his office, that they wish to take her into their home as a secretary-companion as it will advance their social prestige, especially in England, and on their coming trip to England they will be able to meet the people they have never been able to meet before.

He is not very strong for this but says he doesn't care if they want to take her into their home and make her their secretary-companion as long as it won't cause him any further bother. They say it won't and he says he hopes so as he doesn't want to hear any more about her.   FADE OUT.

TITLE   GWEN PREPARES TO TAKE HER PLACE IN THE
         GREAT INDUSTRIAL LIFE OF THE METROPOLIS.

9. GWEN'S BEDROOM (FADE IN). Gwen is at a mirror, getting all dolled up to interview Crowninshield. She picks up a couple of hats from the bed, tries them on, likes the second one best, picks up a hand mirror, looks in it from all angles, then with the mirror in her hand, leaves for the door.

10. GWEN'S SITTING ROOM. Mrs. Armitage is on a ladder fixing some curtains and Eddie is assisting her. In a moment Gwen enters from her bedroom with her mother's hat on and the mirror in her hand, gives herself a final look and says:

SP.   "MOTHER, I THINK I COULD LAND THE JOB
        BETTER IN YOUR HAT."

The mother looks around at her, sizes her up, and says, "All right, you can wear it if you like."

SP.   "BUT IF MY HAT LANDS YOUR JOB, I GET HALF
      YOUR SALARY."

Gwen says she thinks that is fair enough, continues to look at herself in the mirror, fixes her hair and her hat, and then striking a vampish pose, says:

SP.   "DO YOU THINK HE WILL ENGAGE ME?"

The brother looks at her admiringly, sizes her up from head to foot, and says he would like to know why not. The mother goes on hanging up the curtains, smiling to herself.

Gwen thinks a minute, decides that she will rehearse her interview with Crowninshield, and says to Eddie:

SP.   "EDDIE, YOU SIT DOWN AND PRETEND YOU ARE
      CROWNINSHIELD AND I WILL TRY IT ON YOU."

Eddie says all right, that's fine, he likes the idea. He pulls a chair up opposite the table, sits down and takes a very dignified attitude. At the same time Gwen goes out into the bedroom.

11. GWEN'S BEDROOM. Gwen enters, goes to the dresser, puts down the mirror and takes up her letter of introduction, goes back to the door and knocks.

12. GWEN'S SITTING ROOM. Eddie calls, "Come in," the mother looking on. Gwen enters, approaches Eddie at the desk, smiles her sweetest smile at him, and asks if he is Mr. Crowninshield. Eddie in a very dignified way replies that he is, the mother all the time watching. Gwen says she has a letter of introduction to him and hands it to him. Eddie reads it.

INSERT—LETTER OF INTRODUCTION:

San Francisco, 1919

Mr. James Crowninshield,
President,
The Equity Life Insurance Co.,
200 Broadway, New York City.

Dear Mr. Crowninshield:
This will introduce to you Miss Gwendolyn etc. etc.

As Eddie reads the letter, a smile spreads over his face in admiration of the girl. He rises in a very courtly manner, takes her hand, bows to her, and then, motioning to his chair, says:

SP.   "WON'T YOU TAKE MY DESK, MISS ARMITAGE?"

Gwen is quite pleased with this and sits down in the chair vacated by Eddie, Eddie standing beside her, bowing and talking to her in a very courtly and flattering manner. The mother, seeing this, smiles sardonically, raises her hand and says:

SP.   "WAIT A MINUTE. YOU'VE GOT IT ALL WRONG."

They look at her in surprise. She climbs down from the ladder, comes over to Gwen, tells her to go out and try it over, gives her the letter, and Gwen goes out into the other room again. The mother then says to Eddie:

SP.   "NOW YOU ARE THE OFFICE BOY."

She sits at the desk and Eddie sits on a little stool. She then calls out, "All right."

13. GWEN'S BEDROOM. Gwen knocks on the door.

14. GWEN'S SITTING ROOM. Eddie gets up, goes to the door, lets her in, and as she asks for Mr. Crowninshield, he bows and asks her to step over to the mother. Gwen comes to the mother, smiles at her just as she did to the brother before. The mother looks at her frowningly and Gwen continues to smile and smirk more and more. Gwen

hands her the letter, saying, "I have a letter of introduction to you."
The mother takes the letter, opens it, just glances at it, then looks up
frowningly at Gwen, who continues her smiling and smirking. Then
the mother says:

SP.   "YOUNG WOMAN, WHEN I WANT TO SEE
        VAMPING I GO TO THE MOVIES."

Gwen is taken aback at this and the mother, handing back her letter
to her, turns to the boy and says:

SP.   "SHOW THIS YOUNG LADY OUT."

The boy starts to his mother, protesting. The mother comes to
Gwen, puts her arms about her, kisses her. Gwen straightens her hat,
kisses her mother, kisses Eddie, waves the letter of introduction to
her mother and says, "Now, we will see who is right," and starts out,
the mother and boy looking after her.   FADE OUT.

TITLE   BRINGING GWEN TO THE OFFICE OF THE
        EQUITY LIFE INSURANCE COMPANY, JAMES
        CROWNINSHIELD, PRESIDENT.

15. ANTEROOM TO CROWNINSHIELD'S OFFICE with a door at the
back with "Mr. Crowninshield" painted on it.

(FADE IN)

A young man who appears to be quite social is sitting waiting. An office boy ushers Gwen in, telling her to wait there. She gives the boy a
smile which bowls him over. The boy then goes to Crowninshield's
office, smiling back at Gwen and straightening his tie as he goes.

16. CROWNINSHIELD'S PRIVATE OFFICE. Crowninshield is seated at
his desk, Miss Turner (his stenographer) taking dictation. The boy
comes in. Crowninshield finishes dictating the letter, sends Miss
Turner away, and then asks the boy what he wants. The boy says:
"There are a couple of people out there to see you." He asks who they
are and the boy replies:

SP.   "THERE'S A MAN WITH A LETTER OF
        INTRODUCTION AND A GIRL."

Crowninshield, bored at the idea of interviewing them in his office,
decides to get rid of them outside. He goes out, followed by the boy.

17. ANTEROOM, CROWNINSHIELD'S OFFICE. Crowninshield comes in,
followed by the boy, who looks admiringly at Gwen and, with his
gaze still on her, sits down at his little desk. Gwen gives the boy a
smile and then devotes her attention to Crowninshield, fishing in her
bag for her letter of introduction, which she takes out so as to have it
ready when he interviews her.

Crowninshield goes first to the young society man, who introduces
himself and shakes Crowninshield's hand in an extremely social manner. He then says to Crowninshield:

SP.   "I HAVE A LETTER OF INTRODUCTION FROM MRS.
        REGGIE VANDERPOEL."

Crowninshield frowns at this, gives him a disapproving glance, and
then reads the letter, Gwen closely watching all the time. Crowninshield finishes reading the letter, hands it back to the young man,
and says:

SP.   "YOUNG MAN, YOU'LL NEVER GET ANYWHERE
        BY USING SOCIETY LETTERS OF INTRODUCTION.
        WHEN I WENT INTO BUSINESS I PUT FAMILY AND
        POSITION BEHIND ME AND MADE GOOD ON MY
        OWN."

The young man bridles at this and says:

SP.   "BUT ONE MUST BE A GENTLEMAN EVEN IN
        BUSINESS, AND AFTER ALL, WHY SHOULD NOT
        ONE USE ONE'S CONNECTIONS FOR ONE'S OWN
        ADVANCEMENT WHEN ONE CAN."

Taking thorough stock of him, Crowninshield looks him up and
down, and then says:

SP.   "WHAT CAN YOU DO?"

The young man shrugs his shoulders, then says:

SP.   "I THOUGHT I WOULD LEAVE THAT TO YOU."

Again Crowninshield looks him up and down, shakes his head, looks out the door, and says:

SP.   "GOOD-BYE, YOUNG MAN."

Gwen stands aghast at this speech, quickly chucks her letter back in her bag and closes it.

The young man, insulted at this remark, gives Crowninshield a withering look, adjusts his monocle in his eye, puts his hat on his head, freezes Crowninshield with a look, and starts out of the office.

Crowninshield gives him a glance as he goes, then crosses to Gwen. The office boy meanwhile looks on in amusement at the lounge lizard getting the air, perhaps imitates him by sticking a half dollar in his eye.

Crowninshield comes to Gwen, who is quite frightened by this time and rises when he comes. Crowninshield says:

SP.   "WELL, YOUNG WOMAN, WHAT CAN I DO FOR YOU?"

Gwen gulps and swallows and holding her bag with the letter in it behind her, says:

SP.   "I'D LIKE A JOB."

Crowninshield sizes her up in a perfectly gentlemanly way and asks her what she can do. Gwen, who is still fighting to get her bearings, says:

SP.   "I'M A STENOGRAPHER."

Crowninshield turns to the boy, tells him to bring in Mr. Hicks. The boy goes out to the outer office. Crowninshield then turns to Gwen and asks her name. Gwen looks frightened, doesn't quite know what to say, thinks about his objection to social distinction, and finally stammers out:

SP.   "NELLIE JONES."

At this point the boy comes back with Hicks, a middle-aged typical office man, a bit of a character (John Daly Murphy). Hicks comes to Crowninshield and Crowninshield says:

SP.   "DO WE NEED ANY STENOGRAPHERS?"

Hicks scratches his head, shakes it as though he were about to say no, thinking about it. Finally he gets a flash of Gwen, and Gwen has gotten her bearings by now and gives him a sweet ingratiating smile, and old Hicks gradually scratches out of his head the thought that he does need a stenographer. Then he turns to Crowninshield and says:

SP.   "COME TO THINK OF IT, I NEED A STENOGRAPHER MYSELF."

Gwen is quite relieved at this, and Crowninshield says all right, introduces Gwen to him, saying:

SP.   "THIS IS MISS NELLIE JONES. WILL YOU TAKE HER IN CHARGE?"

Hicks says he will. Then Gwen turns and gives Crowninshield a most lovely ingratiating smile of thanks, and Crowninshield, very brusquely and gentlemanly, acknowledges it, says it is all right, he is glad to have her, turns, and goes into his office.

Gwen then turns and gives Hicks just as nice and sweet a smile and then turns and gives a parting smile to the office boy, who smiles back in return. She then turns and gives a final smile to Hicks.

FADE OUT.

TITLE BRINGING US TO THAT EVENING.

18. DINING ROOM OF GWEN'S FLAT, LIVING ROOM AND HALL IN THE BACK (same as in scene #3, except that it is now completely furnished).

(FADE IN)

Eddie has an apron on and is setting the table for dinner. The mother enters from the kitchen with a bowl of flowers, which she puts on the table to indicate that they will observe the niceties of living.

Gwen rushes in from the hall, comes from the sitting room into the dining room. The mother and Eddie stop their work to hear her report. She comes to the head of the table and her mother asks how things are going and she says, "Oh, everything was fine . . ."

SP.   "AND YOU SHOULD SEE MR. CROWNINSHIELD! HE IS THE HANDSOMEST AND MOST MASTERFUL MAN I EVER SAW."

The mother perks up her ears, raises her eyebrows, and looks over at Eddie and says, "Well, well, our Gwen has fallen at last." Then Gwen droops a little bit, shakes her head no, and says:

SP.   "I'M NOT WORKING FOR HIM, WORSE LUCK."

The others are interested, and she goes on to tell how they put her with a nice little man named Hicks and he has been very sweet to her all day and she thinks she is going to like the position very well indeed.

Then she takes out the letter of introduction, says she never used it at all. The mother is surprised at this and also the boy, and she says:

SP.   "MR. CROWNINSHIELD SAID HE HAD MADE GOOD ON HIS OWN AND I DECIDED TO DO THE SAME."

The mother looks at her quizzically, says that's all right if she is able to put it over, she may do better than she ever thought she could.

The boy thinks she is foolish not to have used it. Gwen goes on talking and tears up the letter, telling them how she took the name of Nellie Jones and is going to stand absolutely on her own feet.

FADE OUT.

TITLE   GWEN'S JOB LASTED UNTIL ONE DAY MRS. HICKS
HAPPENED TO DROP INTO THE OFFICE.

19. HICKS'S OFFICE (FADE IN). Hicks is on one side of the desk, dictating to Gwen, who is sitting on the other side, smiling at him sweetly as she takes his dictation. She leans over in order to hear better what he is saying. At last Hicks says:

SP.   "I HAVE A LITTLE SORE THROAT THIS MORNING,
MISS JONES. WOULD YOU MIND SITTING OVER
HERE?"

Nellie jumps up, pulls her chair around close beside him, sits down, goes on taking dictation, smiling at him sweetly. Hicks smiles a bland smile of satisfaction and goes on dictating.

The door at the back opens and Mrs. Hicks suddenly enters, stands quietly in the doorway, and gets an eyeful. She then closes the door. Hicks hears this, turns, sees her, is frightened to death, shows by the expression on his face that his little romance with Nellie is over. He stiffens up in a dignified way, tells Nellie that will do for the present. Nellie leaves, Mrs. Hicks glaring daggers at her.

After Nellie is out of the room, Mrs. Hicks sweeps down upon Hicks in her most dignified manner, sits down, looks at him with a quiet sternness that freezes him, and begins to tell him what is what, fire blazing from her eyes.   FADE OUT.

TITLE   THAT AFTERNOON GWEN HAD BAD NEWS TO
BREAK TO MOTHER.

20. LIVING ROOM, GWEN'S FLAT. Eddie is studying at a table and the mother is sewing. Gwen comes in from the hall, discouraged, slumps into a chair and says:

SP.   "I AM FIRED!"

The mother jumps up, goes to Gwen and begins to sympathize with her. The brother also jumps up but is more angry than sorry. He also comes to Gwen and she starts her tale of woe, saying that she was kicked out this afternoon. They ask her why, what was the matter, and she says:

SP.   "IT WAS ALL ON ACCOUNT OF HICKS'S WIFE."

They ask her how it happened, and she says she was sitting beside Mr. Hicks taking dictation when his battleship of a wife burst into the room and began to raise a row.

The mother nods her head knowingly, raises her eyes to heaven, shakes her head as much as to say "I knew it," then turns to Gwen and says:

SP.   "YOU BETTER GET A JOB IN THE MARTHA WASHINGTON HOTEL."

Gwen looks at her, very much abused to think that her mother would question her modesty and propriety. The brother bridles up, very sore at the injustice done his sister, tells his mother she is all wrong, and says to Gwen:

SP.   "WHY DON'T YOU GO TO THE BOSS ABOUT IT?"

This gives Gwen an idea. She thinks a moment and says to the brother, "Do you think I dare?" The brother says, "Certainly, why not?" Gwen says, "But he is so wonderful he scares me." The brother says, "That's all right but it is always best to go to the big noise. You always get a better deal." Gwen considers this a moment and says to the brother, "I believe you are right. That's just what I will do." Then she thinks about what she will wear, turns to her mother, and says:

SP.   "MOTHER, MAY I BORROW YOUR TAN CAPE?"

The mother, in a half-amused way, turns her head, raises her eyes to the sky, turns to Gwen, and says, "Yes, anything in the world you want."

Gwen goes on making her campaign for the morning.

FADE OUT.

TITLE   BRINGING US TO CROWNINSHIELD'S OFFICE THE NEXT MORNING.

21. CROWNINSHIELD'S OFFICE (FADE IN). Crowninshield is sitting at his desk, very busy dictating to Miss Turner, a hatchet-faced stenographer wearing a shawl.

The boy enters and tells Crowninshield that Nellie Jones wishes to see him. Crowninshield is a little surprised, tells the boy to bring her in. The boy opens the door and Nellie enters, and comes in a rather embarrassed way down to Crowninshield.

He asks her what the trouble is, and she tells him her story, that yesterday she was sitting taking dictation from Hicks when Mrs. Hicks came in and saw her and seemed to be very much upset, and Mr. Hicks sent her out of the room and soon after they came into her room . . .

SP.   "AND MRS. HICKS DISCHARGED ME."

Crowninshield bridles up at this and says, "Mrs. Hicks? What has she to do with it?" Nellie very innocently says she doesn't know. Miss Turner meanwhile gives her a series of dirty looks.

Crowninshield then picks up the telephone and asks for Hicks, telling Nellie he will inquire into the matter.

22. HICKS'S OFFICE. Hicks takes the receiver off the hook and answers it.

23. CROWNINSHIELD'S OFFICE. Crowninshield tells Nellie he is going to ask about her work and she says all right. Then he turns to the phone and says:

SP.   "DID YOU FIND MISS JONES A GOOD STENOGRA-
PHER OR NOT?"

24. HICKS'S OFFICE. Hicks is a little bit embarrassed, doesn't quite
know what to say, finally decides he must do the girl justice and says
into the phone:

SP.   "I AM COMPELLED TO SAY SHE IS THE BEST I HAVE
EVER HAD."

25. CROWNINSHIELD'S OFFICE. Crowninshield is a little surprised
and a bit indignant at hearing this, looks at the girl a second, then
says into the phone: "Then why did you discharge her?"

26. HICKS'S OFFICE. Hicks is very much embarrassed, doesn't quite
know what to say but finally says: "I didn't want to discharge her Mr.
Crowninshield but . . ."

SP.   "WELL, IT WAS A LITTLE DOMESTIC MISUNDER-
STANDING."

27. CROWNINSHIELD'S OFFICE. Crowninshield is sore at the idea of
mixing up business with sentiment and tells him so, reminding him
he knows his ideas on this subject and he will not permit an employee
to be discharged for so trivial a matter, so long as the work is satisfac-
tory.

28. HICKS'S OFFICE. Hicks, frightened at the slating he is getting,
says he agrees with Mr. Crowninshield entirely and thinks he is quite
right but that he couldn't help it as his wife raised such a fuss.

29. CROWNINSHIELD'S OFFICE. Crowninshield tells Hicks to see that
it doesn't happen again, hangs up the receiver, presses a button on his
desk, turns and looks toward the door. The boy enters. Crowninshield tells the boy to ask Mr. Davis to come in. The boy exits.
Crowninshield then turns to Nellie and says:

SP.   "I DON'T BELIEVE IN MIXING SENTIMENT WITH
BUSINESS. YOU HAVE BEEN DONE AN INJUSTICE

AND I WILL SEE THAT YOU GET ANOTHER PLACE
IN THE FIRM."

Nellie gives him a joyful and grateful smile, which fails to register with him entirely. Nellie looks at him soulfully but is disappointed that she makes no impression on him whatever.

At this moment Mr. Davis enters. He wears thick glasses and squints. Mr. Crowninshield asks him first if he has an opening for a stenographer and he says yes, he has, if she is a good one. Crowninshield assures him that Nellie is a good one, introduces her to him, and tells him to put her to work. Nellie smiles at him but he pays no attention. He looks squarely at her, but his face is blank. He tells her to come with him, starts to leave. Nellie leans over and smiles at Crowninshield, thanking him effusively, and he says that's all right, he is only doing what is fair and just, and she again smiles, a little bit flustered, and follows Davis out of the office.

30. GENERAL OFFICE. Room with a continuous desk on each side, running practically the whole length of the room and divided into sections. At each section sits a bookkeeper on a high stool.

At the extreme end of the room is a stenographer's desk.

In the foreground is a flat desk between the rows of desks and at this sits the efficiency man facing front.

Davis enters followed by Nellie, she smiling but he paying no attention at all.

He goes down the aisle between the rows of desks, followed by Nellie, the clerks all turning their necks about to rubber at her. And she flashing a smile at each of them as she passes.

Get inserts of her smiles and also several inserts of clerks craning their necks to watch her.

Davis seats Nellie at the desk at the end of the room facing front. He picks up a letter which he wishes her to copy, holding it right up within an inch of his eyes, examines it to see that it is the right one. Then he hands it to her and looks at her. She smiles.

TITLE   THE REASON NELLIE'S SMILE HAD NO EFFECT
         UPON DAVIS.

CLOSE-UP—NELLIE smiling at him.

CLOSE-UP—DAVIS looking at her, giving her instructions about the
letter.

CLOSE-UP—NELLIE all out of focus and jazzed, looking like nothing
human.

CLOSE-UP—DAVIS continuing his instructions.

SEMI-CLOSE-UP—TWO OF THEM, he giving her the letter and she sitting down at the typewriter and he leaving.

LONG SHOT—ROOM. Davis leaves Nellie and goes down the aisle toward his desk, squinting at each clerk as he passes, and of course each clerk as he passes gets busy but as soon as he has passed the clerks again crane their necks around at Nellie.

Get several inserts of the men craning their necks, also an insert of Nellie doing her work but not forgetting to give them pleasant smiles.

LONG SHOT—Every clerk in the place craning his neck at her, she doing her work smiling to herself and at them.   FADE OUT.

TITLE   THE NEXT DAY EVERY CLERK IN THE
         OFFICE SHOWED UP WITH A STIFF NECK.

31. GENERAL OFFICE. LONG SHOT (FADE IN) Several of the clerks are arranging their books on the desks. They all have stiff necks, which they keep rubbing. Three or four have cloths around their necks. A couple of clerks meet in the middle of the room and compare notes on the stiff necks, one saying, "I have a horrible stiff neck this morning." The other says, "So have I." Then the first one looks around and says:

SP.   "THERE MUST BE A DRAFT IN THIS OFFICE."

A VIRTUOUS VAMP   159

The second one says yes. Then they go to their stools.

All this time Davis has been sitting at his desk in front, going over statements, etc.

Gwen now enters front. Davis doesn't even see her as she goes down the aisle and seats herself at the desk. The men all turn stiffly, holding their necks as they look around after her.

Get several inserts of them turning and looking after her with stiff necks.

She smiles at each one as she goes down the aisle and seats herself at the desk.

CLOSE-UP—GWEN giving a general smile to all of them.

Several inserts of the stiff-necked boys pleased at this smile.

Davis is looking through some papers and wants to verify something. He takes some papers and goes to one of the men and asks him about the account of this person. The man is a little embarrassed and says he failed to make all the entries yesterday and holds up a number of bills which have not been entered. At this Davis is surprised and wants to know what is the matter. The clerk tells him he has a stiff neck and doesn't feel very well. Davis then tells him to enter them right away and goes across to another man.

He asks him a similar question and gets a similar reply. Davis is quite sore at this and tells him to get busy quick and get his work caught up and then returns to his own desk and sits down.

At this point Nellie reaches over her desk to get something and in doing so knocks something else off on the floor in front of her desk. All the clerks make a rush to pick it up for her, each one a little careful on account of his stiff neck. Davis, hearing all this racket, turns and squints his eyes, trying to take it in. The men, seeing him looking at them, quickly return to their desks.

Then Davis thinks a minute, pondering in his mind a new thought. Finally he gets up, goes back to Gwen's desk and puts his face right down within a couple of inches of hers.

CLOSE-UP—GWEN'S FACE, just slightly out of focus but very pretty.

Davis draws back from her, after sizing her up and says:

SP.   "SO, YOU ARE WHAT'S THE MATTER
        WITH THIS OFFICE!"

Gwen is terribly alarmed for fear she is going to lose her job again and tries to talk to him and to cajole him with a frightened smile, saying:

SP.   "BUT, MR. DAVIS, I COULDN'T HELP IT!"

At this Davis gives her a good look at a distance of about three or four feet.

CLOSE-UP—GWEN'S FACE all out of focus, meaning nothing at all.

Davis shakes his head in a puzzled sort of way, not knowing just what to do. Finally he decides to go to Crowninshield and stalks out of the office. Nellie looks after him frightened to death. The minute he is out of the room all the clerks turn again and direct their gaze toward Nellie.

32. CROWNINSHIELD'S OFFICE. Crowninshield is sitting at his desk talking to Kirby about some policies, Kirby telling him that they ought not take such a big risk on this man on account of his propensity for speculating in Wall Street and because of suicide in the family.

Davis now enters, still puzzled and upset about Nellie. He comes to Crowninshield and Crowninshield asks him what he can do for him. He scratches his head and is quite puzzled as to what he ought to do and finally says:

SP.   "IT'S ABOUT THAT STENOGRAPHER.
        SHE HAS UPSET MY WHOLE OFFICE."

Crowninshield is surprised to hear this, asks what's the matter, isn't she a good stenographer. Davis says yes she is a fine stenographer . . .

SP.   "BUT MY CLERKS DON'T GET
        ANY WORK DONE!"

Crowninshield wants to know why. Then Davis explains that they sit
on their stools and look around at this girl all the time and today they
all came in with stiff necks from looking at her.

A smile spreads over Kirby's face and he leans over to Crowninshield, plucks his sleeve, and says:

SP.   "INTRODUCE ME."

This makes Crowninshield sore. He gives Kirby the devil, telling
him it is just that spirit which is making it hard for this girl to hold
a job.

He then turns to Davis and tells him his men are a lot of fools,
sentimental asses. Davis says yes, he knows they are, but shall he
discharge the girl. Crowninshield thinks a minute and then says:

SP.   "NO. I WILL NOT HAVE HER DISCHARGED
        AS LONG AS SHE IS EFFICIENT
        IN HER WORK."

Davis then says, "Well, what am I going to do with her. I can't get
anything done in my office." Crowninshield thinks a moment and
then says:

SP.   "SEND HER UP TO ME."

Davis with a little sigh of relief gets out quick.

Crowninshield then rings the bell and the office boy enters while
Kirby looks smilingly on. Crowninshield says to the office boy:

SP.   "ASK MR. BELL TO COME HERE."

The boy says yes sir, and goes out.

Crowninshield expresses his disgust and anger at the fool men in his employ, then turns to Kirby and says:

SP.   "THIS GIRL IS A FINE STENOGRAPHER BUT THE FOOL MEN IN THIS ORGANIZATION MAKE SUCH IDIOTS OF THEMSELVES OVER HER, I CAN'T KEEP HER IN A JOB."

Kirby laughs, shakes his head, looks at Crowninshield, and finally says, "Well, what are you going to do with her?" Crowninshield says:

SP.   "I'M GOING TO GIVE HER TO BELL. HE'S GOT SENSE AND HE'S ALL BUSINESS." (or "HE WON'T MIX SENTIMENT WITH BUSINESS.")

At this point the door to the anteroom opens. The boy stands in the door and says Miss Jones is there. Crowninshield says to show her in. She comes in, comes over to him. He asks her to sit down, which she does, giving him a very special but frightened smile. Kirby meanwhile is perking himself up and getting a good eyeful of Nellie.

Crowninshield then tells Nellie that Mr. Davis has told him that his fool clerks had been annoying her. Nellie very demurely says that she doesn't understand why they neglect their work as she didn't do a thing.

Crowninshield says of course he knows she didn't do a thing. It is just that the men are a lot of sentimental idiots.

At this point Bell enters and comes to Crowninshield's desk and asks Crowninshield if he sent for him. Crowninshield looks up at him and says:

SP.   "YOU WERE LOOKING FOR A STENOGRAPHER. DID YOU GET ONE?"

Bell nods his head saying yes he did. Crowninshield is a little disappointed, says, "I am sorry. I was going to put Miss Jones in with you." Then Bell looks at Nellie and she flashes a smile at him and he is immediately hit. Bell scratches his chin, gives her a good look, turns and says to Crowninshield:

SP.   "THE GIRL I HAVE GOT ISN'T VERY GOOD . . ."

Nellie smiles in anticipation at this and Crowninshield thinks a second and then says:

SP.   "WELL, PUT HER SOMEWHERE ELSE AND YOU
        TAKE MISS JONES."

Bell gives one quick flash of a smile at Nellie and then turns to Crowninshield, says very well, he will. Then, turning to Nellie, says, "Will you come with me, Miss Jones?" and shows her out the door.

CLOSE-UP—KIRBY rubbering at Nellie as she goes out.

Crowninshield notices Kirby looking after the girl and smiling, sits back in his chair, disgusted, and finally says:

SP.   "I DON'T SEE ANYTHING ABOUT THAT GIRL TO
        TURN MEN'S HEADS."

Kirby looks at him critically and disapprovingly and says, "That's because you're all wrong." Crowninshield looks at him in disgust and thinks of the injustice of the whole situation and finally slams his fist on the desk and says:

SP.   "ANYHOW THESE THINGS OUGHT NOT TO BE
        ALLOWED TO INTERFERE WITH BUSINESS."

Kirby looks at him smiling, nods his head, saying you're quite right, so let's get back to these policies; and they start to look them over.

FADE OUT.

TITLE   HOW MR. BELL GOT ALONG WITH NELLIE.

33. BELL'S OFFICE.

Bell's office is, in importance and luxuriance of fittings, next to Crowninshield's.

(FADE IN)

Bell and Nellie are sitting at the desk. Bell is trying to dictate but as he looks over at Nellie he forgets all about his dictation until she looks up at him from her book, smiling. Then he nervously gets up and starts to walk the floor, finally stopping and continuing to dictate for a moment, she taking it down, then looking up at him smiling. Again he stops, looking at her soulfully and again she looks up at him smiling.

Then he looks at her, swallows, is very embarrassed, tries to go on, looks at her again, and finally impulsively kneels at her feet, grasps her hand, and says:

SP.   "NELLIE, I CAN KEEP IT BACK NO LONGER. I LOVE
        YOU. WILL YOU MARRY ME?"

Gwen is taken aback, utterly surprised at this, can hardly speak. Finally she manages to stammer out:

SP.   "MR. BELL, WHATEVER PUT THAT INTO YOUR
        MIND? I AM PERFECTLY SURPRISED!"

Bell goes on pleading with her, telling her how he adores her, how she has wrapped herself around his heart and that he can't go on without her. She draws her hand away, assumes a very haughty air, and finally says:

SP.   "MR. BELL, I AM SURPRISED THAT YOU SHOULD SO
        PRESUME ON OUR BUSINESS RELATIONSHIP."

He says, "Business relationship? What are you talking about?" and rises to his feet. "Haven't you led me on to think that you cared for me?" She says she certainly has not done anything of the kind. He says, "Well, what have you meant every day when you smiled at me, when you let me hold your hand, when you did everything you could possibly do to let me think you cared for me?" Then she says, "Mr. Bell, you are insulting me. I have done nothing of the kind."

SP.   "IF I HAVE SMILED AT YOU IT HAS BEEN
        ENTIRELY IN A BUSINESS WAY."

He raises his hands to heaven at this, tears his hair, walks up and down the floor, comes back to her and says: "Do you mean to tell me you haven't meant to convey to me that you cared for me?" She says, "Why, certainly not, I have respected you as my employer and that is all." Then he says, "You are a heartless vampire. You have ruined my life. I am through with you and all your kind forever."

She looks at him in mild surprise and a little self-pity, shakes her head, shrugs her shoulders, and then smiles at him a little. He, looking at her, goes crazy, grabs a paper knife off the table, raises it in his hand and says:

SP.   "GOD, WOMAN, YOU MAKE ME SEE RED!"

CLOSE-UP—NELLIE (TINTED RED) looking at him askance and a little frightened but still with a faint smile.

LONG SHOT—BELL slams down his arm with the paper knife in it and, forgetting he has it in his hand, pulls his collar away as if he were choking, at the same time pulling out his necktie, then runs his hand through his hair, and looking front a second resolves to get rid of her and rushes out of the room.

Nellie looks after him, sighs, shakes her head, and sits down at her typewriter to go to work.

34. CROWNINSHIELD'S OFFICE. Crowninshield is at his desk. Kirby comes in with a paper in his hand and sits beside him. Crowninshield signs paper and Kirby starts to go when . . .

In rushes Bell, his hair disheveled, his necktie pulled out, his collar unbuttoned, and the paper knife in his hand. He rushes to the desk, panting; he can't speak for some seconds. At length, he manages to spurt out:

SP.   "YOU WILL HAVE TO GET THAT WOMAN
        AWAY FROM ME. I AM NOT RESPONSIBLE
        WHEN I AM NEAR HER!"

Crowninshield looks at him amazed, asks him what's wrong with
Nellie. Bell says:

SP.   "SHE HAS RUINED MY LIFE! I NEVER WANT TO SEE
        HER AGAIN!"

Crowninshield asks him what in the world is the matter and Bell
waves his arms in the air with the knife in his hand, telling him to
get her out, that he will never go in his office again until she is gone.
He slams the paper knife down on the table. The knife bends double,
being made of lead. Crowninshield then says to be careful of the desk
and then Bell sees the knife, throws it on the floor, tells Crowninshield to get rid of that woman, and rushes out of the office.

Kirby laughs his head off at this but Crowninshield is very much
upset. At length Kirby says:

SP.   "AND THAT'S THE SENSIBLE GUY WHO WAS
        ALL BUSINESS!"
        or
        "AND THAT'S THE ONE MAN WHO WOULDN'T MIX
        SENTIMENT WITH BUSINESS."

Crowninshield looks daggers at Kirby for reminding him of his faith
in this man, is very sore about it and says he doesn't know what to
do. He was the one man who, he thought, was safe from all sorts of
sentimental nonsense.

Kirby says, "Well, how do you know it was his fault? Maybe she
was to blame entirely." Crowninshield says, "No, I don't believe any
such thing. She is a perfectly competent, efficient girl and any girl
who does her work thoroughly has no time for nonsense. I am going
to get her side of it."

Then he rings the bell for the boy. The boy enters, goes to Crowninshield, who says:

SP.   "ASK MISS JONES TO COME HERE."

The boy says yes sir, and exits.

Kirby looks at him, chuckles to himself, leans over to Crown-inshield and says:

SP.   "I WISH YOU WOULD GIVE HER TO ME."

Crowninshield looks in horror at him for this suggestion, says he is the last man in the world he would ever give her to. He thinks a minute, trying to puzzle out what to do, finally turns angrily to Kirby and says:

SP.   "WHAT CHANCE HAS A POOR WORKING GIRL
        GOT WITH MEN WHO ARE SUCH
        BLITHERING IDIOTS?"

Kirby laughs at him for taking the thing so seriously but Crowninshield is very much worked up over the whole thing. At length he turns to Kirby and says:

SP.   "I HAVE A GOOD MIND TO TAKE HER ON MYSELF
        AS AN EXAMPLE TO THE ORGANIZATION!"

Kirby looks at him out of the corner of his eye, smiles to himself, and then tells him to go on and do it, it is just the thing for him to do, in rather a sarcastic way.

At this point the door opens and Miss Nellie walks in. She is a little bit frightened but comes to Crowninshield. Of course she is quite excited and she smiles at him with her heart in her mouth.

Crowninshield turns to Nellie and says, "What was it happened with Mr. Bell, Miss Jones? Why was he so excited?" Nellie, a little embarrassed, doesn't know what to say but finally stammers out:

SP.   "I AM VERY MUCH INTERESTED IN MY WORK, MR.
        CROWNINSHIELD, AND I DON'T WISH TO MARRY
        ANYONE."

Crowninshield is amazed at this and says, "Oh, he wanted to marry you?" She says, "Yes, didn't he tell you? Why, he acted like a madman, frightened me terribly." And she looks frightened. Crowninshield then turns triumphantly to Kirby and says, "See, I told you so. The men have all gone crazy." Kirby smiles knowingly and then Crowninshield turns to Nellie and says:

SP.　"I HAVE DECIDED, MISS JONES, TO TAKE YOU INTO MY OFFICE, WHERE YOU WILL BE ABLE TO WORK IN PEACE."

Nellie, with her heart in her mouth, smiles radiantly at this prospect. Crowninshield then pushes the bell on his desk to call Miss Turner, then turns to Nellie and says, very seriously:

SP.　"I PROMISE YOU, YOU WILL NOT BE ANNOYED BY ANY SENTIMENTAL NONSENSE IN MY OFFICE."

Nellie tries to smile at this but it is rather a wan smile and fades away in disappointment. At this point Miss Turner enters and comes to Crowninshield. Crowninshield turns to her and says:

SP.　"A VERY DIFFICULT SITUATION HAS ARISEN IN MR. BELL'S OFFICE AND I WANT YOU TO TAKE CHARGE OF HIS WORK FOR A WHILE."

Miss Turner is surprised and chagrined at this, gives him a frowning look and then a dirty look at Nellie, as much as to say, "You are responsible for this. I might have known it." Nellie smiles back at her very sweetly.

Then Crowninshield says to Miss Turner, "You better go see Mr. Bell at once. He was a little excited when he was in here. You go and calm him down and get him back to work." Miss Turner, with another freezing look, goes out the main entrance.

Crowninshield, with a little sigh of satisfaction at having settled the thing, turns to Nellie and asks her if she is ready to go to work. Nellie says, "Yes, I will get a book and pencil," and leaves, going out into the anteroom.

Kirby, looking after her, smiling, turns to Crowninshield and says:

SP.   "WILL YOU PUT ME NEXT ON THE LIST?"

Crowninshield bridles at this, turns on him, says this is a serious matter and he doesn't like his levity about it. He picks up the paper Kirby brought, gives it to him, and tells him to get out. Kirby leaves, smiling.

Nellie enters and comes to Crowninshield. She has gotten back her poise and smiles at him, but with more reserve than she showed to the others.

Crowninshield then takes up some papers in a very businesslike way, glances up at Nellie and says:

SP.   "NOW, WE WILL GET TO WORK."

And he looks right back at his papers.

Nellie takes a chair and sits down right beside Crowninshield, unnoticed by him. He, having looked over the papers, is ready to dictate, raises his head to start the dictation, notices Nellie beside him, looks at her. She sits with pencil ready, smiling up at him. He is a little surprised at her nearness and says:

SP.   "YOU BETTER SIT ON THE OTHER SIDE OF THE
        DESK, MISS JONES."

Nellie, surprised and rather chagrined at this, takes her chair and moves around to the other side of the desk, then regains her composure, smiles up again at Crowninshield, and Crowninshield, with the papers in his hand, calmly turns about on his swivel chair with his back almost turned to Nellie and starts to dictate.

CLOSE-UP—NELLIE looking adoringly at him as if he were the most marvelous man in the world and loving him chiefly because he ignores her.   FADE OUT.

[Scene 35 was cut during the filming.]

TITLE INDICATING THAT THE CROWNINSHIELD SISTERS
HAD WAITED ANXIOUSLY FOR SEVERAL WEEKS
FOR SOME WORD FROM THE HONORABLE GWEN-
DOLYN.

35. DRAWING ROOM OF THE CROWNINSHIELD SISTERS. FADE IN.

One is sitting writing notes at a desk when the other enters with a
letter. She rushes in great excitement to her sister and shows her the
letter and they get their heads together over it.

INSERT—LETTER (Same handwriting as letter in scene 5)

San Francisco, Cal., 1919

My dear friends:

I cannot imagine what has become of Miss Armitage.
We have heard nothing from her, but this is not surprising as she is a notoriously poor correspondent. However, it seems quite certain to me that she must have
met someone who offered her a position before she got
to your brother.

Of course, a girl with her charm and unusual social
distinction would be eagerly snapped up by the first one
she happened to meet. I am very sorry you have not met
her, as I know you would have loved her, etc. etc.

The two sisters put down the letter, showing their keen disappointment over the loss of the Armitage girl, and begin to debate with
each other as to what in the world could have become of her. One
wonders whether by any chance Mrs. Jazzbo could have grabbed her,
and the other one says:

SP. "I VENTURE SOME UPSTART HAS SECURED HER TO
PROMOTE HER SOCIAL POSITION."

And the other one then expresses her contempt for anyone who
would do such a miserable thing and they both pan this imaginary
person.   FADE OUT.

[End cut]

36. CROWNINSHIELD'S OFFICE. (FADE IN) Crowninshield is sitting at his desk dictating, Nellie on the opposite side of the desk taking notes. As Crowninshield dictates, he gradually loses interest in what he is saying and his eyes rest on Nellie with unconscious love and caress in them. Nellie notices he isn't talking and looks up at him sweetly, smiling. He quickly gets back to his work and goes on dictating. Nellie, with a little sigh, goes on taking the dictation.

At this point Davis enters with an application for a policy in his hand. He comes to Crowninshield and puts the application before him. Crowninshield asks him what it is and he says:

SP. "IT'S AN APPLICATION FOR A FREAK POLICY.
I THINK YOU HAD BETTER PASS ON IT."

Crowninshield just glances at it and then asks what it is, what's the idea about it. Davis says:

SP. "IT'S A GIRL NAMED BEE PALMER. SHE WANTS HER
SHOULDERS INSURED."

Davis is disgusted with the whole idea. Crowninshield is puzzled at this and wondering what on earth it is all about, asks Davis what it means, why she wants her shoulders insured. Davis, in a very disgusted ways, says:

SP. "SHE IS A SHIMMY DANCER."

Crowninshield, puzzled at this, looks at the application again, studying it, and while he is doing this, Davis looks over and squints at Nellie. Nellie smiles at him sweetly, says, "How do you do, Mr. Davis?" and he, squinting his eyes, says:

SP. "GOOD MORNING, MISS TURNER."

Nellie bridles up at this, says she is not Miss Turner. By this time Crowninshield has finished reading the thing and turns to Davis, says he will look into the matter, and Davis leaves. Crowninshield continues looking over the application. Finally he turns to Nellie and says:

SP.   "I'VE HEARD OF THIS SHIMMY DANCE. DO YOU
       KNOW WHAT'S IT'S LIKE?"

Nellie says, "Why, didn't you ever see a shimmy dancer?" He says no, so she says she will show him. She gets up, starts to move her shoulders. Crowninshield watches her curiously with growing interest as she, increasing the movement of her shoulders, gradually gets into the swing of it. At this point Kirby enters at the back and Nellie stops when she sees him, a little embarrassed, and sits down again at the desk. Kirby stands a moment in the doorway smiling, then comes down, puts some papers on Crowninshield's desk, glances over at Nellie, then turns and whispers to Crowninshield:

SP.   "REMEMBER, I GET HER NEXT."

This makes Crowninshield sore. He grits his teeth, finally turns to Kirby and says:

SP.   "THIS IS BUSINESS, MR. KIRBY."

Kirby says, "Oh, excuse me, I am sorry I spoke," and beats it out the back. Crowninshield looks after him, sore, then returns to the examination of the application, calls Nellie over to him. She comes and looks over his shoulder at the application and he says:

SP.   "THIS BEE PALMER WANTS A $100,000 POLICY."

Nellie opens her eyes as that is rather a large amount. Crowninshield puzzles a moment over it and then says to her:

SP.   "THE QUESTION IN A CASE LIKE THIS IS THE
       MORAL HAZARD."

He then goes on to say he never has seen one of these things and he doesn't know what sort of people they are who do this work, so he is at a loss to know what to do about it. Suddenly Nellie gets an inspiration and says:

SP.   "IF YOU LIKE, I WILL WORK OVERTIME SATURDAY
       NIGHT AND TAKE YOU TO THE MIDNIGHT FROLIC
       TO SEE THIS GIRL."

Crowninshield says, "Well," thinks a second, and then says: "That's a very good idea as long as you don't mind the work. I think we will do it," and then:

SP.   "I AM GLAD TO SEE YOU TAKE SUCH AN INTEREST
       IN THE FIRM, MISS JONES."

She says yes, she is very much interested in the firm, and as they are both kidding each other as to why they are going to see the Midnight Frolic,   FADE OUT.

TITLE   SO NELLIE AND CROWNINSHIELD DID A HEAVY
         NIGHT'S WORK ON THE ZIEGFELD ROOF.

37. ZIEGFELD ROOF. LONG SHOT (FADE IN), showing a part of the show with a vacant table at the ringside.

38. CLOAK ROOM OF THE ROOF. Several people are entering and checking their things. Crowninshield and Nellie enter. Nellie is dressed in a hat and a long cloak. She takes off the cloak, revealing a pretty little dinner dress underneath. Crowninshield is dressed in ordinary business clothes and when he sees Nellie's dress he is somewhat surprised and rather admires her as he has never seen her looking so pretty, but he pulls himself up suddenly and says:

SP.   "HAVE YOU BROUGHT YOUR NOTEBOOK,
       MISS JONES?"

She smiles at him sweetly, fishes in the pocket of her coat and gets out a pencil and book and they start for the hall.

39. ZIEGFELD ROOF. Another shot, showing another part of the show. Crowninshield and Nellie enter and sit at the ringside table and start to order something from the waiter.

CLOSE-UP—OF THEM ORDERING from the waiter.   FADE OUT.

40. ZIEGFELD   ROOF   (FADE   IN)   CLOSE-UP—NELLIE   AND CROWNINSHIELD at their table, perhaps drinking and eating something.

CLOSE-UP—BAND striking up music.

CLOSE-UP—NELLIE looking at her program and saying to Crowninshield:

SP.   "THIS IS BEE PALMER."

Crowninshield is interested and they both turn and watch the stage.

LONG SHOT—NELLIE and CROWNINSHIELD watching the stage and Bee Palmer appears and starts to do her stunt. As she progresses with her shimmy dance . . .

CUT TO—CROWNINSHIELD, very much interested and watching it, then suddenly realizing that this is business and dictating notes to Nellie on it.

LONG SHOT—BEE PALMER finishes her song and retires, all applauding.

Then the orchestra strikes up a dance for the intermission and people get up on the floor and begin to dance.

CLOSE-UP—NELLIE AND CROWNINSHIELD. Nellie looks up at the dancers wistfully as she would like to dance herself. She turns to Crowninshield and asks him if he doesn't dance. He shrugs his shoulder and says he can waltz a little but he isn't much good at it, and she says sweetly, "Oh, I don't mind, I'd love to waltz with you." He says, "Well, all right, if you can stand my tramping on your toes." Then they get up and join the others in the dance.

LONG SHOT—OF THEM ALL DANCING, Crowninshield and Nellie among the others.

CLOSE-UP—CROWNINSHIELD AND NELLIE dancing, and he is dancing very well. Nellie smiles at him and tells him she thinks he is a lovely dancer. He is pleased and says, "Do you think so?" and she says, "Yes, you are fine." Then he goes at it with more of a zest.

FADE OUT.

TITLE SAYING THAT THE CROWNINSHIELD SISTERS, ALARMED AT THE FAILURE OF GWEN TO APPEAR ANYWHERE ON NEW YORK'S SOCIAL HORIZON, DETERMINED TO TAKE DESPERATE MEASURES TO FIND HER.

41. DOOR OF THE SCENTASMELL DETECTIVE AGENCY. (FADE IN)

The two sisters enter, quite ill at ease at the crude surroundings.

42. INTERIOR DETECTIVE OFFICE. The Crowninshield sisters enter the office, state their business, and are assigned a man. They go with him to an inner office and state their business, showing the letters they have received from the lady in California. Perhaps they have a copy of *Burke's Peerage* showing the crest.

The detective is a regular Hawkshaw, a typical conceited self-assertive ass. He tells them that is enough for him to go on, he only needs very slight clues and will get their woman, never worry.

(Either take them out or *fade out* on the scene as they are talking.)

TITLE INDICATING THAT NELLIE AND CROWNINSHIELD SPENT SEVERAL SATURDAY EVENINGS INVES-TIGATING LIVING CONDITIONS IN NEW YORK.

(Illustrate this title by scenes of night life in New York—cabaret, theater, dancing, etc., one moving off as the other comes in or else one fading in after the other.)

TITLE BUT ALWAYS WITH THE SAME RESULT.

43. EXTERIOR NELLIE'S APARTMENT HOUSE, NIGHT (FADE IN)
Crowninshield's car drives up and he helps Nellie out and leads her

up to the door of her apartment house. They stop at the door a moment and Nellie turns to him and bursts out in esctasy:

SP. "HASN'T IT BEEN A GLORIOUS EVENING?"

Crowninshield says very seriously that it has been and he's glad they went out tonight, for . . .

SP. "I GOT A LINE ON A COUPLE OF IMPORTANT RISKS TONIGHT."

Nellie turns on him at this, almost in tears, he paying no attention at all. He takes out his watch, turns to her and says:

SP. "YOU MUST GET TO BED, NOW. WE HAVE A HEAVY DAY'S WORK TOMORROW."

Nellie sighs, looks at him soulfully, which he fails to see. He shakes her hand good night and leaves her, getting in his car and driving off.

Nellie stands on the steps looking after him. She chokes up, finally breaks down sobbing, turns and goes into the house.

FADE OUT.

TITLE   AFTER A SLEEPLESS NIGHT.

44. GWEN'S BEDROOM (FADE IN) CLOSE-UP—GWEN, sitting at the window in her nightie and negligee. She hasn't slept all night and has been crying. She sighs, wipes her nose and her eyes; her eyes plainly show the result of weeping.

LONG SHOT—HER MOTHER enters as though to wake her up, comes toward the bed, sees it is empty, then looks over toward the window, sees that something is wrong, runs to Gwen and kneels beside her. Gwen throws her arms about her mother's neck and begins to sob. Her mother, very much concerned, asks what the trouble is, and at last Gwen controls herself enough to say:

SP. "I'M SO IN LOVE, MOTHER, AND WITH HIM IT IS
NOTHING BUT BUSINESS!"

The mother says in amazement, "You in love at last?" Gwen admits
it and sobs on mother's breast, shivering with hysteria. The mother is
a little alarmed at this, feels her head, which is hot, and her hands,
which are cold, and says, "Goodness, you are going to be ill. Come
and get right back in bed." She leads her over to the bed and tucks
her in. Gwen lies in bed, continuing crying and talking to her
mother about the terrible state of mind she is in. At this point Eddie
enters the door, which the mother has left open, and stands looking
at the mother and Gwen. Then Gwen, continuing her tale of woe to
her mother, says:

SP. "I DON'T SEE HOW I CAN EVER GO BACK TO THAT
OFFICE AGAIN!"

The mother comforts her a little but Eddie pricks up his ears at this,
stalks over to the side of the bed. Gwen looks up at him sorrowfully.
He squares his shoulders and says:

SP. "HAS CROWNINSHIELD BEEN INSULTING YOU?"

Gwen looks up at him sadly, shakes her head no and says:

SP. "NO, I WISH HE WOULD."

Eddie is puzzled at this attitude and quite concerned, not knowing
just what she means, and he asks his mother what she is talking
about, "She wishes he would"; and the mother turns to him with a
wan smile and says, "Our Gwen is in love, Eddie." Eddie is absolutely amazed at this, opens his eyes wide and looks at Gwen and
then at his mother, and finally says:

SP. "IN LOVE WITH CROWNINSHIELD?"

The mother shakes her head yes and Gwen looks over at him sorrowfully, nods her head, and then says:

Eddie is quite upset at this and angry at Crowninshield and wants to know what he has been taking her out nights for. Gwen says very weakly that that has been nothing but business on his part, but on her part it means a great deal more. Eddie is very wroth at this and says no man has a right to lead a girl on that way unless he means business.

Then Gwen says, "Oh, Eddie, keep still, keep still," and then turns to her mother, puts her hands to her head, begins to cry again, leaning her head down on her pillow. The mother leans over her, turns to Eddie and says, "Eddie, Gwen is sick, you better go away." Eddie looks at his mother and at Gwen, very angry, and we see determination growing in his face. At length he stalks out of the room.

45. SITTING ROOM, GWEN'S FLAT. Eddie enters from the bedroom, very determined, gets his hat, slams it on his head, starts for the door, stops, looks back toward the bedroom, and with final determination in his manner, stalks out the front door.

46. GWEN'S BEDROOM. Gwen is still crying with her head down on the pillow. The mother shakes her head sympathetically and finally leans over Gwen and says:

SP.   "I WILL TELEPHONE THE OFFICE THAT YOU
        WON'T BE DOWN TODAY."

Gwen says, no, no, not to do that, that she will feel better in a little while and will go down. The mother argues with her a little, tells her she ought to stay in bed, and Gwen says:

SP.   "NO, WE HAVE A HEAVY DAY TODAY AND
        I MUST GO."

The mother tells her she thinks she ought not go out at all but stay in bed, and Gwen insists that she will be all right when she has had something to eat and a bath. The mother finally says she will telephone that Gwen will be late and leaves the room.

47. SITTING ROOM AND HALL OF GWEN'S FLAT. The mother comes to the telephone and calls a number.

48. GWEN'S BEDROOM. CLOSE-UP—GWEN drying her eyes, sighing, trying to pull herself together, then bursting out again into tears.

49. SITTING ROOM AND HALL. The mother at the telephone speaking in the phone.

50. CROWNINSHIELD'S OFFICE. Crowninshield and Kirby are sitting at the desk, Crowninshield answering the phone.

51. GWEN'S SITTING ROOM. The mother speaks into the phone, saying:

SP.   "MISS JONES IS ILL THIS MORNING AND WILL BE A
        LITTLE LATE AT THE OFFICE."

52. CROWNINSHIELD'S OFFICE. Crowninshield shows some concern over this, says he hopes it is nothing serious.

53. GWEN'S SITTING ROOM. The mother says no, it is nothing serious, that she will be all right in a few hours' time.

54. CROWNINSHIELD'S OFFICE. Crowninshield says he is very glad, to tell her to take care of herself, not to come at all if she doesn't feel able, and hangs up the receiver. Crowninshield then shakes his head as if worried, and Kirby asks him what is the matter. Crowninshield, who is really worried because Nellie is sick, doesn't want Kirby to know this, so he suddenly pulls himself up and says:

SP.   "MISS JONES IS ILL AND I HAVE A VERY HEAVY
        DAY BEFORE ME."

Kirby shakes his head, says that is too bad, and Crowninshield turns to Kirby and says:

SP.   "THE POOR GIRL HAS BEEN WORKING OVERTIME
        WITH ME AT NIGHT AND I AM AFRAID IT HAS
        BEEN TOO MUCH FOR HER."

Kirby then says, "What do you mean, you have been working overtime at night?" as Kirby doesn't know anything about the trips they have been taking. Then Crowninshield explains how she has been to the Follies with him, Churchills, the theater, Coney Island, and a number of other places. And Kirby laughs his head off at this idea. Crowninshield wants to know what he is laughing at and Kirby says, "Nothing, nothing at all," picks up his papers, gets up laughing, and leaves.

Crowninshield looks after him, shakes his head as much as to say the man has gone out of his mind, and then begins to dig hard into his papers. (Note: Maybe a scene of Kirby telling Crowninshield he is headed for the halter and Crowninshield declaring he is a confirmed bachelor).   FADE OUT.

55. ANTEROOM, CROWNINSHIELD'S OFFICE. (FADE IN)

The office boy is there and Eddie enters, very important, and asks if Mr. Crowninshield is in. The office boy asks him who he is, and he says he is Miss Jones's brother. The office boy says he will tell Mr. Crowninshield and goes into Mr. Crowninshield's office.

56. CROWNINSHIELD'S OFFICE. The boy enters, goes to Crowninshield's desk, and tells him Miss Jones's brother wants to see him. Crowninshield is a little puzzled at this and then worried for fear he is bringing him bad news and tells the boy to send him in. The boy goes to the door, calls Eddie, who enters.

Eddie goes at once to Crowninshield's desk. Crowninshield puts out his hand to shake hands with him and Eddie takes his hand very reluctantly. Then Crowninshield asks how his sister is. Eddie says she is very ill; then standing over him like an accusing angel, he folds his arms and says:

SP.   "DO YOU KNOW WHY MY SISTER IS ILL THIS
        MORNING?"

Crowninshield, puzzled at the boy's attitude, shakes his head and says no, he hasn't any idea why. Then Eddie, still belligerent, says:

SP.   "BECAUSE YOU HAVE LED HER ON TO LOVE YOU
        AND HAVE BROKEN HER HEART!"

Crowninshield is absolutely astounded at this and asks Eddie what in
the world he is talking about. Eddie says, "Haven't you taken her out
night after night?" Crowninshield says but that was a matter of business. Eddie sniffs at the idea that this was business and says anyhow it
might have been business for you but it wasn't business for her. She
thought of course that your intentions were serious and the result of it
is that she is ill in bed and I, her brother, do not intend to see her
suffer for the misdeeds of any man.

Crowninshield shakes his head in despair and then turns to Eddie
in a patronizing way and says:

SP.   "MY BOY, I KNOW YOUR SISTER BETTER THAN
        YOU DO AND I KNOW HER FEELINGS ARE EX-
        ACTLY THE SAME AS MINE."

Eddie draws himself up in a superior manner and says:

SP.   "YOU ARE VERY MUCH MISTAKEN. MY SISTER'S
        HEART IS BROKEN AND IT IS UP TO YOU TO DO
        THE RIGHT THING BY HER."

Crowninshield looks at the boy in surprise and amusement, then
begins to laugh, saying:

SP.   "DO YOU THINK I OUGHT TO MARRY HER?"

Eddie, pulling himelf up to his full height, then looking at Crowninshield accusingly, says:

SP.   "THAT'S EXACTLY WHAT I DO MEAN; YOU OUGHT
        TO MARRY HER."

Crowninshield, trying to suppress a smile at the boy's earnestness,
says:

SP.   "BUT SHE DOESN'T WISH TO MARRY ME."

Eddie, raising his eyebrows in a superior manner, and looking down on Crowninshield, says:

SP.   "HOW DO YOU KNOW SHE DOESN'T?"

Crowninshield shrugs his shoulders, says:

SP.   "WELL, SHE HAS NEVER GIVEN ANY SIGN OF
        SUCH A THING."

And Eddie, pulling himself up to his full Armitage height, says:

SP.   "MY SISTER HAS SOME PRIDE."

Crowninshield shakes his head and says, "No, my boy, you are mistaken. Let's forget all about this nonsense." Eddie bridles at this and very angrily demands:

SP.   "THEN YOU REFUSE TO ASK HER TO MARRY YOU?"

Crowninshield reiterates that it wouldn't do any good, that she doesn't want to marry him. Eddie says he is convinced that is not true, that his sister would never have gone out with a man as she has with him unless she were in love with him. Crowninshield is getting tired of this by now, shakes his head as much as to say "Boy, you are a fool," then turns to Eddie and says:

SP.   "ALL RIGHT, I WILL PROPOSE TO HER IF THAT
        WILL SATISFY YOUR ROYAL HIGHNESS."

Eddie says very well, that is all he wants and now he knows he is a real man and will shake hands with him. He puts out his hand and shakes his hand firmly, says, "You will do it soon?" Crowninshield says smilingly:

SP. "I WILL DO IT AS SOON AS SHE COMES TO THE OFFICE JUST TO PROVE THAT YOU ARE WRONG."

Eddie says that is very fine of him, gives his hand another grip, bids him good-bye and leaves.

Crowninshield raises his hands to heaven, then turns again and digs into his work. FADE OUT.

TITLE BRINGING GWEN TO THE OFFICE. INDICATE AFTERNOON IN TITLE.

57. CROWNINSHIELD'S OFFICE. (FADE IN) Crowninshield is at his desk, dictating to a strange stenographer. The office boy opens the door and Nellie walks in. Crowninshield immediately gets up from his chair, comes over to her, helps her off with her hat and coat, and then dismisses the other girl, who leaves.

Then Nellie sits at his desk to start work. He asks her if she is sure she feels well enough to work, and she says yes, she is all right, she is well again; and he is just about to start dictating a letter when he thinks of Eddie and his promise and he smiles a little, then turns to Nellie and says:

SP. "MISS JONES, THERE IS SOMETHING I WANT TO ASK YOU BEFORE WE START TO WORK."

Nellie looks at him wanly, and asks him what it is. Then he says:

SP. "IT IS GOING TO GIVE YOU A GOOD LAUGH. ARE YOU WELL ENOUGH TO STAND IT?"

Then she, more and more puzzled, says yes, she is all right. What is it he wants to ask her. Finally Crowninshield smilingly says:

SP. "ARE YOU IN LOVE WITH ME AND DO YOU WANT TO MARRY ME?"

Nellie's eyes widen. She weakly drops her hands to her sides and slumps back in her chair, with her eyes closed. Crowninshield, alarmed, gets up and goes to her, asks her what is the matter, is she ill, his arm around the back of her shoulder. As she opens her eyes she looks up at him with a wan smile and says:

SP.   "YOU DARLING, HOW DID YOU GUESS?"

At this Crowninshield is flabbergasted, stammers and stutters and looks at her, she still smiling at him. He is hardly able to speak but finally manages to get out:

SP.   "YOU DON'T MEAN THAT, DO YOU?"

She says yes, of course she means it, you darling thing.

SP.   "I LOVED YOU FOR WEEKS AND I THOUGHT YOU
        DIDN'T CARE."

She holds his hand and continues smiling and talking to him, perfectly at peace, with a tremendous feeling of relief and joy, while he doesn't dare look at her. He is bewildered, not knowing what the devil hit him, occasionally gives her a little sickly smile, and then the office boy enters, which gives him an excuse for drawing away from her and sitting down at his desk.

She looks disgusted at the interruption. The boy is a little surprised at the situation, comes over to Crowninshield with four or five visiting cards in his hand and tells him these people are all waiting to see him. Crowninshield takes the cards, looks them over. The boy glances over at Nellie who gives him a sweet, satisfied smile. Crowninshield finishes looking at the cards and says he will see them in a few minutes, and the boy goes out.

As soon as the boy has gone, Gwen, having regained her poise by now, smiles sweetly over at Crowninshield and says:

SP.   "OF COURSE, WE ARE NOT REALLY ENGAGED
        UNTIL YOU KISS ME."

Crowninshield, very much embarrassed and frightened, not knowing what in the devil to do, finally gets up, comes over to her, she all anticipation. He looks down at her, hesitates a moment, then takes her hand, raises it to his lips and kisses it. She throws his hand off and says, "No, silly, not like that, here," and raises her mouth to him, all ready to be kissed. He, still more embarrassed, hesitates, doesn't know what the devil to do, when the door opens and Kirby enters with another man, sees the situation for a second, smiles but passes it off, comes to Crowninshield's desk, and introduces the man to Crowninshield.

Nellie is very much disgusted by this interruption. Kirby speaks a moment to Crowninshield, then goes to the door of the anteroom and calls another man, who enters. Kirby takes this man, introduces him to Crowninshield, and they start to draw up chairs to engage in what seems to be an important conference. Gwen is looking at them with supreme disgust. The men begin their conference.   FADE OUT.

TITLE   CONFERENCE LASTED TILL CLOSING TIME. SAYING IT WAS INDEED A HEAVY DAY AND NOT UNTIL NEARLY CLOSING TIME DID THEY HAVE A MOMENT ALONE.

58. CROWNINSHIELD'S OFFICE. Crowinshield, Gwen, and a man are sitting near his desk. Crowninshield is just finishing his conversation with the man. He rises, escorts the man to the anteroom door, shakes his hand, and lets the man out, then closes the door.

He stands by the door and now that business is over, he realizes he must settle the girl problem. He goes over to Nellie, takes her hand, looks down at her, thinks a second, and then says:

SP.   "I SUPPOSE WE OUGHT TO HAVE A LONG ENGAGEMENT IN CASE YOU SHOULD CHANGE YOUR MIND."

She looks up at him, startled, and a little bit alarmed, thinks a second, and then asks him if he wants to change his mind. He protests no, no, he doesn't but he thought perhaps she might. Then she, relieved, says no, no, she will never change her mind, rises and snuggles up against him, looking up into his face and smiling, sighs deeply and contentedly, and then looks up again and says:

SP.   "YOU KNOW, WE ARE NOT REALLY
        ENGAGED YET."

Then holding up her mouth suggestively to be kissed. Crowninshield is very much embarrassed, not knowing what to do but seeing he is in for it, finally leans over and kisses her, giving her a little peck on the mouth, but she smiles in a deprecating sort of way at his ignorance, tells him he doesn't know anything about making love, slowly reaches up her arms, pulls his face down to hers and holds him in a long, lingering kiss. After having held this a sufficient length of time, let Kirby enter and stand amazed at the situation.

Nellie, realizing he is there, suddenly draws away from Crowninshield, looks at Kirby, laughs half hysterically, goes and grabs her hat and coat and rushes out through the anteroom, Kirby looking after her in amazement.

Crowninshield stands dazed for a moment and then slowly rubs his hand across his forehead, bats his eyes, and then as in a sort of half daze, turns and goes toward the door where she went out, opens the door, looks out, sees she is gone, turns back, closes the door, comes back to his desk, and sinks down into his chair, Kirby watching him in amazement during the whole time.

Kirby comes over to the desk, stands beside Crowninshield, looks at him, and says:

SP.   "MY CHANCES OF GETTING MISS JONES SEEM
        TO BE PRETTY SLIM."

Crowninshield, with a little sigh and a beatific smile, looks up at him and says determinedly:

SP.   "YOU WILL NEVER GET HER. I AM GOING TO
        MARRY HER."

Kirby is amazed at this, asks if it is really true. Crowninshield insists that it is true, that he has been a fool all along not to recognize that he was in love with the girl, but that he has finally discovered he loves her and they are going to be married.

After he has finished his ravings, Kirby nods his head, smiles his own approval, but suddenly thinks of the sisters and says:

SP.   "WHAT ABOUT YOUR FAMILY? WHAT WILL
        THEY SAY?"

Crowninshield shakes his head as much as to indicate he doesn't care what they say, makes up his mind he will tell them right now, and picks up the phone and calls a number.

59. DRAWING ROOM—CROWNINSHIELD SISTERS. Maid brings in detective to Minerva. Flora comes from other room. He is quite elated over discoveries he has made. She asks what they are.

He says:

SP.   "SHE LEFT S.F. WITH HER MOTHER ON MAY 3."

Minerva says:

SP.   "THAT'S FINE."

He says:

SP.   "ALL WE HAVE TO DO NOW IS TO LOCATE HER."

60. CROWNINSHIELD'S OFFICE. Crowninshield is talking to Kirby with the receiver to his ear when he gets an answer to his call and speaks into the phone, asking if that is his sister.

61. DRAWING ROOM, CROWNINSHIELD SISTERS' HOME. One of them is at the phone answering it, saying yes it is Minerva.

62. CROWNINSHIELD'S OFFICE. Crowninshield at the phone says to Kirby that it is Minerva and he is going to spill the beans to her. Then he turns to the phone and says:

SP.   "I WANT TO TELL YOU BEFORE YOU HEAR IT FROM
        SOMEBODY ELSE THAT I AM GOING TO MARRY
        NELLIE JONES, MY STENOGRAPHER."

63. DRAWING ROOM, CROWNINSHIELD SISTERS' HOME. Minerva is absolutely appalled at this, asks him what on earth he means, and calls the other sister to her.

LONG SHOT—OF THE ROOM, showing the other sister running and joining Minerva at the telephone.

64. CROWNINSHIELD'S OFFICE. Crowninshield talking into the phone, telling them he is going to marry Miss Jones and their expostulations won't do any good, that they might as well accept the thing gracefully as it is all settled, and he hangs up the receiver.

65. DRAWING ROOM, CROWNINSHIELD SISTERS' HOME. They wiggle the hook trying to get him back on the phone but there is nothing doing. Finally they hang up and begin to chatter about this terrible scandal and what on earth they can do to stop the marriage, for it certainly must be stopped as this girl has simply led their brother on and into this terrible misalliance. Finally one of them gets an inspiration and says to the other:

SP.   "GET OUR WRAPS. I'LL GET HER ADDRESS FROM
        MISS TURNER IN THE OFFICE, AND WE WILL GO TO
        HER HOUSE AT ONCE AND SETTLE THIS."

She goes out and the other starts to get the girl's address.

                                                    FADE OUT.

66. GWEN'S BEDROOM. (FADE IN) Gwen and her mother are sitting on the bed, the mother dressed in apron and cook cap as though she had just started to get dinner. Gwen is going into ecstasies about the events of the day, telling her mother that this wonderful man has proposed to her and they are going to be married and she is just the happiest girl in the whole wide world.

In the middle of the tirade Eddie enters through the door from the sitting room. Gwen continues her rhapsody, telling her mother that somebody interrupted them all day long so that they hardly had a moment together but when he kissed her good night it made up for everything. The mother smiles in a comprehending sort of way, nods her head and says:

SP.   "WELL, YOU ARE LUCKY. YOU DON'T DESERVE IT."

Gwen bridles a little at this and wants to know why she doesn't deserve it. The mother looks at her with a mock frown and then bursts into laughter, leans over, throws her arms around Gwen and kisses her.

Eddie then takes a few steps into the room, folds his arms, stands proudly and says:

SP.   "SO, HE PROPOSED TO YOU, DIDN'T HE?"

And Gwen nods her head yes, smiling happily. Eddie then puts his thumbs in his armpits and struts up and down the room like a conquering hero. Gwen and the mother look at him askance and Gwen asks him what is the matter with him. Eddie leans over, looks at her like the cat who swallowed the canary, and says, "Nothing, nothing." Gwen shakes her head as if to indicate he has gone off his head.

67. HALLWAY, OUTSIDE GWEN'S APARTMENT. The two Crowninshield sisters enter, look at the number on the door, and ring the bell. (Note: There must be no name of any kind on this door.)

68. GWEN'S BEDROOM. Eddie, still strutting up and down; the mother and Gwen, thinking he is a nut, hear the bell. The mother tells Eddie to go answer it, and Eddie goes out.

69. SITTING ROOM, GWEN'S APARTMENT. Eddie enters from bedroom, goes to the hall door and opens it. The two sisters outside ask him if Miss Jones is in. Eddie thinks a second, represses a smile, and then says, "Yes, will you come in?" and they enter the room. Eddie asks them to be seated, which they do, and he leaves.

70. GWEN'S BEDROOM. Gwen and the mother are still sitting on the bed. Eddie enters and closes the door, when he comes to Gwen, tells her there are two grand-looking women in the other room who want to see her. Gwen is puzzled, wants to know who they are. Eddie says he didn't get their name. Gwen turns to her mother, asks who she supposes they are. The mother says:

SP.   "WHY DON'T YOU GO IN AND FIND OUT WHO
THEY ARE. I HAVE TO GET THE DINNER READY."

So she calls Eddie and they go out the back door.

Gwen then primps a little before the mirror and finally goes out to meet the two women.

71. GWEN'S SITTING ROOM. The two sisters are sitting waiting as Gwen enters. She greets them rather awkwardly as they rise with great dignity, look her up and down insultingly, then turn to each other and nod their heads as much as to say: "Just as we supposed, a very common person." Then one of them turns to Gwen and says:

SP.   "WE ARE THE SISTERS OF MR. JAMES
CROWNINSHIELD."

Gwen is quite taken aback at this and does not quite know what to make of it, whether they have called to felicitate with her or to make trouble, but trouble seems the more likely and she is immediately on her guard against them. She forces a smile and asks them to sit down, but they say they prefer to stand as the interview will be very short. This gets Gwen more on edge and she asks them what she can do for them and one says:

SP.   "WE HAVE JUST LEARNED OF THIS RIDICULOUS
ENGAGEMENT BETWEEN OUR BROTHER AND
YOURSELF."

This makes Gwen still more angry and she bridles up and asks them what is ridiculous about it. They smile at her in a supercilious way and one of them says:

SP.   "YOU MUST REALIZE, MISS JONES, THAT OUR
BROTHER IS A SCION OF ONE OF THE OLDEST AND
MOST ARISTOCRATIC FAMILIES IN NEW YORK."

At this Gwen looks at them out of the corner of her eye, indulges in a little smile to herself at the idea of their boasting of their family, then turns to them and quizzically says:

SP.   "DO YOU KNOW ANYTHING AGAINST MY
        FAMILY?"

The sisters shrug their shoulders, give her another look up and down,
and then turn to each other, and then one of them says of course they
have no doubt her family is a perfectly respectable one . . .

SP.   "BUT IT IS OBVIOUS, MISS JONES, YOU ARE NOT OF
        OUR CLASS."

Gwen now begins to boil inwardly at these insults and the unspeak-
able snobbery of these women. She is almost on the verge of telling
them where they get off, who she is and what she thinks of them, but
she suppresses this inclination and says to them:

SP.   "WHEN I MARRY YOUR BROTHER, I MARRY HIM
        AND NOT HIS FAMILY."

The sisters try to think of further argument but they are at the end of
their resources so far as persuasion goes. They look at each other and
decide to change their tactics. One of them comes to Gwen and says
that she must realize this is a misalliance, that it would not mean
happiness to either party, that she of course understands the great advantage it would be to Gwen in a financial way, and says:

SP.   "IF YOU WILL RENOUNCE THE ENGAGEMENT, WE
        WILL GLADLY PAY YOU ANY REASONABLE
        AMOUNT."

This absolutely exhausts Gwen's endurance. She looks at them with
fire in her eye, then goes to the door, opens it and says:

SP.   "GOOD DAY, LADIES."

They look at each other, shrug their shoulders in admission of temporary defeat, and go to the door. At the door they stop and one of
them turns to Gwen and says:

SP.   "YOU'D BETTER THINK OVER OUR FINANCIAL
        OFFER, MISS JONES, AS WE INTEND TO SEE TO IT
        THAT THIS ALLIANCE BRINGS YOU NO SOCIAL
        ADVANCEMENT."

Gwen looks at them, hardly able to contain herself, raises her eyes to
heaven as much as to say, "God deliver me from your social advance-
ment," finally controls herself enough to say:

SP.   "GOOD-BYE."

They give her a last look and go out with great dignity. Gwen slams
the door shut and rushes out through the sitting room toward the
dining room.

72. DINING ROOM, GWEN'S APARTMENT. The mother and Eddie are
just spreading the cloth on the table for dinner when the door opens
at the back and Gwen rushes in from the sitting room. She is almost
hysterical from rage and wounded pride. She comes to her mother and
says:

SP.   "WHO DO YOU THINK THEY WERE?"

The mother is surprised, says she doesn't know, and asks who they
were, and Gwen says:

SP.   "THE CROWNINSHIELD SISTERS—THE OLD CATS."

The mother is still more surprised to hear this and Gwen says they are
the most insulting pair of snobs she has ever seen. They want to break
off the engagement. They even wanted to buy her off with money.
She then looks at her mother and says hysterically:

SP.   "DO I LOOK LIKE A COMMON HUSSY THAT THEY
        SHOULD INSULT ME IN THAT WAY?"

Then she begins to sob hysterically and sits at the table.

The mother takes it more philosophically, smiles at the idea of their ostracizing Gwen because of their social position. She goes to Gwen and tells her to buck up, not to mind what they say, but Eddie is very wroth at the insult to his sister and tells her that she should have put them right in their place and that this hiding of her identity has gone on long enough and . . .

SP.   "IT IS ABOUT TIME THESE PEOPLE FOUND OUT WHO YOU ARE."

Gwen angrily says no, she wouldn't give them that much satisfaction after the way they insulted her. Eddie says that doesn't make any difference.

SP.   "THEY'VE GOT TO KNOW. OTHERWISE THEY MAY TALK THEIR BROTHER OUT OF MARRYING YOU."

This makes Gwen angry at Eddie for thinking their brother would listen to his sisters about anything against her, and she tells him she will not tell them under any circumstances whatsoever. Eddie then says: "I am not going to have things spoiled at this late date."

SP.   "I'M GOING TO TELL THEM MYSELF."

And he stands with his arms folded in a determined, defiant manner. Gwen sighs, shakes her head in a discouraged sort of way, looks up at her mother, and finally says:

SP.   "MOTHER, PLEASE DON'T LET HIM MIX UP IN THIS."

This makes Eddie very sore and he says: "Oh, I'm not to mix up in it, ain't I?" Then he turns to her and says:

SP.   "I'D LIKE TO KNOW WHERE YOU'D BE IF I HADN'T MIXED UP IN IT."

The mother and Gwen both turn on him amazed at this statement and ask him what in the world he means. Eddie squares his shoulders and says with great pride and defiance:

SP.   "I'D LIKE YOU TO KNOW THAT I AM THE ONE
       WHO WENT TO THE OFFICE AND FIXED THIS FOR
       YOU."

Gwen in absolute amazement rises to her feet, and she and her mother stare at Eddie while Eddie, now having gotten a good start, goes on boastfully to tell how he went down to the office, told Crowninshield his sister was sick and heartbroken over her love for him, that he had led her on until she fell in love with him and now it was up to him to marry her, and that is the way he fixed it for her.

Gwen is dumbfounded at this revelation and angered to the quick, as is also her mother. Gwen rushes to Eddie, shakes him by the shoulders and says, "You didn't do that, you didn't do that." He jerks away from her and says you bet he did. He'd like to see anyone fool with his sister and what's more, Crowninshield is going through with it, he will see that he does. He starts to leave the room, going toward the sitting room. The mother rushes to him and stops him and puts him down in a chair and says:

SP.   "YOU STAY RIGHT WHERE YOU ARE, EDDIE.
       GWEN WILL SETTLE THIS THING HERSELF!"

Meanwhile, Gwen is stunned by the revelation that Eddie has made. She stands staring ahead of her in absolute bewilderment, dismay, and disillusionment, and finally sinks into a chair, broken-hearted, and sits there dull and stupefied. At length her mother comes to her, stands over her sympathetically. Gwen shakes her head wanly and says:

SP.   "IT'S ALL OVER, MOTHER. YOU WERE RIGHT.
       I DIDN'T DESERVE IT."

The mother is sorry for ever having said that, puts her arm about her, sympathizes with her very sweetly.   FADE OUT.

TITLE   BRINGING CROWNINSHIELD TO GWEN'S HOUSE
THAT EVENING.

73. GWEN'S SITTING ROOM. The mother goes to the hall door and
opens it, admitting Crowninshield. He comes in all smiles but a little
bit embarrassed, as is natural under the circumstances. The mother is
also slightly embarrassed, not having expected him, and although she
has never seen him, she guesses from Gwen's description that this is
Crowninshield and Crowninshield guesses that this is the mother.

He says that he assumes that she is Nellie's mother and she says
yes, she is, and Crowninshield says, "Well, I am Mr. Crowninshield." The mother asks him into the room and they sit down.

Crowninshield says that he presumes Nellie has told her about
their engagement. The mother says yes, that she has, and Crowninshield says he hopes she approves, and the mother shakes her head,
saying that she is afraid that there has been a misunderstanding.

Crowninshield is alarmed at this and wants to know what is the
matter and the mother after a little hesitation forces a smile and says:

SP.   "TAKING EVERYTHING INTO CONSIDERATION,
MR. CROWNINSHIELD, WE HAVE DECIDED THE
WHOLE AFFAIR IS A PIECE OF FOLLY."

Crowninshield is dumbfounded at this and doesn't know what to say,
asks her what she means, what it is all about. The mother says that
her daughter has asked her to say good-bye to him for her and to ask
him to forget the whole incident as a foolish mistake. Crowninshield,
still utterly dumbfounded, says:

SP.   "DO YOU MEAN THAT YOUR DAUGHTER DOESN'T
LOVE ME?"

And the mother, trying to save Gwen's pride, smiles in a sort of patronizing way and says:

SP.   "OF COURSE ALL GIRLS HAVE THESE LITTLE INFAT-
UATIONS BUT THEY DON'T LAST LONG AND MY

DAUGHTER'S GOOD SENSE HAS COME TO HER RESCUE."

Crowninshield, hurt clear to the heart by this, has a little struggle with himself but as a gentleman he hasn't very much more to say, so he rises and starts to go, then suddenly stops and says:

SP.   "COULDN'T I SEE NELLIE, MRS. JONES?"

And the mother smiles in a kindly way, shakes her head no and says:

SP.   "I THINK IT IS BEST THAT YOU SHOULD NOT SEE HER AGAIN. IT WOULD ONLY BE EMBARRASSING TO BOTH OF YOU."

Crowninshield, feeling deeply that his whole romance is shattered, says good-bye and goes out, still dazed.

The mother closes the door after him, stands a moment, thinking, realizes what a splendid match it would have been for Gwen and for a moment is quite serious over the matter. Then she pulls herself together, realizing that she must cheer Gwen up, goes through the sitting room to the bedroom.

74. GWEN'S BEDROOM. Gwen is lying on the bed, crying quietly. The mother comes in, cheerful, sits down beside her, tries to comfort her and cheer her up.   FADE OUT.

TITLE   AFTER A STORMY VISIT FROM HIS SISTERS, CROWN-INSHIELD APPEALS TO HIS ONLY HOPE.

75. KIRBY'S BACHELOR APARTMENT. A very attractively fitted up man's sitting room (FADE IN)

Kirby is in a dressing gown, sitting on a couch before a fire, smoking and reading, when his servant enters and announces Crowninshield, who follows the servant in almost directly.

Crowninshield is very excited. He rushes to Kirby, who asks him what in the world is the matter. They both sit down on the couch and Crowninshield tells him that his romance has been smashed. Kirby asks how and Crowninshield says:

SP.   "THOSE PRECIOUS SISTERS OF MINE HAVE BEEN TO NELLIE AND SPOILED EVERYTHING."

He then goes on to tell how they went to Nellie's house, insulted the poor child, and she is so upset she has refused to see him, that the mother has told him everything is off . . .

SP.   "AND NELLIE HAS DECLARED SHE WILL *NEVER SEE ME AGAIN.*"

Kirby is naturally upset by this because he knows that Crowninshield really loves the girl, and he tries to figure out some way to help him. He asks Crowninshield why he doesn't go back to the house again and try to see Nellie, and Crowninshield says:

SP.   "I DID GO BACK AND HER MOTHER WOULDN'T EVEN LET ME IN."

Kirby is upset by this news and realizes that there is nothing in that scheme and tries to figure out some way to help his friend. At last he hits on the thread of an idea and says:

SP.   "IF WE COULD GET NELLIE TO COME TO THE OFFICE, YOU MIGHT BE ABLE TO PUT THINGS RIGHT."

Crowninshield says yes, he thinks possibly he might, but she has declared she will never come near the place again. Kirby figures around and finally digs out a scheme which he thinks will more or less force her to come back. At last he turns to Crowninshield and says:

SP.   "DID SHE TRANSCRIBE THE NOTES SHE MADE OF THE CONFERENCE IN YOUR OFFICE TODAY?"

Crowninshield thinks a moment, says no. Then he sees a little light in this scheme. His face brightens up and he says:

SP.   "I WOULD HAVE TO GO OVER THAT REPORT
         WITH HER."

Kirby says, yes, of course he would. I think if I tell her how important it is and that these men came from a long way off, that they have left town and no one else can transcribe the notes but her, that she will come.

Crowninshield is quite hopeful over this little plan.

FADE OUT.

76. GWEN'S SITTING ROOM. (FADE IN) Eddie comes to the hall door and opens it, admitting Kirby. Kirby asks if Miss Nellie Jones is there and the boy, wanting to say no but Miss Gwendolyn Armitage is here, swallows his pride and his palate at the same time and says yes, that she is and will the gentleman come in; they enter the sitting room and Kirby says to the boy, "Please tell Miss Jones that Mr. Kirby wants to see her." Eddie says all right and leaves, going out toward the dining room as Kirby sits down.

77. GWEN'S DINING ROOM. Gwen and her mother, dressed in morning house dresses, are finishing their breakfast. Eddie opens the door at back and enters. Eddie is now of course in disgrace and very much on his dignity. He comes to his place at the table and standing by his own chair, says to Gwen:

SP.   "MR. KIRBY WISHES TO SEE YOU."

And then he sits very dignified and goes on with his breakfast.

Gwen looks at her mother inquiringly and a little alarmed, wondering what Kirby wants. The mother is puzzled, doesn't know. Gwen asks if she thinks she ought to see him. The mother thinks a minute and then says yes, she must. There is nothing else to do. Gwen then says, "Well, you come with me." The mother says, "Well, all right," and they both go out to the sitting room.

78. GWEN'S SITTING ROOM. Kirby is sitting when Gwen and her mother enter. He immediately rises, comes over, and cordially shakes hands with Gwen. Gwen of course is very sad and rather dignified and on her guard. She introduces Kirby to her mother and then asks him to sit down. They all sit.

Kirby then tells Gwen that he understands she has left Mr. Crowninshield's employ. Gwen says yes, she has, and Kirby says he is sorry to hear it and he has come to ask her a great favor. She wants to know what it is and he says:

SP.   "THE NOTES FROM YESTERDAY'S CONFERENCE
        HAVE NOT BEEN TRANSCRIBED AND NO ONE CAN
        DO THAT BUT YOU."

Gwen immediately bridles up a little at his suggesting that she should come to the office. Kirby then says he knows he is asking a very great favor, but it means a great deal to him and then goes on to say:

SP.   "THE MEN IN THAT CONFERENCE WERE FROM
        CHICAGO AND THEY HAVE RETURNED HOME."

So of course you can see what a difficult situation it leaves me in and if you will only come down to the office just a few hours and put these notes in shape so that a report of the meeting can be gotten out, I will be tremendously obliged. Gwen considers the matter seriously, says of course she would be glad to do anything to be of service to Mr. Kirby. Kirby says that is very nice of her, but Gwen, a little doubtful about coming to the office, finally says:

SP.   "SHALL I HAVE TO SEE MR. CROWNINSHIELD?"

Kirby shrugs his shoulders and says yes, he is afraid she will because . . .

SP.   "MR. CROWNINSHIELD WILL HAVE TO GO OVER
        THE NOTES WITH YOU."

This doesn't please Gwen at all and she is very much in doubt as to what she ought to do. She turns to her mother for advice, and her mother says that of course she understands she doesn't want to see Mr. Crowninshield but it would seem that simply as a matter of fairness she would have to go and finish her work. Gwen then considers the matter a moment further and finally decides that she will go. Kirby is very much pleased and rises as if to go. Gwen rises and stops Kirby as he is going, thinks a second, and then says to him:

SP.   "I WILL COME ON CONDITION THAT MR. CROWN-
        INSHIELD PROMISES NOT TO SPEAK ONE WORD
        TO ME ON ANY PERSONAL MATTER."

Kirby says yes, he understands what she means and he will give his word of honor that Mr. Crowninshield will not speak one syllable to her concerning anything but the business in hand. She says very well, she will go. Kirby thanks her, bids her good-bye and bids her mother good-bye, and leaves. Gwen closes the door, then comes to her mother, shakes her head sadly and says:

SP.   "YOU SEE, MOTHER, IT IS AS I TOLD YOU—
        NOTHING BUT BUSINESS WITH HIM."

The mother nods her head, sighs a little, says yes, she understands, but she mustn't let it ruin her life; she has to go on living and she must keep her word and go down. Gwen says yes and they start for Gwen's bedroom.   FADE OUT.

TITLE   INDICATING THE END OF GWEN'S WORK FOR
        CROWNINSHIELD.

TITLE   CROWNINSHIELD KEPT HIS WORD. HE NEVER
        SPOKE A SYLLABLE OF ANYTHING BUT BUSINESS.

79. CROWNINSHIELD'S OFFICE. (FADE IN) Crowninshield is sitting at one side of the desk and Gwen on the other. Crowninshield is looking over some papers and Gwen is correcting the last few sheets, or is

looking over the last few sheets, which she hands to him a sheet at a time as she sees it is correct.

Finally he examines the last sheet, sees it is correct, straightens up the whole report, and looks up at Gwen and says he is very much obliged indeed for her having come down and finished this work for him.

Then he rises and she rises as if she were going. He takes her hand, agaiñ thanks her and bids her good-bye. She looks up at him with one quick, soulful look, hardly able to keep back the tears in spite of her pride. She breaks away from him suddenly and rushes off into her own little office.

Crowninshield stands a moment, pretty well satisfied by now that she cares a whole lot for him. Then he quickly goes out to her little office.

80. GWEN'S OFFICE. Gwen is in her little office, just starting to put on her hat when Crowninshield enters. She stops and looks at him, questioningly, and he says:

SP.   "EVERYONE ELSE HAS GONE. WOULD YOU MIND TAKING A SHORT LETTER ON THE TYPEWRITER FOR ME?"

She looks at him, rather pained at having to go through any more, but doesn't know just how to refuse and finally she acquiesces and says she will and sits down at the machine. He sits beside her. (Note: This must be a visible typewriter and the whole letter must be visible at one time.) She gets paper and everything ready and looks at him to begin. Then he starts to dictate and Nellie starts to take it down.

INSERT—TYPEWRITER, with the typing appearing letter by letter on it as follows:

N.Y. July, 1919

Miss Nellie Jones,
New York City.

Nellie stops typing, looks at him sharply and he says:

SP   "I AM AN UTTERLY HOPELESS, BLITHERING
       IDIOT . . ."

Nellie takes this down on her typewriter as though she agrees with
the sentiment, and Crowninshield, looking at her, is a little discon-
certed at this. However, he gathers his wits together and goes on,
saying:

SP.   "FOR NOT REALIZING LONG AGO THAT I WASN'T
       HAPPY A MINUTE OUT OF YOUR SIGHT."

He looks down at Nellie expecting a little compassion, but she looks
up at him coldly and tells him to go on with the dictation. He then
says:

SP.   "I'VE LOVED YOU FROM THE VERY BEGINNING."

Nellie takes this down in a very businesslike way and Crowninshield
walks back and forth and continues:

SP.   "AND I NEED YOU SO THAT I CANNOT THINK OF
       LIVING MY LIFE WITHOUT YOU."

Nellie takes this down, still in her calm businesslike manner.

   Crowninshield stops by her side and finally, forgetting the game he
is playing, he takes her hand impulsively and says: "Nellie, why keep
this up? Can't you give me an answer?" Nellie in her businesslike way
gently but firmly takes her hand away from him and goes on typing.

INSERT—TYPING:

   Hoping to have an early reply, I remain,

                                          Yours truly,

She then takes the paper out of the machine, picks up a pen, hands it
to Crowninshield and says:

SP.   "NO DOUBT YOU WILL HAVE MISS JONES'S AN-
       SWER IN DUE COURSE OF TIME."

He looks at her, sighs, realizes that she is going to play the thing out.

She then walks out of the office and Crowninshield looks after her, partly doubtful but mostly feeling that the fact that she is kidding him may mean that she is going to yield.

TITLE SAYING THAT MISS CROWNINSHIELD'S DETECTIVE AT LAST FOUND SOMETHING OUT

81. LIVING ROOM, CROWNINSHIELD SISTERS' HOME. One of the girls is in the front room and the other in the back room. The maid shows into the front room the detective, who carries a morning paper in his hand and comes to the Crowninshield sister.

She looks up, interested, and asks if he has anything to report. The detective swells up with importance, says you bet he has something to report, that he has found his woman. This sister excitedly calls to the other sister, who rushes in from the other room, and the detective takes from his pocket a morning newspaper, probably *The American,* which he hands to one of the sisters. The two sisters eagerly lean over the paper as the detective points to his discovery.

INSERT—Section of the newspaper with a picture of Gwen, a picture of Crowninshield and a reproduction of the family crest of the Armitage family.

Then a little article with the headline saying:

INTERNATIONAL WEDDING A SURPRISE
TO SOCIETY.

Member of English aristocracy marries plain American businessman.

Society on both sides of the water will be interested to learn of the sudden marriage of the Honorable Gwendolyn Diana Beaufort-Beaufort Armitage to Mr. James

[balance missing]